RUN ON RED

Noelle W. Ihli

Published 2022 by Dynamite Books

www.dynamitebookspublishing.com

ISBN: 9798360715627

Any references to historical events, real people, or real places are used ficti-
tiously. Names, characters, and places are products of the author's imagina-
tion.

Cover design by Dynamite Books, LLC

First printing, November 2022

For the ones who made it out alive.
For the ones who didn't.
For the ones still fighting somewhere in between.

This novel includes non-explicit references to sexual violence. Please read with care.

1

"They're still tailgating us," I murmured, squinting into the lone pair of headlights shining through the back windshield. The sequins on my halter top caught on the lap belt, snicking like ticker tape as I shifted in the passenger seat.

"Maybe it's the Green River Killer," Laura said evenly, keeping her eyes on the road.

I snorted but kept watching as the headlights crept closer. "They caught the Green River Killer. I thought you read that blog I sent."

"It was twenty pages long. Anyway, why do I need a crime blog when I have Olivia Heath in my car?" she asked. As she slowed down to take the next hairpin turn, the watery yellow headlights behind us turned a pale orange where they mingled with our brake lights.

I ignored her and kept staring at the headlights that had been tailgating us relentlessly for miles on the dark rural highway.

Everything is fine, I chided myself. There were "No Passing" signs posted every other switchback on the narrow road, and our ancient Volvo was going ten miles under the speed limit as we chugged uphill. Of course they were tailgating us.

When I blinked, two mirror-image red spots flashed behind my eyelids. It was impossible to see the drivers—and I was getting carsick. I glared into the headlights a little longer and committed the license plate to memory: 2C GR275.

"Liv? Earth to Liv. They're probably late to the bonfire. Same as us." Laura was the Scully to my Mulder: ever the optimist, ever reasonable. Ever the one who talked me down from my imaginary ledges. But the question always tapped at the back of my mind: What if there really *was* a ledge?

"The license plate *does* say GR," I grumbled, but turned around, smoothing down my wonky sequins and drawing in a slow breath to calm my sloshing stomach.

"GR?" Laura prodded, glancing at me as we came out of the curve.

"Green River," I clarified with an exaggerated sigh. "Or Gary Ridgway, same guy. Go easy on the turns." I rested one hand out the uneven window ledge, so the cool night air hit my face in a slap that smelled like sage.

The Volvo's passenger-side window had collapsed inside the doorframe a few weeks earlier. Laura's sister Tish had talked about taping up a sheet of plastic in the hole, but since the car didn't have air conditioning, the window just stayed open. I rubbed at a smattering of goosebumps on my bare arms. I should have brought a jacket. The hills were at least twenty degrees cooler than the city, but I'd been too rushed—and too sweaty—after work to care.

The bonfire at the reservoir had started more than an hour ago, and as far as I could tell we were the only car on the road—aside from the tailgaters. Laura had waited until my shift ended at the Pie Hole to make the tedious, winding drive through the hills.

The interior of the Volvo grew brighter as the headlights edged closer. Laura glanced in the rearview mirror. When I craned my neck to do the same, she sent me a warning glare. "Stay facing forward. The only thing you need to worry about is not getting barf on Tish's car." She flicked the fuzzy dice hanging from the mirror. "I can't believe she bailed on us again tonight."

"I'm fine," I insisted, even as my stomach lurched dangerously. I inhaled slowly through my nose to stave off the nausea. "But—"

"Breathe, Liv," she soothed. "They just want to pass us. I'll find somewhere to pull over."

"There's nowhere to pull over," I mumbled, wishing I'd gone to the library with Tish instead of "putting myself out there" tonight. "And this is definitely a no-passing zone." The isolated two-lane rural highway made me nervous, even in the daytime.

"Look, right there." Laura signaled and angled the Volvo toward a shallow gravel pullout carved into the hillside to our right.

The headlights stayed behind us, moving toward the same shoulder at a crawl.

"Why aren't they passing?" I demanded, even while I scolded myself for overreacting. I didn't trust my anxious brain to correctly identify a real threat. It had steered me wrong way too many times.

As soon as the words left my lips, a vehicle with one headlight out—only the second car we'd seen since leaving city limits—whipped into view. It passed us from behind, going way too fast and nearly clipping the driver's side mirror of the Volvo. Once its brake lights disappeared around the next bend, the tailgaters eased back onto the road and zipped past us as well.

Within a few seconds, the hills were dark and quiet again, except for the Volvo's idling mutter.

"See? They were just letting that idiot pass," Laura insisted triumphantly, flashing me a grin before hitting the gas and easing back onto the road. "No serial killers."

When I didn't respond, her eyes flicked toward me. "Have you heard anything from Tish?"

Shaking off the useless adrenaline rush, I sighed and reached down the front of my high-waisted denim cut-offs to open the slim traveler's pouch where I'd tucked my cell phone. Laura snickered at the sound of the zipper.

I ignored her and flipped open the phone. "You know she hasn't texted. You just wanted to see me open the magic fanny pack." I snapped the elastic of the traveler's pouch, tucked just beneath the top button of my shorts, for emphasis. "My pockets can hold half a Saltine, at most. Where the hell am I supposed to put my cell phone when I go out?"

"And your rape whistle, and your pepper spray," Laura chirped.

I rolled my eyes and laughed. "You really should read the blog."

My phone screen showed one service bar. I didn't have any new messages, but I took the opportunity to text Tish the car's license plate: 2C GR275. *Just in case.*

She wouldn't see it until she got home from the library later tonight. And even then, she wouldn't think anything of the text unless the apartment was still empty in the morning. Tish—like Laura—had come to expect the occasional license plate number—or blurry photo of some rando at the gas station who looked like a police sketch I'd seen on Twitter.

Laura shifted in the driver's seat to face me. "You know, we can turn around if you want," she offered gently, the bright white of her teeth slowly disappearing with her smile. "If you're not feeling up for the bonfire—"

"I'm good," I insisted more gruffly than I intended, avoiding her eyes. I could deal with jokes about my red-alert texts and travel pouch and rape whistle. But any hint of sympathy for the underbelly of my social anxiety ... not so much.

I zipped my cell phone back into the slim travel pouch, refusing to imagine the last bar of cell service flickering out as we drove deeper into the hills. Then I reached over and turned the volume knob on the ancient boombox propped between us, where the glove box in the old Volvo used to live. It was an indestructible monstrosity, like the Volvo itself. I absolutely loved it.

"I did not wear scratchy sequins to turn around and go home," I sang off-key over Britney Spears. Laura had spent hours making this party mix, first downloading the songs, then burning them to a CD, then recording the CD onto a tape that would play in the ridiculous boombox.

Laura's smile brightened. "Atta girl."

2

The music pumping through the old boombox lasted until we approached the final turnoff onto the long dirt road that led to the reservoir.

The tape turned over with a loud click right as the Volvo clunked over a shallow pothole. When Britney's voice reemerged, it was slow and distorted, like the song had been dunked in syrup.

"Brit? Stay with us," Laura coaxed as the song subsided to a tinny whine. The boombox made a sudden, harsh buzzing noise, coughed out a burst of static, then went completely silent.

"I guess not." She laughed and wiggled the volume knob one more time.

I smiled and rested my arm on the edge of the open window, dipping my hand down, then up, then down in the breeze. *The bonfire will be fun,* I reassured myself. *You always have fun once you get there. Just stay with Laura.*

The nervous fizz deep in my stomach remained wary. I leaned out the open window a little and followed the smoky trail of the Milky Way until it disappeared behind the hillside looming to our right. The sounds of night creatures worrying among themselves took center stage in the quiet night as the Volvo slowly chugged up the incline.

A muted scratching coming from the dash suddenly broke through the geriatric drone of the engine. The seatbelt caught as I shifted in my seat, leaving a drooping curl of fabric across my chest.

There it was again: a soft skittering. "Do you hear that? I swear there's something inside the dash."

Laura let go of the wheel with one hand to rap on the plastic of the dash. The sound stopped. "I think there might be something living in that hole, gnawing on the wires," she said, then shrugged as if she'd just made a comment about the weather. "Sometimes I hear that same scurrying sound while I drive. Tish said she does too. It's probably a mouse."

I looked at her in disbelief. "If I see a damn *mouse* come out of your dashboard, I am hurling myself out of the Volvo." I shuddered. "I still can't believe Tish spent money on this thing. It's amazing that it runs."

Laura shrugged again, unfazed. "She got it cheap from Tony's friend. It was like, five hundred bucks." Then she added, "The guy actually said he'd give it to her for two hundred if she threw in a blow job."

"Okay, pull the car over." I mimed gagging and grabbed the door handle.

"Olivia!" Laura shrieked and hit the brakes.

I laughed. "I'm kidding. Mostly. He actually *said* that to Tish?"

She rolled her eyes dramatically. "Yep."

"While Tish and Tony were together?"

"Uh huh."

"Gross." I sat forward in my seat, studying the sloping hills looming in the distance. If I remembered right, we were about twenty minutes away from the reservoir once we turned onto this dirt road.

"How is Tish doing, anyway?" I asked after a minute. "If I didn't see her cereal bowl in the sink, I wouldn't even know she'd been sleeping at the apartment lately."

Laura sighed. "She's okay—I think? I've hardly seen her lately either. Ever since the breakup, she's been weird."

I nodded, still half-listening for the mouse scurrying around in the dash, but Tish's drama was a welcome distraction. Tish and I were friends—but we'd never been especially close. Not like me and Laura, who had been inseparable since the seventh grade. "I thought she was definitely coming tonight," I pressed. "She even RSVPed on Facebook. Why did she stay home?"

Laura slowed the car down to skirt another pothole in the dirt road. "No idea. She texted a few minutes before you got home from work, saying she was staying at the library late." She shrugged again. "I think she just doesn't want to risk running into Tony at the bonfire."

I nodded slowly. "Do you think he'll be there? It's not really a Delta vibe."

"A Delta vibe?" Laura giggled. "You mean like, an AXE Body Spray commercial?"

I burst out laughing. "Pretty much."

Laura raised her eyebrow and smiled. "Are *you* hoping Tony will be there?"

Heat rose in my cheeks. "No way. Tish was *engaged* to him, dummy."

I'd seen plenty of photos of Tish's boyfriend—briefly fiancé—on Facebook, but I'd only really met him a couple of times. Once across the room at a party, and once on the apartment couch in passing. We didn't actually know each other. Not really.

I pictured the smiling, sun-kissed boy I'd seen on Tish's Facebook profile, wearing a Band of Horses T-shirt. He was incredibly good-looking.

Laura sighed and brushed her bangs away from her face. "It's true. He's ruined for all of us now."

"I'm surprised Tish …" I trailed off, not totally sure how to finish that sentence. Both Laura and I had been surprised when Tish started dating Tony last year. He was what my dad would call a "big man on campus." Handsome, charming, and one of the chosen ones who had been accepted into the Delta fraternity freshman year. As much as I loved Tish, it was impossible to deny that she was Tony's polar opposite: quiet, shy, and maybe a little boring if I was being mean. Basically, she was like me. Laura had always been the designated social butterfly of our little cadre.

Laura giggled. "Hey, at least you've got *Ziggy*."

I snickered, but my stomach tightened at the mention of his name. "Stop it. We aren't discussing him tonight."

"Ziggy," which I now knew was short for "Zachariah," was the supremely awkward humanities TA who stared at me during class. Laura and I had found his Facebook profile one night and learned, to our horror and delight, that he was a member of the Pen and Quill Society: a LARPing group on campus. Ziggy was a "mage": which Laura and I had to Google. It meant he was some kind of magician.

Last week, in an effort to "put myself out there," I'd made the horrifying mistake of accepting a date with a cute guy I'd met on MySpace. His profile photo bore almost zero resemblance to the tall, painfully quiet, acne-covered senior who wrote things like "me likey" and "bomb diggity" on the margins of my papers. I didn't realize it was Ziggy until we met up for happy hour at SpaceBar that night. Things went from bad to worse when I learned he had recognized *me* from my profile photo. I'd made an excuse about a family emergency and booked it out of the bar, vowing to delete my profile the second I got back to the apartment to lick my wounds.

"Did you hear back from your professor?" Laura prodded.

I nodded slowly. Laura had convinced me to email my humanities professor about what had happened, but I still felt weird about the whole thing. "Yeah, forgot to tell you. He wrote back yesterday with a long apology about how this happened earlier in the semester to someone else. Long story short, Ziggy's not the humanities TA anymore."

Laura shot me an impressed look and took a turn in the road a little too fast. "Nice job, killer. What a creep."

I held my breath as our wheels edged toward the thin shoulder that petered off into the darkness beyond our headlights. I tugged on my seatbelt again, hoping it had been engineered to outlast the rest of the car despite its obvious fatigue. "I haven't been up to Coffee Creek in forever. How much farther is it to the reservoir?"

"Coffin Creek," Laura corrected me sternly.

I rolled my eyes. "I hate that name. Do we have to call it that? There's no coffin. Just muddy water and beer cans."

"Because it's fun. And because the freshman who went missing is buried there." She shrugged, then flashed me a wicked grin.

I sighed. "Her name is Ava Robles. And if they knew where she was buried, she wouldn't be missing, would she? If you had read *that* blog post, you'd know they never found her body."

Incoming freshman Ava Robles had gone missing near Coffin Creek three years earlier. The same year Laura and I had started at University of Idaho. I hadn't known her. Neither had Laura. We weren't on the guest list for that particular party.

Ava had been one of the few freshmen who attended the exclusive sorority party that night, at the end of Rush week. Her story had been firmly embedded in campus lore almost as soon as the news broke that she had gone missing. For weeks at the start of the semester, cops stalked sorority and frat houses to interview anyone who had attended the huge toga party.

When rumors—and a few bloggers—started to spread that her body had been dumped in Coffin Creek, the detectives even sent divers to troll the murky waters. They'd found absolutely nothing. From the blog I'd read, the police believed that the rumors might have been intentionally started as a way to throw off the investigation. It worked. And the rumors—as well as the unfortunate nickname—stuck like glue around campus ever since.

The only things they'd ever found of Ava's were her purse and phone, tossed into the sagebrush at the edge of the reservoir. They'd trolled it too, with zero success. All anyone really knew was that Ava had been at that party one minute—and the next she hadn't.

There were no traces of blood. No signs of a struggle. No witnesses who had noticed anything strange.

Everyone assumed she was dead. There was even some speculation that maybe she'd been pulled into the hills by a cougar. It wasn't likely, but it wasn't impossible. Despite the university nearby, this part of Idaho was mostly wild. The hills went on for miles and miles in all directions with sportsman's access.

I shivered. Thinking about Ava Robles was not helping my state of mind. "How much longer until we get there?" I asked.

Laura shrugged. "We'll be there in fifteen minutes, give or take. Is your stomach feeling better?"

"All good," I insisted, not counting the anxious bubbles. "But I'm freezing." I rubbed my arms, wishing again that I had brought my jacket. The last bonfire we'd attended—stoked by overeager freshmen— had burned so hot that somebody's bumper had melted by the end of the night.

"Me too, but this top looks like an old paper bag if I cover up my arms." She gestured to the high-neck cotton blouse that looked nothing like a paper bag. "I never learn. See if you can get the heater to work. Tish swore it did."

I turned my attention to the large knob next to the radio dial, cranking it all the way to the red side. It made a clicking noise, followed by a soft *pop*. "That's a no. It might be time to take the Volvo to a farm." I patted the window frame. "We love you, but you're falling apart."

Giving up on the heater, I settled against the bucket seat, reaching up to touch my hair. I'd cut it from waist-length to a trendy lob with bangs a few days earlier, and my head still felt weirdly untethered without the extra weight.

I shifted slightly to study Laura's long hair in my peripheral vision. It hung down her back and was such a pale white-blond that it seemed to glow against the gray seat. The summer before sixth grade, we'd both tried highlighting our hair with a combination of Sun-In and peroxide. Laura's hair had turned an ethereal white. My dark brown hair had turned Sunny-Delight orange in splotches I hadn't fully eradicated until eighth grade. I made a face and asked, "Was it a mistake to cut my hair?"

She smiled and tapped on the brakes as a deer's eyes glowed white near the side of the road before it bounded into the night. "Stop it right now. I keep telling you, it's gorgeous. And it makes your eyes look huge." She reached up to grab a hunk of her blond hair. "Mine feels like straw lately—how do you get yours so shiny?"

I flipped my short hair dramatically. "Thanks. It's probably from the Pie Hole. All that oil in the air—it's like pizza-scented deep conditioner."

Laura sighed loudly. "Another reason I should've taken summer semester off to get a job. I can't get over the idea that physical education is an *actual* college requirement. Are we not adults now? How am I being forced into running?"

I wound my cold hands into the soft underside of the halter top, keeping my gaze on the shoulder of the road to watch for more pairs of ghostly eyes. "Are you sure we took the right turnoff?"

I glanced at the Volvo's dash clock out of habit, even though I knew it would read 3:03 no matter how long we drove. This far into the hills, it felt like we'd been swallowed up by the night itself.

I didn't hear her response. As the dirt road crested a rise, we passed a skinny ATV trail ducking into the hills. A dark, hulking shape sat angled in the weeds like a black hole in the pale, dry grass.

A truck.

Everything is fine, I told myself firmly, channeling my inner Laura.

The moment we drove past, the truck's high beams blinked on, blazing into our rearview mirror as it roared to life and pulled behind us.

3

"It's the same car," I mumbled in disbelief.

"What? How can you tell?" Laura asked distractedly, navigating a pothole.

I squinted through the back windshield into the blinding headlights. "Same license plate: 2C GR275. I texted it to Tish earlier."

Laura shot me a look. "Liv, everything is okay. Even if it is the same car, it's fine. If they took this turnoff, they're definitely on their way to the bonfire. Maybe it's a couple that decided to mess around on the side of the road for a while." She grinned then cranked down the driver's side window, signaling for the other vehicle to pass us.

I stared at her in bewilderment as she calmly motioned out the window.

When the headlights in the rearview mirror didn't disappear after a few seconds, Laura slowed the Volvo to a crawl and motioned more dramatically, her pale skin illuminated in the foggy beams. "Go around, dumbass," she said in a soft singsong.

I quietly unzipped the travel pouch beneath my shorts and pulled out the flip phone with shaking hands. No service, as expected. And the battery had dipped to just five percent. Berating myself for not turning off roaming sooner, I quickly navigated to Settings then snapped the phone shut.

"Dick," Laura mumbled, her lips turned down in a frown. Her purple lipstick looked black in the darkness. "Why don't they turn off their brights, at least? They're blinding me. I'm going to find somewhere to pull over all the way. The road is super narrow here."

She hit the gas and brought the Volvo slowly back up to speed.

The other vehicle accelerated behind us.

"They could back off our ass a little," Laura grumbled, hunching in her seat so the glare of the headlights didn't hit her directly. "The good news is that if we get rear-ended, Tish's car won't be the one going in for repairs. It's probably been totaled for the past ten years."

The truck began flashing its brights on and off in rapid succession as if transmitting a message in Morse code.

"Give me a hot second," Laura exclaimed, tapping on the brakes as the road curved and emptied into another steep straightaway. The Volvo decelerated quickly, laboriously crawling up the incline.

"There should be—" I began as the other vehicle abruptly swerved left and pulled up alongside us on the narrow straightaway. It was so close to us that if Laura reached her hand out the window, she could have touched the passenger's side mirror.

"Who is it?" she asked, keeping her eyes glued to the road as we approached the next curve. "They're going to get plastered if they stay in the left lane and someone comes around that bend," she added lightly, as if that might be a favorable outcome.

I didn't answer right away as I stared into the darkness beyond Laura's open window. I had been secretly hoping to see someone we knew. Or at the very least, a car packed with random frat boys, their teeth flashing white as they laughed at our wide eyes. But as the truck came even with the Volvo for a brief moment, I could see the silhouettes of two men inside, facing forward. Each wore a dark-colored hoodie pulled up over his head, concealing all but the barest outline of his profile. Neither one turned to look at me.

I felt like I'd just been dunked in ice water, even though the cell phone in my hand was slippery with sweat. *This is bad,* my gut screamed. *Are you sure?* my brain fired back.

"Who is it?" Laura asked again as both vehicles crawled along in tandem. A hot trickle of adrenaline chipped away at the ice in my veins. "Do we know them or something? Maybe they recognize the Volvo. It's hard to miss."

"We don't know them," I whispered, clutching the seatbelt across my chest. Both men were still facing forward. Neither had even glanced in our direction. "Should ... I call the police?" I asked shakily, hoping Laura would reassure me that the answer was *no.* That there was some reasonable and innocuous reason these men were toying with us. For all the times I'd repeated the catchphrases from my favorite bloggers—"Be vigilant, stay alive," "Screw polite-ness," "Stay safe, get weird," I knew deep down I'd only call 9-1-1 if I was actually in the process of being murdered.

I moved one finger to hover over the Emergency Call button, glancing between the glowing red text and the headlights. Still no service.

"I—I don't know. What do they look like?" Laura demanded. For the first time, she sounded rattled.

The truck stayed alongside us a moment longer. Then it roared ahead violently, the smell of dust and rubber filling the air as it dart-ed past the Volvo, moved into our lane and disappeared around the approaching bend with mere inches to spare.

I shook my head, already second-guessing what I'd seen. "I—I couldn't tell very much, but I really think we should turn around. There's two guys. Neither one of them would look at me, and they were both wearing hoodies pulled all the way up over their—"

Laura gasped as we took the curve.

Red brake lights blazed just a few yards away.

4

Laura shrieked and slammed on the brakes. Her blond hair flew forward in my peripheral vision before I squeezed my eyes shut and braced for impact.

As we lurched to a stop, I kept my eyes closed tight, focusing on my own pulse throbbing loudly in my ears and the sound of Laura drawing in fast, shallow breaths next to me. I quickly took inventory. There was no broken glass. There had been no squeal of twisted metal.

We'd stopped just in time.

I opened my eyes and saw that the Volvo's front bumper was so close to the truck's back bumper that I couldn't have walked between the two cars. The glow from their taillights combined with our headlights created an eerie vignette around the Volvo's front end.

In the dim red light, I saw that Laura hadn't released her death grip on the steering wheel. "Fuckers," she hissed quietly, but her voice shook as she spoke.

When she reached for the door handle, I grabbed her sleeve. "No, don't get out of the car. I don't know what they want, but I have a bad feeling—like, really bad. Stay in the car."

For a moment, it looked like she might argue with me. She opened then closed her mouth.

The truck still hadn't budged. It was like the passengers were waiting for us to make the next move. "Let's just turn around and go home, okay? Screw the bonfire," I begged. "I'm really scared."

"Breathe, Liv," she whispered, her eyes fixed on the brake lights. "We're almost there."

She was right: Home was almost an hour in the other direction. Would it be safer to try to get to the bonfire after all? Cold dread curdled in my gut, making my body feel heavy and slow, even as the adrenaline pumping through my veins made my legs itchy to run.

"Please, Laur," I choked out, no longer sure what I was asking her to do. My voice sounded too loud and too fast and somehow naked in the open window beside me. I held my breath, straining to hear the sound of someone else, anyone else, coming up the road behind us.

There was nothing.

"Maybe …" Laura trailed off, then tried again. "Maybe," she tried again but let the sentence die there. We stared at the two blocky, black silhouettes in the truck.

She swore softly. "Screw this. Let's just turn around."

My relief was short-lived as I scanned the boat-like frame of the Volvo. The road was so narrow we'd have to do a three-point turn— at least—to safely turn the clunky vehicle around without skidding past the shoulder of the road. "Okay, back up as far as you can against the hillside, then ease forward," I whispered shakily, imagining the grade on the other side of the road. There was no railing this far into the boonies. "We'll be able to go faster once we start driving downhill, but—"

I stopped talking as the brake lights blinked off. The truck slowly pulled forward at an angle until the front half of the vehicle nosed into the left lane. Laura glanced at me quickly. I kept my gaze on the driver, still just a bulky silhouette in our headlights.

Get out of here, my gut screamed. I watched in frozen fascination. The truck now blocked both lanes of traffic.

"Are they trying to turn around?" Laura asked in confusion.

No. We couldn't get around the truck—or get to the bonfire—even if we wanted to.

"Are they serious right now?" Laura's voice was high and incredulous as she yanked on the gearshift to put the Volvo into reverse. "Do you still have your cell phone?"

"We—we don't have service," I stuttered.

"Maybe 9-1-1 will go through," she replied slowly.

Another wave of adrenaline hit my bloodstream, making my heart pound even harder. Laura was scared too. She thought we should call 9-1-1. For reasons I couldn't understand, this scared me even more than the men in the truck.

I flipped open the phone and shook my head in frustration. "I only have five percent battery left. It's about to die. Hand me your cell instead," I hissed and shoved my own phone back into the zippered pouch. The truck hadn't moved.

Laura took one hand off the steering wheel but kept her eyes on the truck. She inched the Volvo into the first point of the turn then gestured toward the backseat. "My wristlet is behind you. Hurry, grab my phone."

I twisted around and ran my hands over the debris on the backseat. A fast-food wrapper, a pair of shoes, some large gym shorts that must have belonged to Tony. I finally landed on Laura's leather wristlet.

My fumbling fingers closed around the cold rectangle of Laura's flip phone. As I turned my body to face forward, I saw movement from the corner of my eye.

The truck's driver's side door had just opened.

"Hurry, hurry!" I urged, flipping her phone open. I dialed three numbers, making sure my fingers found the right keys despite their shaking.

Laura floored the gas. The Volvo made an abrupt lurch forward then stopped precariously close to the edge. I braced and held onto the phone, finger frozen over the Send Call button.

A man was getting out of the truck. There was something strange about his face. It wasn't shaped right.

The open passenger-side window suddenly felt less like an inconvenience and more like a chink in the Volvo's armor.

"Go, Laura!" I shrieked, feeling the panic rise like bile in my throat. I tore my eyes from the smoky red glow of the taillights. From the encroaching shadowy figure.

I forced myself to focus on the phone in my hand. *Dial 9, then 1, then 1.*

Part of my brain screamed at me that this was how we would die. Part of it still insisted that this was all a misunderstanding or a bad joke we'd laugh about later.

"It'll be okay," Laura hissed, jerking the car into reverse.

I finally hit Send Call, then pressed the phone to my ear. I strained to hear any indication that a connection had been made.

The phone beeped quietly, and I looked at the screen.

No service.

Whether we needed it or not, help would not be coming.

The Volvo pitched backward then stopped moving altogether.

"I stalled it—I—" Laura gasped in disbelief, turning the key again hard as she pressed down on the clutch. I didn't know how to drive stick shift, so I didn't really know what this meant. All I knew was that the throaty growl of the engine was gone, replaced by the sound of footsteps thudding toward us.

I looked up. The driver of the truck had already crossed half of the short distance between us. The passenger-side door had opened as well. Both men were moving toward the Volvo. The hunch of their shoulders and the position of their arms made my blood run cold. They weren't coming over to say hello. They were coming for us.

Finally, I saw their faces in the periphery of our headlights. Were my eyes playing tricks on me? Was the adrenaline getting to me? They were barely faces at all. Both were misshapen, with identical bruise-black circles framing their eyes. The face on the left was a sickly white. The one on the right was a deep reddish-brown color. Both of their thick, ropy lips were pulled back in grotesque grins.

It took a second for me to register what I was seeing: not human skin, but latex masks. It didn't temper the white-hot fear pumping through my veins.

"Laura," I whispered, voice hoarse, vision suddenly swimming with little black dots. Was I going to pass out? I thought of every *Dateline* episode I'd ever watched, every crime blog I'd ever read. So many started just like this. And they all ended in predictably similar ways.

Our episode would start with two college girls wearing impractical party clothes—right down to my ridiculous sequined halter top and Laura's flowy sleeveless top—heading out into the middle of nowhere for a night of body shots and hookups in the hills. In the dramatization with B-list actresses, they would show us laughing about boys and summer school. Maybe they'd even feature the old boombox in the Volvo, if the producers had done their research.

They wouldn't know about the men in masks. Nobody would know the full terror of those latex faces in our last moments.

Whatever the episode did or didn't show, it would end with our blood on the side of the narrow highway. I played the scene out like a movie in my mind, seeing how it would all happen with perfect clarity.

I couldn't move. This was actually happening.

What were our chances on foot? Was there any way we could outrun them?

No. My sparkly, strappy shoes were as ridiculous as my sequined top.

In a few seconds, Red Mask would reach my open window.

"No, no," Laura whimpered as she cranked the key again and again, her eyes wide and fixed on the man in the white mask, still a few yards from her window. Unlike Red Mask, he was just standing there—staring back at us.

Red Mask's footsteps landed on the dirt in loud thumps. I could see the headlights reflected in his eyes, set deep in his sickly mask.

"*Go,* dammit!" Laura screamed, turning the key as she released the clutch yet again.

The Volvo obeyed.

5

Sputtering into reverse, the Volvo jolted violently backward.

Gravel crunched beneath our back wheels on the narrow shoulder, warning that we were about to hit the hillside. Laura cranked the wheel again, shifting forward quickly. Were we going to overshoot the road and plunge into the hills?

"Stop, stop!" I screamed. Laura slammed on the brakes, hurling us against our seatbelts.

I gasped for breath and jerked my head back up. My loose belt had failed to catch me all the way, and I had dropped Laura's phone onto the floorboards. "Shit, shit, shit," I mumbled. It didn't really matter what happened to the phone at this point. Even if I had it next to my ear, I wouldn't be able to make a call.

The bloated reddish mask hovered beside my open window.

"Go!" I screamed again at Laura, recoiling backward against the seatbelt. It only loosely held me in place. There was nowhere to run.

Red Mask grabbed the passenger door's handle. He shook it roughly, but it didn't budge. Despite my terror, I felt a surge of love for the Volvo. The passenger door handle had completely stopped working soon after Tish bought it from Tony's friend. It didn't open from the outside *or* the inside. You either had to crawl through the window or the driver's side.

Distantly, I could hear Laura next to me, struggling with the gears. Each movement felt syrupy and slow, like we had been plunged underwater. Why weren't we moving? Had we stalled again?

With one last rattle of the useless passenger door handle, Red Mask gave up. He reached through the open window. I recoiled, screaming as his fingers closed around my loose seatbelt. They brushed against the bare skin of my collarbone. I arched back as far as I could without ramming into Laura. A whiff of his sour breath hit my face, hot and acrylic from the mask.

Go for the groin, the eyes, the nose, my brain shouted. *Fight back.*

Before I could settle on a way to strike, his other hand snaked into the car. It grabbed hold of my short hair, digging into my scalp. He gripped and twisted with one hand while pulling the floppy seatbelt over my shoulder with the other.

Next to me, Laura screamed and let go of the wheel to pummel the arm gripping me by the hair.

The sound went mute beneath the pulse booming in my ears. I clawed at his arm, arching backward as far as the lap belt would allow. He held on, grasping for a better hold in my hair. He snapped my neck back violently toward the open window, sending needles of pain through my scalp.

My fingernails dug into the exposed flesh of his hand and forearm. I fought harder, digging for bone, anything to make him let go. Cursing, he twisted and let go of the seatbelt. His hand roamed to my lap in search of my seatbelt buckle.

The pain was blinding. But the idea of being pulled outside the car with him was worse.

In the corner of my eye, I saw that White Mask had finally reached the Volvo now as well. He slammed both fists against the hood of the car in a thick smack.

The belt buckle clicked open.

The lap belt went slack, and the pressure on my hair intensified. I felt the familiar pitch of the Volvo shifting into gear.

With as much force as I could gather, I jerked my body forward against the dashboard. Then I slammed my head against the seat back —and his hand.

His grip gave just a little, so I twisted sideways. My elbow smashed into Laura's right arm as the Volvo shot backward toward the hillside. Its tires screamed beneath the sound of my own shriek. My hair ripped at the roots as he finally lost his grip.

In my peripheral vision, White Mask stumbled backward from the driver's side of the Volvo, then tripped and fell hard onto the shoulder of the road.

Red Mask screamed something unintelligible, then jumped backward to avoid the car's sudden momentum.

Please, please, please. The words raced through my head, a mantra or a desperate prayer—for another pair of headlights, divine intervention, anything but the feel of those clammy, grasping hands on my skin again.

The Volvo's bumper hit the hillside with a loud thunk, but Laura didn't hesitate as she yanked the steering wheel and shifted gears.

I realized that a three-point turn had been optimistic. Maybe the boat-like Volvo could have done it under the best of circumstances. But panic had replaced precision. We were going to have to shift forward, then back, at least one more time before we could fully clear the turn.

My scalp throbbed and a trickle of something wet ran down the back of my head. I didn't reach up to touch it. I knew it was blood.

Laura swore and cranked the steering wheel as tight as it would go. I braced myself, praying again that we wouldn't overshoot the ledge. We were nearly perpendicular to the road now.

"Bitch," Red Mask hissed through his swollen, grinning lips. White Mask was on his feet now too, brushing dust off his hoodie. I shrank away from the open window on the passenger's side as both men closed in. Any second, they would grab me again. This time, they would pull me out of the car.

"Hurry! Get in the backseat!" Laura shrieked. She hit the gas and the Volvo jerked forward another few feet, dangerously close to both men—and the cliff ledge.

I scrambled over the tangle of wires and debris between the two front bucket seats, desperately trying not to touch the gearshift. I pushed one foot against the console and dove into the backseat. The boombox caught on my sandal straps and clanked hard against the shell of the missing glove box.

When I whipped around, Red Mask was leaning into the passenger-side window again, grasping the inside door handle—which didn't budge. God, I loved the Volvo.

Red Mask swore again as the Volvo lurched backward one more time. He lost his grip on the inner door handle. This time, instead of backing away, he kept pace with us until the bumper of the Volvo brushed the hillside and Laura was forced to brake.

From the backseat, I watched in terror as Red Mask abruptly gave up on trying to get inside the passenger-side door. He took a step back then suddenly dropped to the ground. I couldn't see him anymore. What was he doing? "Laur," I stumbled. "Is your door locked?" I glanced between the doors in the backseat, reassuring myself that both locks were down. I craned my neck to see where he'd gone.

"Locked," Laura gasped as she successfully shifted into drive. "Hang on," she hissed. This was it: the final point of the turn. It would be close, but we would barely clear the turn. We had to.

My eyes flicked to White Mask, who was just standing there, staring at the place where Red Mask had been. The thought zipped through my mind that he wasn't sure what to do now—that they didn't have a cohesive plan. This wasn't an organized attack. They were winging it—and White Mask had lost his place in the script.

If there was a silver lining, that was it.

Laura cranked the steering wheel and hit the gas. I squeezed my eyes shut and held on tight, wishing I'd had time to scramble for a seatbelt in the backseat.

The Volvo flew forward only a few feet before Laura slammed on the brakes and screamed. I opened my eyes to see that she'd let go of the steering wheel again. I could still hear the soft rumble of the engine. It wasn't stalled, but we weren't moving.

I followed Laura's terrified gaze to see that Red Mask had reappeared near the front of the Volvo. This time, he was holding something in his hand: a large, jagged-looking rock.

Before Laura could duck for cover, he slammed the rock down on the windshield. I felt the impact as much as I heard it. The glass took the rock's blow with a deafening crack, webbing into a spidery hematoma that covered most of the driver's side windshield.

I knew that any second, he would reach through the window again and grab the keys. Laura wasn't even holding onto the gearshift anymore.

I watched in mute horror as he lifted the rock again. Would he use it on us, too? How much would it hurt to die that way? Would every blow register, or would that first strike be the last thing I felt? I pictured his real eyes, set deep in the mask, as he balanced the rock in one hand, studying the damage he'd done. I couldn't see his real lips either, but I imagined them twisted into that same exaggerated, latex smile.

Apparently satisfied that we weren't going anywhere, Red Mask dropped the rock and muttered something over his shoulder. Then he walked around to the passenger side of the Volvo. This time, he leaned all the way inside and grabbed hold of Laura's shirt, grunting as he tried to pull her toward him.

Gathering every ounce of courage I could, I felt for the boombox wedged into the missing glove box. I gripped the handle tight in one hand, lifted it up, then rammed it toward his arm.

Laura screamed again, and for a moment I thought that I had hit her, not him.

The force of impact had pushed him—and Laura—roughly forward toward the front of the car. He let go of her for just a moment and stumbled away from the car. And then, impossibly, Laura released the clutch and pushed on the gas.

The Volvo shot forward one more time and finally cleared the turn, moving onto open road.

6

We were free.

For a few seconds, neither of us said anything. The two men stood in the middle of the road as we drove away. They were both screaming obscenities—at us, and at each other. I watched them until the dirt road dipped, then curved, and the only thing visible through the back windshield was the endless hills.

I drew in a ragged breath and collapsed against the backseat, fumbling for a seatbelt. My hands shook violently as I tried to make sense of the tangled belts and receivers. Nobody ever rode in the backseat—and now I remembered why. Where seatbelts should have been, I found one empty metal receiver and a broken lap belt instead.

I stopped pawing for a seatbelt, realizing for the first time that one of my fingernails was throbbing. It had been partially torn off. In the dark, it looked like a broken seashell, clinging to my pointer finger by a thread. For a second, I thought I might throw up. I stopped looking at it and sat back in the seat, careful not to let the back of my head rest against the dirty fabric. My scalp hummed with a hot, prickly ache.

"Liv, are you okay? Do you still have my phone?" Laura asked from the front seat, her voice stretched and uneven. She brushed at her right arm violently as she clutched the wheel and moved her head back and forth, trying to see out the smashed windshield as she drove. "Do you still have the phone?" she asked again. She leaned closer to the steering wheel and tilted her head to see through another pocket of unbroken glass as the road curved.

"I dropped it when he grabbed me." The last word came out as a whisper. I couldn't believe what had just happened. "I'll find it," I added quickly, careful not to look at my finger as I scrambled over the glove compartment's exposed hole and back into the passenger seat. I clicked the semi-functional seatbelt into place then started feeling around on the floorboards.

"Are you okay?" Laura asked again, her voice nearly lost in the wind rushing through the open window. "When he had you by the hair, I thought ..." She trailed off.

I blinked back the tears that suddenly prickled behind my eyes, unwilling to let myself feel the full horror of the situation. I needed to find that phone. "I'm okay," I managed. "Are you?" When I glanced up at her, I saw a volley of deep scratches running from her bare shoulder to her elbow. They looked angry and bloody, even in the dim light.

She grimaced as we hit a pothole in the dirt road head on. "I'm fine—but I can barely see through the windshield." She unclipped her seatbelt, tucking one leg underneath her and leaning forward in the driver's seat so that her face was nearer to the windshield—and one of the small clear patches among the glass webbing. "There, that's better."

She hit the gas harder, and the Volvo flew faster down the dirt road. We were still miles from civilization, but we were headed in the right direction. "Do you hate me?" she asked after a moment.

"Why would I hate you?" I asked incredulously, pausing my search for the phone to glance behind us, scanning the shadowy hills for any sign of approaching headlights. There was nothing.

"I dragged you out here tonight, even though you had to work, and then I didn't listen to you. You knew something was wrong, and I kept telling you everything was fine."

I shook my head. "No. I have to be dragged everywhere. And I always think something is wrong. You know that."

"But this time you were right," she choked. "What if they'd gotten us out of the car?"

"They didn't," I said firmly. Those words sent a shudder of relief through me. "They didn't," I repeated. "That's all that matters."

I kept rummaging along the floorboards, feeling for the outline of the flip phone until I heard Laura whisper, "Shit."

I sat up and whipped around to look behind us. Just before we rounded a curve, I caught a glimpse of headlights.

7

"Maybe it's not them," Laura stammered. "It could be…"

She trailed off. It was them.

The tires crunched on the road through the open window. In a matter of seconds, the truck's brights filled our rearview mirror.

"Hurry, find the phone," Laura begged. "I'm going as fast as I can, but I don't want to overshoot a turn."

My fingers felt a rectangular edge on the floorboards. I seized it —only to realize it was a tape deck. Not the phone.

"We just have to make it to the paved road. Then it's only a few more miles until we get service, right?" she said in a rush. "Do you remember where we were when you sent that text to Tish?"

I shook my head miserably, wishing I'd thought to look for a landmark when I saw that last flickering bar of service. "I don't know."

The Volvo picked up speed as we moved downhill into a straightaway.

She took the next curve without braking, which pushed my shoulder hard against the base of the gearshift. A metallic thud sounded next to my feet and I quickly reached down to grab hold of the phone that had thunked against the console.

"Got it," I said hoarsely, trying to calm my shaking hands, trying to focus.

The brights behind us blazed into full view, and Laura floored the gas again. "Keep redialing," she prompted, shifting the Volvo into second gear.

The phone's dim screen lit up as I opened the flip phone and redialed 9-1-1.

The number blinked on the screen as the cell searched for a signal.

Then, like before, the call failed.

I tried again and again. This time the call would connect. Dispatch would answer. Someone would find us and help us. I rehearsed what I would say when they answered. *When.*

Call failed.
Call failed.
Call failed.
Battery low.

I clutched the seatbelt and set the phone on my lap as Laura took another turn. My head hurt, and my stomach was roiling again. Gingerly, I reached up to touch my disheveled hair and felt something slick and raw beneath it.

I wiped my hand against the side of my halter top, watching the sequins turn dark with my blood.

Laura began to cry as the truck blinked its brights on and off in that maniacal Morse code. It nosed closer. Her soft, snuffling tears grew into loud hysterical sobs, but her hands stayed glued to the steering wheel. Her gaze flicked steadily back and forth between the road and the rearview mirror.

My throat tightened as I heard the steady roar of the truck's engine behind us, its flashing brights filling up our mirrors.

The turnoff to the paved road suddenly appeared in our headlights.

"Okay, we made it this far, now if we can just get back to—" Laura choked out.

The truck stayed right behind us, slowing down just enough to take the turn onto the paved road in pursuit without flying over the ledge on the other side.

The paved straightaway that stretched out before us was long compared to the meandering curves of the dirt road. I clenched one hand around the seatbelt at my waist. Would we make it to one more switchback? Let alone to the point where we'd have cell reception again? I brought the phone back to my ear, dialing and redialing, watching the dark road for any sign of another car.

The headlights closed in quickly, even though we had picked up speed so that the air rushing inside the passenger window drowned out everything but the engine's drone and the down-notes of Laura's sobs.

The Volvo suddenly rattled hard. Was something falling apart? The bumper? Part of the undercarriage? The engine itself? I couldn't see the speedometer, but I was certain that nobody had ever gone this fast in the Volvo for a very long time. The ancient car maxed out at fifty-five on a good day—and we were going much faster than that on the downhill now.

The car shuddered so hard that my seatbelt caught.

I jolted forward.

The men in the truck had hit us from behind.

Before I could process what had happened, they hit us again, more forcefully this time. The pathetic boombox tumbled against my leg and clattered to the floorboards. The sound of metal colliding with metal punctuated the rush of air outside the car.

"What the hell are we supposed to do now?" Laura choked out. The truck backed off slightly then gunned its engine again and barreled toward us. She shot me a panicked look, as if I really might know the answer.

My brain spun through every worst-case scenario I'd ever imagined. Nothing like this had ever crossed my mind as something I might need to prepare for. I had absolutely no idea what to do next.

Laura drew her shoulders up, bracing for impact. I grabbed hold of the window frame and planted my feet against the floorboards.

"Just keep going," I screamed over the wind. "No matter what, keep going." The truck was a beast, but the Volvo was a tank. As long as the wheels didn't come off, it would keep us safe.

As I braced for the next hit, something in the distance made me forget about the blood in my hair and the *failed signal* message on Laura's phone.

More headlights.

8

The truck didn't ram us again.

The driver must have seen the set of approaching headlights, too. He fell back to a safe following distance and turned off the truck's brights, looking like just any other vehicle on the road.

A knot of determination grew out of the fear churning in my stomach. We had to get the other car's attention—let them know we needed help.

"How do I turn on the Volvo's hazards?" I barked, trying to find the little orange triangle on the console.

"They don't work," Laura wailed, flashing her brights erratically.

"Then slow down. Roll down your window! Hurry!" My voice was hoarse, thin. I swallowed, getting ready to scream as loudly as I could.

Laura was already rolling down her window and screaming, flashing the brights again and again while she waved her arm wildly, even though the oncoming vehicle was still several cars' lengths away.

The Volvo weaved dangerously on the road while Laura struggled to keep the car in position, poking her head out the window to see instead of peering through the shattered windshield.

Leaning as far as I could next to her on the driver's side, I cleared my throat and tried to make my voice carry over the wind, too. "Help, we need help!"

I made out the silhouette of the lone driver in a white suburban as it drew closer.

Time seemed to expand as our vehicles approached one another and Laura leaned farther out the window, causing the Volvo to wobble violently in our lane. For a moment, before Laura could correct our path, we veered over the centerline, toward the Suburban.

I felt more than saw the other driver's eyes rest on us and on the shitty Volvo weaving out of its lane. His attention was on us—not on the truck that had fallen back a significant distance behind us. My stomach sank.

"Help us!" I screamed again at his closed driver's side window, willing him to look at the broken windshield, to understand that something awful had happened. That something worse would happen if he didn't intervene.

The driver was an older man with a short gray beard and bushy eyebrows. His mouth was turned down in a deep frown. Our eyes met for a fraction of a second, and he shook his head in disgust.

Then, raising his middle finger, he was gone.

Laura left her arm hanging limply over the edge of the driver's side door for a few seconds before she slowly pulled it back inside and rolled up the window, tucking her leg beneath her once more and leaning forward so she could see through the windshield. I twisted around in my seat and stared through the back windshield, my hand at my throat.

The white suburban passed the truck without slowing down, its red taillights disappearing around the bend. I imagined the driver, still indignant, still shaking his head. *Drunk kids driving down the canyon at night, going to kill somebody.*

I watched with morbid expectancy as the truck flashed its brights at us and picked up speed again.

"No," I whispered. Laura kept silent. The tears on her cheeks had dried in the wind.

The sound of the truck's engine grew steadily louder. In no time, their front bumper was inches from our tailgate again.

Laura slammed the gas, and for the next half a mile we somehow stayed just ahead of them.

If we could make it a few more miles, we'd get cell service back. I dialed 9-1-1 again and again, losing track of how many times I had heard the beeping message. *No service.*

I touched my hair again. Some of the blood was starting to dry against my scalp, but I could still feel a wet trickle down the back of my head. What else would Red Mask do if given the opportunity?

I was pretty sure I already knew the answer to that question.

I opened the glove box then thrust my hand into the shallow storage area beneath the arm rest, searching for anything sharp. Anything we could use to arm ourselves. The boombox at my feet had worked once, but it was so heavy and unwieldy I wasn't sure how useful it really was.

I found a bottle of ibuprofen. A book. Insurance papers. Pens. Everything and nothing.

"We have to be close," Laura said desperately, flicking her gaze from the windshield to the cell phone pressed against my ear. "Just keep trying, Liv."

We slowed down a little to take another sharp curve, skidding dangerously close to the drop-off. The truck veered sharply into the left lane alongside us.

I kept the phone to my ear and concentrated, counting to ten between each redial in an effort to save the remaining battery life. Laura floored the gas and edged in front of the truck. She wasn't about to let them pass us again. I held my breath, straining my eyes for any sign of headlights in the distance. In the center of the road, we were playing chicken with a head-on collision, but that idea wasn't nearly as scary as the possibility of letting them stop us again.

If we could stay ahead of them a little longer, we'd get service back and the call would finally connect. I gritted my teeth and redialed, listening for the beep above the wind rushing through the open window and the sound of the papers and wrappers in the backseat skittering like nervous animals.

Instead of attempting to pass us again, the truck stayed even with our back tires. As we entered the next short straightaway, I brought the phone away from my ear to check on the battery on Laura's phone. Fifteen percent.

I looked through the back windshield just in time to see the truck nose into the left lane, then swerve toward us, hitting the Volvo's back left bumper with a grating squeal and a dull *thunk*.

We were already moving way too fast—barely in control, barely able to see through the webbed windshield. Laura gasped as the Volvo pulled hard toward the right side of the road, pumping the brakes and jerking the steering wheel to the left in a frantic attempt to correct the Volvo's forward path.

Thunk. Another strike to the edge of the bumper.

The rush of blackness outside my window seemed to fill the car as the truck veered toward us again, hitting our rear passenger side. My head whipped forward as I desperately tried to follow what was happening. The phone, still blinking *No Service* in my hand, slipped out of my grasp once more and hit the dash with a *crack*.

I braced for the next impact and tried to tug the seatbelt tighter. I could no longer see the grade of the hillside to our left.

We'd overcorrected.

My vision swam with dots. The gravel under our tires crunched out a warning that we were crossing onto the narrow shoulder.

The tires scrambled for purchase on dirt as Laura tried to pull us back into the center of the lane. Her voice was thick and syrupy in my ears, like it came from underwater. "They're … trying to run us off the road."

The truck struck our rear fender this time, and the Volvo's back tires spun as Laura cranked the wheel again.

Another blow.

I suddenly remembered that Laura wasn't wearing a seatbelt anymore.

Our front left tire dipped over the edge. The sharp edge of the boombox, then the light tap of the phone, clunked against my foot. I didn't reach down to grab it. Instead, I clung to the floppy seatbelt, afraid to move, afraid to look out the window at the slope of the dark hillside yawning much too close.

"Laura!" I gasped. "Put on your seatbelt!"

Her eyes widened, and she let go of the wheel with one hand to reach for the seatbelt.

Before she could click it into place, the truck hit us again.

It was more of a nudge than a blow. A careful, almost gentle tap.

A whiff of exhaust drifted through the window as the headlights backed away from the ledge. And then the Volvo began to slide downhill.

9

I braced for the car to flip end over end, like a scene from *Mission Impossible*. Instead, we slid a few feet then stopped when the tires sank into the soft dirt at the top of the grade.

The Volvo made a metallic groaning noise.

I twisted to unbuckle my seatbelt, and the tires slid another few inches.

Laura gasped. I froze. Had I done that?

The headlights behind us grew fainter as the truck pulled away, plunging us back into complete darkness aside from the Volvo's dim headlights, obscured by a tangle of feathery sagebrush smashed against the front grill of the car.

Move, I told my legs. *Do something,* I screamed at my hands, willing them to unbuckle the seatbelt so I could hurl myself through the open passenger window. Anything seemed preferable to careening down the slope toward the murky valley in the foothills below. Even taking our chances on the road.

But I couldn't move. I could barely even breathe, terrified that any tiny movement would send the car sliding again.

Laura met my gaze in horror. In one hand, she held her own detached seatbelt buckle. In the other, she held the driver's side door handle. Her eyes met mine, asking the same unanswerable question slamming through my brain: *What now?*

* * *

At the end of Tish's senior year, Laura, Tish, and I had taken a road trip to Silverwood, a theme park in Northern Idaho. A last hurrah until we joined her at college.

Tish and Laura spent weeks mapping out the entire park, starting with Roller Coaster Alley.

I spent weeks fretting about whether I would chicken out on the very first ride and asking Jeeves to investigate whether anybody had ever died at Silverwood.

They hadn't. But there was always a first time.

"Tremors," a wooden roller coaster that arced above the highest treetops, was the first stop on the map. The wooden track was an enormous tangle of complicated joists and beams. Some of the wood on the support beams was splintering just a little. When was this thing built? How much did engineers know back then?

I put on my best smile until the creaky metal bar came down across my lap and the ride attendant—a gum-popping kid with a greasy center part—walked back to the control deck.

The lap bar was a full six inches above my waist. My hands, slippery with sweat, were not going to be able to hold on tight enough when I passed out. I knew with every cell in my body that I was going to fall out of the coaster cart. My body, caught in the momentum of the twisting coaster, would be smashed into the tracks. The jolt would derail the entire coaster. I would die, and so would everyone else.

"Laura," I begged, not wanting Tish—who had agreed to ride solo in front of us—to hear me. "I can't. I can't do this. I'm sorry. I can't. I shouldn't have come."

She let go of the lap bar with one hand to link one arm through mine, anchoring me tight beside her. "I've got you, Liv," she said simply.

The rickety coaster cart was already chugging up the first steep incline.

My vision blurred. The Life cereal I'd eaten for breakfast churned. Laura squeezed my arm, whispering something about *fun*.

The gears pulled the line of faded sky-blue coaster carts steadily up the first hill. With each tick of the chain, I watched the cars in the parking lot and the trees shrink. I darted my eyes across the track, trying to determine our path. All I could see was the dark tunnel at the bottom of the first hill: a tiny black mouth that disappeared underground. It looked way too small to accommodate the long line of coaster carts.

I imagined myself flopping to the side of the cart, where my head would hit the edge of the tunnel and explode in a mess of brains.

Laura squeezed my arm harder. The first coaster cart had crested the top of the slope and was hanging over the other side, inching forward while the back cars struggled to the top.

Laura and I were in the middle. The tipping point. As soon as our car reached the slope, gravity would take over and pull the entire line of coaster cars down, down, down into the tunnel.

Our car ticked to the top of the slope, and I let go of the bar for a split second to wipe my sweaty hands on my pants. I tore my eyes away from the impossibly tiny black mouth at the bottom of the slope to look at Laura.

Her eyes were squeezed shut. "Don't let go, okay, Liv?" she whispered.

It wasn't until that moment that I realized she was scared too.

The surprise jolted me out of my panic just long enough that when the cars tipped forward and began their race down the first hill, I stopped thinking about my body getting ground into the track ties like hamburger.

Instead, I locked my arm into Laura's as tight as she was holding onto me and squeezed back.

That was the last time I rode a roller coaster. Laura and Tish rode the Panic Plunge, Stunt Pilot, Timber Terror, and Corkscrew together, while I stood in line for Elephant Ears and cotton candy. Neither of them teased me about being a chicken or a baby.

We rode the Ferris wheel together at the end of the day, arms linked tight while the enclosed gondolas drifted above the park and the sun melted into the trees.

They've got me, I told myself when the flutters in my stomach turned to pinpricks of doubt over the structural integrity of the bolts holding our gondola in place.

They've got me.

Sometimes, in my nightmares, I still found myself balanced precariously at the very top of a rickety wooden track set to plunge into a tunnel.

I always woke up, sweaty and breathing hard, before the coaster cart tipped.

10

The Volvo's headlights blinked erratically. It moaned and slid a few more feet, pitching Laura and I forward roughly.

"Liv?" Laura whispered, her voice small and shaky.

It unfroze something in me. If we didn't get out of the car now, things were going to get much worse.

"Come on, we have to get out—" Before the words had left my mouth, before I had committed to pressing the button to unbuckle my own seatbelt, the Volvo began rolling downhill again.

The coaster cart had reached its tipping point.

The wheels clunked faster as the front tires hit packed dirt and gained traction on the incline.

"No," Laura shrieked. "No, my seatbelt—"

We hit a large rock with a sudden *bang* that flung both of us against the dash.

I gasped, pushing myself back against the seat. Our headlights illuminated a line of scraggly pines before we made impact.

The tree trunks were small enough that I could have wrapped both hands around them, fingers touching. Gawky mountain transplants that managed to grab a foothold in the sagebrush-dotted hills and crumbling, dry dirt. They weren't enough to stop our flight. When we hit the trees, the loose lap belt snapped tight against my waist with a sudden vise grip while the shoulder belt went slack. The impact flung me forward as the airbags deployed.

The seatbelt strap dug tighter into my stomach, forcing the air from my lungs while the airbag enveloped my head, covering my nose and mouth, making it impossible to draw a breath.

The vehicle bucked and shuddered like a spooked horse, picking up speed as it ran down the hillside, clanging and screaming each time it collided with a new hazard.

I couldn't see. I couldn't breathe. I couldn't hear Laura's screams anymore—just the sound of air rushing through the open window and the vehicle itself banging and squealing, moving faster and faster downhill.

Bam, bam, BAM. We hit something substantial with a teeth-rattling slam, mowing it down in a series of rapid-fire blows to the undercarriage.

With each hit, the impact threw me against the seat, then forward against the airbag.

I managed to push myself back from the airbag and tried to draw a gulp of air.

All I got was a fresh mouthful of dust. I coughed violently, desperate for oxygen as the Volvo crashed forward. White dots prickled through my vision, and I was sure I was going to pass out.

Protect your head. Protect your neck. Brace for impact. Keep fighting, my brain demanded on repeat, grasping at fragments I'd heard again and again on *Secrets to Survival.*

I tried to reach my hands up to the back of my neck, screaming Laura's name before my face pressed into the dusty air bag yet again.

Brush and dirt from outside the vehicle flew inside the open passenger window like shrapnel, slicing at my arms, catching in my hair, and filling my mouth, eyes, and nose as I gasped and coughed.

I pushed back from the air bag again and clawed at the tight lap belt, drawing in another ragged, dusty breath before being jerked forward like a rag doll.

The useless shoulder belt flopped around my chest. My lungs were on fire, and my vision swirled with indecipherable shapes of light and dark as the headlights bounced and cut out.

Bang.

Slam.

Clang.

When would we hit the tree trunk thick enough to kill us?

Impossibly, the car kept sliding—either smashing across or through everything in its path like the tank it was.

Laura hadn't screamed again. I couldn't see her. I couldn't tell how far we'd slid—and whether we were moments from plunging into the river on the valley floor or over a ledge that would finally tip us end over end.

The undercarriage groaned and the wheels caught as soil turned sandy beneath us. I pushed myself away from the air bag, fighting with the pillowy fabric and trying desperately to see through the smashed windshield.

The Volvo slowed to a crawl, tires sinking into the soft dirt. The body of the car was nearly level with the ground beneath now.

And then, abruptly, everything stopped moving.

The car moaned as if in pain when we finally ground to a complete stop where the foothills leveled off on the valley floor. I coughed violently in the sudden stillness. It felt like my lungs were filled with more dust than air.

The ringing in my ears slowly subsided, and the quiet rush of water a short distance away drew my attention. The air was thick with the smell of sage. I blinked and wiped my eyes, trying to see through the stinging sand and filth that had pelted my face. As my vision cleared and I squinted through the open passenger window, I saw we had come to a stop in a clearing right beside the river's edge.

In a haze, I turned to Laura, who was leaning against the driver's side window. Her face was mostly obscured by a billow from the airbag. Her body was turned away from me, twisted at an awkward angle against the window.

I blinked hard, realizing that the driver's side airbag wasn't nearly as full as mine. It had only partially deployed.

My relief that we had made it to the valley floor alive turned sick and sour.

"Laura?" I whispered, my voice raw and unsteady. "Are you okay?" In the darkness beyond the narrow beam of light cast by the Volvo's one surviving headlight, a bird shrieked in the night.

Laura didn't answer. I unbuckled my seatbelt and gently nudged her shoulder, pressing down on the corners of the airbag so I could see her face.

Her eyes were closed and her mouth hung slightly open, the deep purple lipstick that had been flawless earlier was now smeared across her chin like blood.

Was she dead? "Please, no," I whimpered, straining to hear her breathing. I couldn't stop myself from coughing violently again.

I pressed two fingers gently against her throat. She suddenly groaned, rolling away from me onto the inflated portion of the airbag. My shoulders slumped with relief, and I shifted to a kneeling position on the passenger seat. When I brushed the pale strands of hair away from her face, she mumbled something.

"Laur? What hurts? Can you move? Can you hear me?"

She moaned in response but didn't try to move again.

The Volvo's remaining headlight flickered erratically then went out, wrapping our wreck in a blanket of darkness. The vehicle made a tired-sounding sigh, followed by a loud bang somewhere in the bowels of the undercarriage, then quivered into silence. I hadn't even noticed that the Volvo was still running until the hum beneath my seat went still.

11

"Laura," I whispered again, my voice catching as the buzz of adrenaline threatened to spill into tears. Something acrid wafted through the open window. Was it smoke? Fluid from the vehicle? Were we safer inside the car or out? Was this what the men in the truck had wanted all along?

I squeezed my eyes shut, pushing the unanswerable questions away.

Right now, I really needed to know how serious Laura's injuries were.

As my eyes adjusted to the dark, I leaned close to Laura, trying to see how badly she'd been injured. There was a lump the size of a plum swelling on her forehead, near her left temple. She shifted in her seat again but kept her eyes closed.

She was moving. That must mean no spinal or neck injury, but I wasn't a doctor. I wasn't anybody. The only thing I knew for certain was that I should keep her as motionless as possible until help arrived.

If help arrived. The only people who had any idea that our car had crashed were the two men in masks who had run us off the road.

I stared out the open passenger window, looking up the hillside. *At least they're gone.*

As quickly as the thought materialized in my mind, a dim beam of light flickered then disappeared so briefly I wondered if I'd imagined it.

My mouth went dry. Surely that wasn't their headlights. But what if it was?

Had the men in the truck sped off into the night the moment the Volvo started rolling into the foothills? Had they watched the entire horrifying descent from the edge of the road until our headlights were swallowed up by the valley? Or were they up there now, waiting, on the off chance we had survived and would try to make our way back up the hill?

The flickering light didn't appear again. There was only darkness and the quiet rush of the river.

Whatever they were doing up there didn't matter right now. What mattered was Laura.

The unfamiliar emotion prickling through my veins wasn't panic anymore. It was something like outrage. I replayed the memory of smashing the boombox onto the man's arm and hoped I'd done at least a little damage.

The indignation stunned me enough that I stopped worrying about the bump on Laura's head and the fact that we were alone in the middle of the hills without any chance of rescue. I'd been bracing for something bad to happen for as long as I could remember. Ever vigilant, ever anxious, Olivia Heath.

The bad thing had finally happened. But—for now at least—both Laura and I were still alive. If I played my cards right, it would stay that way.

I decided this wasn't a *Dateline* episode about two silly, scantily clad college girls going missing on their way to a party at Coffin Creek after all. This was an episode of *Secrets to Survival.*

Laura shifted in her seat and took a raspy breath, drawing me back to the present. "Laura?" I whispered. "Can you hear me?"

Even in the dark, without a clear view of Laura's injuries, my stomach turned a little when I thought about the bump on her head. And that bump probably paled in comparison to whatever internal wounds I couldn't see. "Stay still, okay Laur? It's going to be okay. I just need to think for a minute."

I pictured Tish at the library, cell phone on airplane mode, dutifully cracking open another textbook. When she finally left, she'd see my text with the license plate and smile. *Typical Olivia.* Then she'd go to bed, thinking we were at the bonfire.

When she found our beds unmade in the morning, surely she'd know something was wrong. She'd call her and Laura's parents. She'd text my mom. Maybe she'd even enlist Tony to find out whether any of his fellow Deltas remembered seeing us at the party.

Someone would call the police. Tish would give them the license plate number. They would find us.

We would survive.

But none of that would happen tonight.

I wrapped my arms around myself in the chilly air, suddenly hyperaware of the goosebumps on my raw skin. It was much colder down here than it had been on the road, and it couldn't be much later than 9:00 p.m. The temperature was only going to drop as the night deepened.

Just how cold would it get? Cold enough to freeze? I thought of the camping trips I'd taken at Blue Lake with my parents when I was younger. Even with a sleeping bag, I'd shivered all night long, zipping the flap over my head and curling my knees to my chest.

The irony that we might have escaped the psychopaths on the road only to freeze to death in the canyon felt razor sharp. I couldn't let the story end this way.

Laura hadn't moved again. I watched her chest rise and fall as reassurance that at least she was breathing easily while I took inventory of our options.

When someone drove up the canyon looking for us—tomorrow, most likely—they would eventually find the place where the Volvo went off the road. With all the brush and dirt that was now inside the car—and stuck to my clothing—we must have left some kind of trail. There might even be skid marks and tire tracks on the road where the pavement met the soft dirt at the top of the grade.

My mind spun as I tried to remember who else had RSVPed to the bonfire tonight.

A bunch of drunk college students, came the easy answer. Nobody would bat an eye if Laura and I didn't show up tonight.

A faraway howl, followed by a volley of answering yips, broke through the steady burble of the river. Coyotes? I shrank against the dirty seat, feeling a sharp branch dig into my back. It sounded like they were just past the wreck.

Despite the dim light, I could see my breath as it came in fast, shallow puffs.

I refocused my attention on the rise and fall of Laura's chest, desperately wishing she could help me think through our options. Thankfully, the acrid smell I'd detected earlier had all but disappeared. The ancient Volvo felt like our safe haven again.

Laura should stay where she was in the car. She wasn't in any condition to bushwhack. But what about me? Should I stay with her until help arrived? Find a way to keep warm? Should I leave her and hike until I could call 9-1-1?

Laura's phone.

I froze. Where was it?

My own phone was still tucked safely inside the travel pouch at my waist. I pulled it out, bracing to see a black screen—but it lit up as soon as I flipped it open, the screen blinking a low-battery warning of one percent. There was every reason to think it might die after one more call.

I frowned. Laura's phone had substantially more juice left—but only if I could find it.

I remembered the feel of the little rectangle hitting my foot right before we went over the edge of the road. But I had no idea whether it was even inside the car anymore. Plenty of debris had flown into the open window as we careened down the hillside in a horrifying roller coaster ride. Had the phone been thrown out, too?

The car hadn't flipped. Some of the papers and trash were still scattered around the vehicle. The phone had to be nearby.

Unbuckling my seatbelt, I leaned down and began frantically running my hands along the grimy car floor and into every crack and crevice, repeating the same desperate dance I'd done earlier.

All of it could have been avoided if I just had some goddamn pockets.

This time, no matter how many times I swept my hands between the crack and around the debris on the floor, I couldn't find the phone. It simply wasn't there.

Laura moaned, but I didn't look up this time. In the darkness, my fingers ran along sharp, leafy, unidentifiable objects that would have made me draw back in disgust an hour earlier. The fingernail on my pointer finger must have come off at some point during the chaos earlier, but I barely felt it anymore. I just wanted to feel the familiar shape of Laura's tiny flip phone in my hand again.

"Shit. Please, God. Please, please, please," I prayed, even though I hadn't been to church all year. Not since Christmas, when my mom had dragged my dad and me to midnight mass.

I forced myself to slow down, methodically feeling the nasty carpet under my feet, even underneath Laura's feet, crouching and then carefully reaching past her, running my hands along the dirty driver's side.

I climbed over the console and into the backseat, carefully inching past Laura's slumped frame so as not to jostle her.

A chorus of yips and howls started up again, close enough this time that I paused to look out the open passenger window for glowing eyes.

Nothing.

NOELLE W. IHLI

I kept my hands crawling over every surface, slow and desperate.

No phone. And nothing even remotely useful to keep us warm —except maybe Tony's mesh gym shorts. I grabbed the slippery material and slid it over my arms, catching a whiff of cologne.

Teeth chattering, I finally pulled my legs up to my chest in the backseat, hugging myself and mumbling the same rambling prayer. From somewhere beyond the Volvo, there was another shriek and another chorus of yips and howls.

I blinked back tears of frustration and lay my head on my knees. I would make one more pass of the car, and if I couldn't find it, I'd take my chances with the one-percent battery. "Dear God, help me find that fucking phone," I prayed aloud to whoever might be listening.

From the front seat, Laura coughed. Then, to my amazement, she laughed softly. "Can't swear ... in a prayer, Liv. Cancels ... the whole thing."

My head snapped up. Laura had pushed herself upright in the driver's seat. One of her eyes drooped a little, and she swayed slightly as she touched the lump forming near her temple, but she was conscious. She smiled wearily.

For a moment, I couldn't speak past the lump in my throat. I leaned forward and touched her arm, wanting to throw my arms around her but too afraid to touch her. "You're okay?" I finally choked out.

Laura winced as she shifted in the seat and lifted something up for me to see. "I don't know about 'okay,'" she said, her words thick and slow, "but my phone is right here."

12

Laura's phone had bounced off the dash and landed on her lap when we hit the first bump on our flight down the hillside. She'd managed to tuck it under her legs before her head hit the window and she lost consciousness.

At first, I couldn't stop shaking and crying. I still wasn't sure what we should do next, but I wasn't alone anymore. And we had a phone with enough battery power if we could just get it to connect.

"There might be blankets … in the trunk," Laura managed as she shifted in her seat, wincing as she tried to peer outside the car. The cracked, dirty windshield had fogged up and was starting to crystallize as the moisture froze. It was impossible to see much of anything now, except through the open passenger-side window. "They're gross. But better than those shorts."

I let out a choked laugh, pushing aside the memory of the howls I'd heard a few minutes earlier, and grabbed the keys Laura passed to me.

It took some effort to open the backseat doors. One wouldn't budge at all, and the other was wedged against the skinny trunk of a small pine the car had demolished before coming to rest on the loose soil in the clearing near the riverbank. I finally managed to kick it open with a hollow-sounding *clank* and the crack of snapping branches.

My flats sank into the sandy soil and dirt poured inside my shoes. Keeping one hand on the dusty Volvo, I turned in a slow circle, trying to orient myself in the consuming darkness outside the car. The sound of the river burbled quietly, and a breeze whispered through the brush flanking the river on both sides. For now, the coyotes were quiet.

One more time, I strained my eyes for any sign of headlights from the road tucked somewhere above the sloping hills. But all I could see were stars, burning impossibly bright in the velvet sky. The night was silent now, except for the soft coo of an owl in the distance. I took a deep breath of cold, fresh air.

Shivering hard, I hurried to the trunk and inserted the key. It opened easily enough—and inside I found not one but two blankets shoved into the very back. From the way they peeled like Velcro from the coarse fabric lining the trunk, they might have been there as long as the car had existed.

I squealed softly with delight then made a quick retreat to the safety of the Volvo, climbing in through the backseat then over the console next to Laura.

I shrugged off Tony's gym shorts then carefully tucked one of the scratchy flannel blankets around Laura's shoulders. I wrapped the other around myself, already feeling warmer.

We just reset the clock, I told myself.

Any time the host of *Secrets to Survival* covered a wilderness survival story, he repeated the same advice. It went something like, "You just have to remember the rule of threes. You can survive three minutes without air. Three hours without shelter. Three days without water. Three weeks without food. First things first, and you'll survive."

I wrapped the blanket tighter around my body. What was the rule of threes for the terrifying chase with the men in the truck that had sent Laura and me plummeting to the valley floor?

Three seconds before he pulls you from the car by your hair.

Three minutes of sliding through the hills without a proper airbag or seatbelt.

I shivered and hugged the blanket tighter, unwilling to imagine what three hours might have brought if Laura hadn't been able to restart the Volvo.

I pushed the memory of their grinning masks away. We could both breathe again. We now had some kind of shelter—and even water if we got desperate enough to risk drinking from the river. Tish would realize we were missing in the morning and send help. There was no need to think past the morning. We just had to sit tight.

For the first time, a tentative blossom of hope ignited in my chest.

As long as the rule of threes held out, we still had a fighting chance.

Laura lay her head down on the partially inflated, dusty airbag like a pillow. I leaned over the dash so I could snuggle up against her side.

The coyotes bickered in the distance, farther away than before, and I relaxed a little more. Neither of us were shivering quite so violently anymore, even with the open window. I flipped open Laura's phone and studied the bright screen, in case the deceptive service bar had suddenly appeared. It hadn't.

Before I closed the phone, I turned the light toward Laura, reminding myself that the dark smears on her face were lipstick, not blood. "Hey, open your eyes for a second."

She squinted into the light. "Why?"

I snapped the phone shut. One of her pupils was significantly larger than the other. "Does your stomach hurt?"

She frowned. "Yeah, a little."

"You definitely have a concussion," I said as matter-of-factly as I could, not wanting her to worry. I could worry enough for both of us.

"Maybe I should take the phone and try to get a signal, so I can call for help," I said slowly. I really didn't want to get out of the Volvo or walk through the darkness by myself, but Laura's injury had me worried. What was the rule of threes for concussions?

Laura grunted. "Tish will ... realize something is wrong," she murmured. "Let's sleep while we wait."

"Laura, no," I said quickly. "If your head ..." I didn't want to verbalize the worst-case scenarios running through my mind about brain bleeds and swelling and skull fractures, as if that would make all of them true. "Never mind. I just don't think you should sleep," I managed.

"Everything is okay. But ... stay with me," she mumbled, reaching for my hand under the blanket.

I squeezed my eyes shut and tried to believe her.

"Just stay," she repeated again. "Don't ... leave me."

"I will," I promised, focusing on the rise and fall of her chest and the sound of the river.

That was when I heard a branch snap in the distance, followed by a muffled clatter of rocks.

I stiffened, listening harder.

The sound that came after was so faint I wanted to believe I'd imagined it: A deep yelp that didn't sound anything like a coyote.

13

I held my breath, listening for the sound to come again.

Laura's eyes were closed, and her breathing was already steady and deep. She hadn't heard the noise.

I tried to replicate the sound in my mind. A startled, deep yelp. Wordless. But distinctly human.

I started to shake again, trying to control my breathing and think it through. The part of me that was at least marginally warm and safe told me that the sound had been nothing. But the part of me that had my hair pulled out by the roots screamed for me to leave the car behind and hide along the trees by the riverbank.

Three seconds to exit the car and start running.

"Laura?" I whispered. "Laur, we have to go." I gently squeezed her shoulder.

She exhaled heavily and opened her eyes. Both of her pupils were huge and black, and she blinked several times as if trying to focus. "What? No." She fumbled with the door latch half-heartedly.

I glanced over my shoulder into the darkness beyond the open passenger-side window. The night was still and peaceful. The sound hadn't come again, but it was difficult to tell over the quiet burble of the river. My mind spun. What was the right move? What choice led to a happy ending—and our survival?

The distant sound of clattering rocks came again, followed by what sounded like a grunt.

We had to move—now.

Bypassing the useless passenger-side door handle and climbing through the window, I made my way around the vehicle to Laura's side as quickly and quietly as possible.

More dirt and sharp pebbles spilled into the sides of my zero-traction flats. With each step, I tripped over uprooted debris. I was making too much noise, but moving any slower wasn't an option.

I glanced over my shoulder to stare at the gouges the Volvo had left in the dirt, ending in our tires. We'd basically created a map right to our location. I could only see a short distance, but I knew that our trail wouldn't be difficult for someone to find if they were looking for it.

"Laura, can you stand up?" I whispered and tugged open the driver's side door.

She winced but managed to get to her feet, sinking into the loose dirt beside me and leaning against my shoulder. "Yeah, I'm good," she mumbled.

The weight of our situation settled into the pit of my stomach as we stumbled forward, keeping the blankets wrapped around our shoulders. We were slow. Laura was injured. And we'd be easy to find—if we didn't get out of here fast.

Laura sighed as I shifted her arm around my other shoulder and kept moving. As we stepped away from the car, she tripped over something and pitched away from me. I thought we were both going to fall, but just as quickly Laura managed to catch herself—and me —before we hit the dirt. "Sorry," she whispered. "I feel dizzy."

We wouldn't get very far walking like this. She was too woozy, and I was too weak to support her.

More branches snapped in the distance and I froze. "It's okay," Laura whispered. "Come on. I'll be fine if we go slow. Just hold my hand." I reluctantly shuffled out from under her arm and grasped her hand tight under the blankets.

She took an unsteady step forward. Then another. "I'm okay," she repeated, sounding more like herself. "Let's go."

"Oh my god, yes, you're doing great." The words tumbled out in a rush, to Laura or God or both.

"Thanks for staying with me," she whispered in a choked voice and squeezed my hand.

I squeezed back. My grip tightened as I heard a twig snap in the brush, closer now. It had been much longer than three seconds. We were running out of time.

Think. Survive.

If we followed the river downstream, we would eventually make it back to cell service. The scrubby trees and brush by the riverbank were denser than the rest of the sparse desert fauna, and I was positive we weren't that far—maybe a mile or two—from where we'd have reception again.

Laura's cell phone was now safely tucked into my travel pouch. We just had to get somewhere we could use it. Every instinct warned me to put as much distance between ourselves and the Volvo as quickly as possible. But we couldn't run. And I wouldn't leave Laura behind.

The breeze picked up, rustling through a feathery stand of sagebrush to our left and drowning out subtler noises for a few long seconds.

We shuffled toward a thick outcropping of trees near the riverbank. If we could make it there, we'd be completely hidden in the darkness.

More movement from behind us. Closer now.

I forced myself to draw slow breaths while my heart hammered in my chest. Every few seconds, I looked over my shoulder to stare blindly into the night. Laura's breathing was ragged in my ears, but the closer we got to the riverbank, the more difficult it would be to hear any noise we made over the rush of the water.

At last, we reached the treeline at the bank of the river. Laura nodded toward the other side. "I think we ... should cross."

"You think we should cross?" I whispered incredulously, staring at the swirling black water. The shallow river was littered with small boulders and rocks—an easy hopscotch under other circumstances, where a misplaced step wasn't a matter of life or death. It was already cold outside. If we got wet, it would be far worse. And if one of us stumbled, the sound of a splash would carry.

Crossing would be easy enough for me. But Laura was another story. What if she slipped? It would be a disaster.

I darted my eyes around, trying to identify the best path to take along the river.

My heart sank. Laura was right. Most of the trees along the riverbank were growing so close to the water's edge that we'd have to get our feet wet—and risk splashing—to cut around them. Either that, or we'd have to weave back into the open, where we'd be spotted. If we crossed to the other side of the river, we could cut through the treeline. To anyone looking across the river, we'd be hidden from view.

I swallowed. "Let's do it," I said finally. The water wasn't deep —maybe three or four feet in the middle, judging from the boulders dotted throughout the center. At its widest point, it was maybe fifteen yards across.

A small animal shrieked nearby, and we froze, waiting. Something scuffled in dirt then quickly moved away from us in the underbrush.

I exhaled slowly.

"Come on," Laura whispered. "If you go first, I can hold onto your—"

More twigs cracked, undeniably closer, and we shrank toward the sandy ground. A rock popped beneath my shoe as I crouched lower, and I wondered frantically how far the sound had carried in the stillness.

A grunt.

Then a distant, hissing "Shh."

14

What had felt like a dense cover of surrounding sagebrush and scraggly trees a moment earlier now felt bare and exposed as the footsteps approached the Volvo, maybe twenty yards away, and stopped.

I had been staring at the prickly weeds matted on the ground, where I had planted my hands as I crouched next to Laura. I looked up as indistinct voices drifted toward us. In daylight, we likely would have been spotted pretty quickly with a glance around the riverbank. It was only the thick cover of darkness combined with the brush and the blankets that was keeping us hidden.

I could make out the Volvo's tank-like silhouette in the distance.

Laura grasped my arm, digging her fingernails in hard enough that I winced. Neither of us moved. Running wasn't an option. If they heard us and followed—which they would—it was only a matter of time before one of us tripped and fell in our flimsy shoes. And then there was Laura—who I wasn't even totally sure should be walking or sitting upright, let alone running for her life.

Tugging at the hem of my halter top, Laura slowly stood and began moving in the opposite direction of the deep voices, toward the sandy shore of the sloping riverbank. She froze again as the voices suddenly rose in volume, becoming just audible over the sound of the river.

"They're gone." A spark of recognition flared in my mind then died. I'd heard that voice before. Laura nudged me in the side urgently. I got the message—she recognized the voice too. "Let's go back —"

"Nah. They're here. I can tell." A second, unfamiliar voice. This one was deeper, coarser.

More footsteps.

"Someone is going to hit your truck in the dark," Familiar Voice insisted.

A rattling door handle. Creaking metal. More footsteps. "There's not even any blood in the car," Deep Voice responded, ignoring him. "That PIT maneuver was sick, right?"

I couldn't tell if Deep Voice was pleased or upset by the discovery that there was no blood in the Volvo. My skin crawled with anger as I remembered the feel of his hands in my hair, grabbing and tearing. Laura leaned next to my ear as if to whisper, but when the men spoke again, she froze.

"But what about—" Familiar Voice began.

"It'll take us five minutes to find them," Deep Voice insisted. "Stop being dead weight and help me look."

The wind whispered through the nearby trees again, and the voices drifted out of earshot. I looked at Laura, who nodded toward the river. "Let's go," she mouthed.

I hesitated, listening intently. Quiet footsteps were branched out from the Volvo. What would happen when they found us?

When.

One set of footsteps moved steadily closer, coming in our direction.

Laura pushed herself up to a raised crouch and began moving slowly, silently through the brush toward the water's edge without me. With the flannel blanket still humped around her shoulders, she looked like a moving rock.

The footsteps were closing in.

Survive.

Ahead of me, Laura picked her way closer to the water's edge. I wanted to call her back, tell her to slow down, to wait until the footsteps went the other way. Instead, I pushed past the ice water in my veins and followed her. The drumming of blood in my ears made it difficult to tell how much noise either of us was actually making. Every scritch of my jean shorts and blanket against the undergrowth sounded like a dead giveaway.

The men hadn't spoken again. Either they had drifted back toward the road or they were closing in behind us, waiting for the right moment to pounce.

I grabbed Laura's arm and we crouched by the edge of the water. I could hear her breath near my ear, fast and erratic, above the quiet rush of the black water as it swirled among the scattered boulders. The lazy riffles in the surface winked as they reflected the star-filled sky.

My eyes followed the rocky path we would need to take to cross the river without getting wet. There was only one section—in the middle—where the boulders disappeared altogether for a couple of feet. We'd have to jump at that point. If either of us fell, it would be disastrous. In daylight, in warm weather, without a head injury, the leap would have been laughably easy. But right now, it felt almost impossible.

I listened harder, trying to locate the footsteps again. Had they moved on? Were the two men standing a few feet away, scanning for our silhouettes? It was difficult to tell while we were still crouched at the river's edge, this close to the gurgling water. The only way to know would be to stand up and step out onto the first boulder, into the open. If either of the men were close by, they would see—or hear—the movement.

As I steeled myself to take the first step, Laura pressed something into my hand: a baseball-sized rock. The weight of it gave me an unexpected glimmer of confidence. Unlike the awkward, heavy boombox, this was a weapon I could use.

I didn't let myself dwell on what it would feel like to actually smash the rock into someone's skull. I knew I would do it in a heartbeat, but all I really wanted was to get the hell out of here alive.

I grabbed onto Laura's hand. "Come on, let's go."

As we rose from a crouch, there was another clatter of rocks from the hillside, followed by a hiss that sounded like "shut up."

Both noises came from farther past the Volvo. They must have circled back toward the hill—probably thinking we were trying to make our way up to the road.

If we were going to cross, we had to move now.

I glanced from rock to rock again, reconfirming the path we would take. Then I shifted the blanket to my neck like a scarf, and tightened my grip on the rock. Laura wrapped her own blanket around her neck and let go of my hand. "Grab onto me," I whispered, moving in front of her.

I planted one foot onto the first boulder, then the second. Right behind me, Laura wrapped her fingers through the belt loops on my shorts. I gritted my teeth and fought to stay balanced—for the both of us.

We moved surprisingly quickly at first. One step at a time, we crept from boulder to boulder. Each time I moved my foot to a new rock, Laura placed hers where it had been a moment earlier, shadowing my every step.

Laura tugged on the belt loops and stopped moving. "Hold on … I'm worried I might throw up," she whispered as I inched my left foot forward toward another rock. She leaned her head against my back and drew in a deep breath. "Just give me a second."

Don't throw up. Not here. Not now, I begged silently. "Deep breaths," I told her, echoing what she'd said to me earlier in the evening, a lifetime ago. "Just a little farther," I added, but the truth was that we weren't even halfway across yet.

We stood frozen in silence for a few seconds as the water rushed around our feet. I had no idea if we were visible from the hillside, but I chose to believe we were little more than dark specks in the inky night.

"Okay, it passed," Laura finally whispered. "Let's go."

Each step was agonizingly slow as I felt for the right foothold that would keep us both on balance. "Just one more step," I murmured again and again, unsure whether she could even hear me as we kept moving. But each time I took another step, she followed behind.

When we reached the middle of the river, I couldn't help imagining both of us tipping into the waist-deep black water with a splash. Would the sound carry all the way to the hillside behind us, like we'd heard the miniature landslide of rocks earlier?

"Getting close," I whispered a little louder. This time it was true. We were making progress. We were almost there.

Suddenly, Laura sagged against me.

My center of gravity thrown off, I lurched toward the next boulder, twisting to support her. I bit back a yelp, bracing for the sound of the splash and the bite of the freezing water.

In the scramble, I let go of the blanket that had been precariously wrapped around my shoulders. It slipped into the current and was gone before I could balance myself to snatch it back.

Laura inhaled sharply and managed to right herself on the boulder behind me. "I'm sorry," she whispered, "I'll give you mine. I'm so sorry—"

"It'll be okay," I whispered back, trying to convince myself that was true. Without the blanket, the night was freezing. Already, a sheet of goosebumps were popping up across my bare arms. "Just a few more steps. Hang on, Laur."

She repositioned her fingers through my belt loops and took a painful-sounding breath. "I'm good. Let's go."

Before I moved to the next boulder, I turned my head and chanced a look behind us.

The other side of the riverbank was, mercifully, still empty.

* * *

When my feet sank into the mucky sand on the other side of the river, I wanted to cheer. Or cry. Instead, Laura and I quietly linked arms and huddled underneath a spidery thicket of sagebrush to rest.

My breath came in shaky gasps as the adrenaline thumped through my veins like a victory march. *We did it. We did it. We did it.*

I felt like I could run for miles without stopping—even in my flats. But I forced my breathing to stay measured and strained my ears, trying to tell whether or not we'd been seen.

Nothing.

After a few seconds of stillness, Laura leaned close to my ear. "That guy's voice sounded familiar to you too, right?"

I nodded, still scanning the other side of the river. "Definitely."

"The guy with the higher voice, right? I ... I keep running through everyone I know, trying to think of anyone who would want to hurt us. Because if we know them, this wasn't random. They were waiting for us ... they knew we'd be at the bonfire tonight."

I tried to imagine an RSVP list on the Facebook event. Maybe thirty people had RSVPed, but it was a public event. Anyone could see the list.

Laura inhaled sharply and turned to look at me. "Liv. Could it be ... Ziggy?"

I felt the blood drain from my face as I remembered the email I'd sent our professor. I'd thrown him under the bus completely. He'd lost his TA position because of me.

I shook my head slowly. He was a small-c creep. I'd never felt afraid of him, just annoyed. Still, even small-c creeps could surprise you. Then I remembered something: "It can't be Ziggy. You've never heard his voice."

Laura picked a leaf out of her hair, flicking it onto the sand at our feet. "We watched his video."

"Shit." She was right. We'd both watched the LARPing video Ziggy had posted to his Facebook account—several times, actually. Laura had pulled it up again after the MySpace disaster, laughing hysterically as Ziggy introduced himself as a "mage," whatever that meant, before turning the camera away from himself to show two guys pummeling each other with foam swords in the campus quad.

"I don't think Ziggy is the type to do something like this, but I really don't know him that well," I whispered back. "What about the other guy? Did you recognize his voice at all?"

She frowned and wiped some of the lipstick off her chin. "I don't think so. He seemed ... scarier, though."

I nodded in agreement. I somehow felt sure he was Red Mask.

Neither of us put forward any more guesses about who the men might be. Right now, it mattered less who was on the other side of the river than how quickly we could get away from them. "How's your head?" I asked hopefully. She sounded more like herself, but I knew both of us were headed for a crash at some point. Adrenaline would only get us so far.

Laura reached up to touch the lump on her forehead. "A little better? I feel okay right now, but as soon as I stand up, I get dizzy and nauseous again."

"We'll go slow," I promised. The blanket would cover both of us if we stayed together. And if we just kept moving, little by little, we could cover a lot of ground. "You told me you ran the mile in ten minutes the other day, right?"

Laura laughed softly. "Yeah, that is not happening right now."

"I know, but even if it takes us five times longer—and it's two miles until we get cell service back—that's only two hours." Another zip of adrenaline prickled through me. Help could be less than two hours away.

Laura smiled—a real one that showed her perfect teeth. "You're right. And you've still got my phone?" she asked as we shifted to a crouch and got ready to start moving again.

I tugged at the elastic of the travel pouch under my shorts and grinned. "Damn right—and mine too, although the battery's going to die any second. Here," I said, unzipping the pouch and pressing Laura's phone into her right hand.

To my surprise, she pushed it away. "Keep it for me. My pockets are useless, and if ..." She stopped talking then took a couple slow, deep breaths, reaching up to touch her temple again. "If we get separated or whatever, you need to keep the phone so you can keep going. There's no way you'll be able to drag me if I can't keep up. I have total confidence in your scrappy little brain, but you have zero upper body strength."

I smiled weakly but didn't press the issue. She was right about the poor upper body strength, but the jury was still out on my scrappy brain.

15

We crept along the riverbank at an agonizingly slow pace. Partly to stay quiet, partly to stay warm with the shared blanket, and partly because it was impossible for Laura to move any faster without getting dizzy.

As we navigated the sagebrush and gnarled trees that snaked along the river, I kept my mind blank, focused on our goal: survival.

Every time my thoughts tried to drift to the creepy masks or the way the man's hands gripped the back of my head without letting go, I reminded myself that we'd gotten away. No matter how scary the masks had been, no matter what they'd been planning, we'd outsmarted them. And soon we'd be warm and safe and reporting their asses to the police.

We had their license plate. We had the cover of darkness. We had the upper hand.

When we came to a fork in the river, Laura tapped my shoulder, motioning for us to stop so she could lean against an outcropping of boulders. "Hold on. I think I'm going to hurl."

She let go of the blanket and clutched at her stomach, kneeling by the riverbank as she quietly retched into the water. I knelt beside her and covered her back with the blanket while she stayed on her knees. "You're doing good, Laur. Let's rest, okay?"

She shook her head and wiped her mouth, scooping up a handful of dirty water and staring at it for a moment before flinging it back into the river. "Nah, not that desperate." She flashed me a weak smile then took my arm and stood. "I'm okay now," she insisted, shivering as I pulled her tight into the blanket.

She didn't look okay. The adrenaline rush was wearing off for me, too—and I didn't have a head injury. "Try the cell again?" she prompted.

I opened my travel pouch and hit the call button, cupping my hands over the screen so the light wouldn't show in case someone happened to be watching. I'd been doing the same thing every few minutes. The result was the same every time. *No service.* I zipped the phone carefully into my pouch, letting my fingers linger over the rape whistle and wishing I'd brought the pepper spray tonight. It was sitting on my dresser right now—too bulky for my party outfit.

We'd been steadily picking our way forward for around twenty minutes, but I had no idea how far we'd actually traveled. Our pace was agonizingly slow. Maybe half a mile, I decided optimistically.

The battery dipped a little lower with each set of calls. How many more tries did we have before the phone went dead?

Laura sighed in frustration. "I can walk a little faster. Let's keep—"

She inhaled sharply and stopped walking. As she did, I felt my foot sink into something soft at the same time a crunching sound prickled through the darkness.

The carcass of a deer lay inches away from my left foot. I'd just stepped on its decomposing leg.

A glint of grayish skull protruded through the mangy looking head, and a long tear in its belly spilled black entrails. The doe had clearly been dead for a while, and its eye sockets stared blindly up at us.

A pungent, sickly sweet smell filled the air. Laura doubled over and retched loudly.

"I'm sorry," she gasped, pulling away from the blanket. She stumbled a few steps past the deer carcass and threw up again.

I tore my gaze from the carcass and followed Laura, folding her back into the dirty blanket and whispering that everything would be all right, that the sound wouldn't carry, that the call would connect the next time we tried.

But in that moment, all I could see when I blinked were the doe's dead eye sockets staring up at me.

* * *

This time, Laura didn't hesitate to scoop up a mouthful of river water to swish. She spit the water out and stayed crouched on her hands and knees at the bank for a few minutes before wiping her mouth on her arm.

"Hurry, get back in the blanket," I coaxed, trying not to let my teeth chatter as I helped her get to her feet.

Even in the moonlight, her skin looked much too pale—except for the angry lump near her temple.

The breeze whispered through the brush, carrying a new chorus of howls in the distance and making me shiver harder. Above us, the stars winked brighter, dazzling in their clarity. The view would have been stunning if I wasn't worried it might be the last thing we'd ever see.

Laura shook her head slowly, muttering a string of expletives under her breath. "I'm fine now. I just need to rest for a second longer. That smell ... I couldn't keep—"

"It's okay," I told her, swallowing back the tremble in my voice, wishing I had more reassurances to offer. I wasn't used to being the one with a cool head, the one who saw the silver linings. That was Laura's role.

Laura shook her head again, her white-blond hair falling into her eyes but not quite covering the mottled, baseball-sized lump. It looked worse than it had earlier, more swollen. I knew she should be in a bed with an IV, being examined by a doctor. Not stumbling through the foothills, running for her life.

While I waited for her to catch her breath, I redialed 9-1-1 and moved the cell phone to my ear for the hundredth time. The phone beeped. Still nothing. I shoved it back inside my pouch, gritting my teeth in frustration.

In a survival situation, everything is inconvenient. Stay focused on your top priority. Resist panic. The words found their way to the front of my memory. I couldn't remember which rugged TV host said them, but they rang true. We could breathe. We had shelter—or at least shelter enough to get us through the night. We were safe—for now. That had to be enough.

"It'll be okay," I told Laura more firmly, this time believing the words.

"That doesn't sound like you," Laura murmured, but she smiled a little as she said it.

We'd only gone a few steps before she stumbled, crashing forward to catch herself then stepping right into a pile of dead brush on the ground with a series of loud *snaps*. We both froze, listening. The crickets and the soft cooing of a mourning dove went quiet before slowly resuming their chatter.

Laura sighed. "I'm sorry, Liv. I can't feel my toes anymore."

Neither could I. "Come on, let's warm up a little." I gently tugged Laura's arm. "A few minutes won't hurt. We'll move faster if we rest." When she didn't argue, I guided us to the water's edge where an outcropping of tall boulders loomed along a narrow stretch of sandy shore. There was an alcove between two of the boulders just wide enough for both Laura and I to sit with our backs to the rocks. I tucked the blanket tight around us from the front.

"This is … almost warm." Laura shivered violently and lay her head on my shoulder.

I rested my head on top of her head, keeping my eyes on the murky shapes and spidery brush for any sign of movement on the other side of the river.

Laura shuddered again. It took me a moment to realize she was crying.

I swallowed past the lump in my dry throat. "Hey, do you remember the time we tried to make our own demo tape in high school?"

Laura snuffled then laughed softly. "Yeah … we thought we sounded amazing."

We'd spent months writing the songs our freshman year of high school—then recording them on the bathroom floor using my mom's old tape recorder. We made three copies of the demo. One went to the address on the back of my Gloria Estefan tape, one went to an address we found in the phone book for Boise Talent Search, and one copy stayed in Tish's car—which was an elderly Honda Civic at the time. Whenever Tish let us borrow the car, we'd turn the music up loud and sing along with our own badly written lyrics, dreaming of the day Gloria's agent would call us in to sign a deal.

"You can never be my dream boy if you don't see me, boy," I crooned quietly. A coyote howled in the distance, as if joining the chorus. "I'm still in shock that nobody ever called us. Boise Talent Search at least."

Laura laughed quietly. "Oh my god …" she trailed off.

I couldn't remember any more of the lyrics, but it didn't matter. Laura had stopped shaking, and her breathing was turning slow and deep. Her head felt heavy on my shoulder. I tucked the blanket tighter around both of us. I didn't have the heart to wake her up yet, concussion or not. There had to be a point at which exhaustion and stress was worse than getting a few minutes of sleep. We both needed to get warm, and Laura desperately needed to rest.

I wouldn't let her sleep long. Just enough to reset so we could make another push. I closed my eyes and listened to the sound of the river prattling peacefully, drawing in slow breaths through my nose.

That was when a terrifying thought wormed its way to the front of my mind: What if we were too far down in the canyon to get cell reception?

16

I didn't know how cell signals worked exactly; however, I'd seen enough people on campus lift their phone up like baby Simba in the dead-spot near the dorms that the thought sent a new wave of anxiety through me. If that was the case, we might walk for miles past the point where a call would go through up on the road. Hell, it was possible a call might go through now if we cut back up the hill toward the road.

My breathing sped up while I studied what I could see of the river. It was as shallow and rocky as before. I felt pretty confident that I could make it to the other side just fine, but I wasn't sure how Laura would fare. Why risk another treacherous crossing out in the open—or losing another blanket?

I closed my eyes and focused on the rise and fall of Laura's chest. If I left her here with the blanket, I could cross the river by myself and pick my way back up the hillside toward the road, then test the signal. If it worked, I would call for help. If it didn't, I would come back and we would hunker here until Laura had time to rest.

Don't leave her, part of my brain warned.

She won't even know you're gone, another argued.

You could keep walking through the valley all night if you don't, the deciding voice insisted. *Laura won't make it.*

"Laura?" I whispered. She didn't stir. I tried a little louder. "Laura? I'm going to leave you with the blanket. I'll be back in a little while, okay? Hang on."

I nudged her in the side, and she finally murmured something in response and waved me away. I gently shifted her head from my shoulder and lay her on the ground next to the rocks, tucking the blanket underneath her shoulders.

The cold night air stung my arms again as I stood on the riverbank, steeling myself to step out into the open, wondering how long it would take me to negotiate the hillside in the dark. What if the coyotes found Laura? What if they found me?

My shoes sank into the wet muck at the waterline as I wavered.

I would just have to hurry.

I counted to three in my head then stepped onto the first boulder, carefully picking my way across the river. My cheap flats were falling apart in earnest now, splitting at the sole and flapping a little with each movement. They weren't built for these conditions, and neither was I. Every step took precious seconds of planning. Each footfall was a near-miss with a loud splash into the cold water.

When I was halfway across the river, I glanced back at the other bank. As I turned, I noticed the sequins on my halter top glinting in the starlight like a poor man's disco ball.

I was basically wearing a blinking sign to anyone who might be watching that read, *Here I am.*

Please don't let anyone be watching, I prayed. Then I quickly whipped the shirt up and over my head, turning it inside out. The scratchy sequins were going to tear up my already raw skin, but I'd survive it.

By the time the other riverbank was within reach, I was exhausted and shaking from the cold. And I hadn't even started the climb up the slope toward the road.

I studied the second-to-last boulder for a flat spot, lifting my shredded shoe forward carefully when I found it.

That was when I heard Laura shriek in terror.

I whipped around in a panic, losing sight of the flat spot on the next boulder and nearly tumbling into the shallow water. I dropped to a crouch, catching myself with my hands and squinting into the murky darkness on the other riverbank.

Laura had scrambled to her feet, an eerie silhouette still partly wrapped in the flannel blanket. She was swaying back and forth, frantically darting forward, then back, then stumbling to her knees on the sand. I suddenly realized she was looking for me.

She thought I'd left her behind.

Idiot, the vindictive voice—the one that told me not to leave her—hissed.

Guilt curdled in my stomach. "Laur," I whisper-shouted, knowing I was making too much noise. "It's okay. Just stay warm. I'm right here. I'll be back in a few minutes, okay? Everything is fine."

Laura stopped trying to get to her feet. I couldn't hear what she said in response over the quiet rush of the river, but after a few moments she held up one hand in a small wave then shrank back against the boulders, out of sight.

I relaxed a little and hesitated. Should I keep going? Was this the priority right now?

I watched the pale lip of sand along the shore for another few seconds then turned around. If my theory was right, we might keep wandering down the middle of the valley, following the river for way too long. If I could get to the top of the hill and try again to connect to cell service, help could be here within the hour.

I was about to make the last leap onto the shore when Laura screamed again.

I froze. This sound was different—a ragged, vulgar sound that sent adrenaline pouring into my veins again.

The shallow breath of relief I had drawn a second earlier whooshed out in a gasp.

When I turned around, I knew immediately that something was very wrong. There were now two tall shadows looming on the other side of the river.

One of their faces was too dark to see. The other glowed a faint, pale white.

It was them. They'd found us.

My slippery flats wobbled on the rocks as my brain tried to process the impossible options: Go back for Laura or keep going.

One of the shadows standing on the riverbank had broken apart from the tangle of brush and was moving toward me across the rocky path cutting through the river.

My mind went blank as the adrenaline took over, pumping through my legs before I could make a conscious decision to run.

As I pushed off the boulder and leaped for the riverbank, one of my shoes lost purchase on a soft spot of moss. I landed hard in the muck on the other side then slipped again when I tried to pull myself up to standing.

The chaos behind me was getting louder. The slick *thud* of a shoe hitting a rock sounded above the rush of the river. Laura screamed again. "Olivia!"

The word was enough to cut through the panic that told me not to look back.

I turned around as I finally managed to pull myself upright in the cold mud.

This time, I could see the outline of the mask on his face. He was even closer than I'd expected, closing the gap between us as he neatly jumped to the next boulder in the river.

The panic grabbed hold, and I bolted.

He dove for the riverbank—miscalculating the distance from the last narrow rock to the muddy shoreline. One of his feet plunged into the icy water with a loud splash, sending him off balance. He rolled into the shallow water lapping at the shore. He swore loudly, and the sound echoed in my ear above the screams and the muddy slurping sounds. I scrambled uphill as fast as I could possibly move.

The adrenaline that had pooled in my limbs over and over for the past hour finally ignited. I pounded through openings in the underbrush, not caring how many twigs snapped or what I might trip over. Each time I fell, I pushed myself up and clawed my way forward. Part of one shoe ripped as it caught on a fallen branch, pushing a sharp twig into one toe. I didn't stop.

The chemical rush and white-hot fear were like rocket fuel. Branches lashed at my face and stung my arms and legs as I ran. Every inch of my skin crawled, waiting to feel his fingers in my hair at any moment. I pushed myself to move even faster, farther away from the chaos behind me.

I ran like that for maybe five minutes before forcing myself to stop beneath a rocky shelf, finally able to make sense of the thought slamming around inside my head like a pinball.

What have you done, what have you done, what have you done.

I had left Laura behind. That's what I'd done.

The guilt ate away at the adrenaline like acid. I listened, gasping for breath, but the only sounds I could hear confirmed what I already knew: Laura didn't stand a chance. Unlike me, she couldn't get away, she couldn't run, and she couldn't hide.

One more scream echoed through the valley then cut short, followed by a barking command that I couldn't make out.

Then nothing.

In the sudden silence, my mind screamed louder with guilt and regret.

Laura. Laura. Laura. Her name repeated like an alarm.

All the awfulness of the night up to this point—the terrifying chase on the road, the crash down the hillside, Laura's injuries, the cold—seemed suddenly bearable in comparison to this new reality.

We'd been together before. Now, we were both alone, and all because I'd done exactly what I said I wouldn't do: I'd left her behind.

My legs, which felt like speed machines a few seconds earlier, now felt like tree trunks rooting me to the shifting hillside. A forceful breeze slapped a webby sagebrush branch against my bare legs and sent a violent shiver down my back.

If I kept going, I felt pretty certain I would survive. I'd gotten away. There was nobody behind me anymore.

But what good was survival if Laura wasn't with me?

If this really were an episode of *Secrets to Survival,* I knew what I'd be shouting at the girl on the screen—the one who had already been through hell and back, and who ran for her life because it was the only choice—even though it meant leaving her best friend behind.

You did what you had to do, I'd be thinking while she wavered, torn up with guilt and regret. *Keep running. Don't stop. Don't be stupid. Make the smart choice, not the emotional choice. Get that damn cell phone to connect. That's all you can do now. You're no match for those creeps.*

I knew Laura herself would probably tell me the same. After all, what could I really do that wouldn't end this nightmare with two missing girls instead of one?

But I also knew what Laura would do if it were me on the other side of that river, fighting for my life.

She'd never leave me. And it wasn't just because she'd never read any of the blogs I sent her way about death and survival, or because she was an eternal optimist. It was because she cared about me enough to make the stupid choice. And because she'd never be able to live with herself if she walked away.

Neither could I.

On shaky legs, I leaned back and looked up at the slope. It was impossible to tell how far I was from the road. Without a stream of cars driving by, it was just a strip of lonely, silent pavement cut into the hillside. It might be a ten-minute hike, or it might be much longer.

I squeezed my eyes shut tight. Then I crouched, felt around for another rock, and began to pick my way quietly downhill toward the river.

17

The deep voices floated toward me in spurts while I carefully back-tracked down the hillside.

They weren't trying to be particularly quiet anymore.

The hunt had been successful.

I couldn't make sense of the words yet, but I didn't care. All that mattered was finding out that Laura was alive, and then figuring out how to keep it that way.

Digging my fingers against the rock so it wouldn't slip out of my hand, I approached the thick line of brush flanking the riverbank. From this vantage, I could just make out Laura's dark silhouette on the other side of the river. She was lying prone, face down, beside the water's edge.

One of the men was straddling her, facing away from me. I caught a flash of movement from his arm and heard the scratchy squeal of duct tape. He bent and then wound it around Laura's hands several times. She didn't move, didn't make a sound.

I clenched the rock tighter and picked my footing carefully. The other man, standing a few feet away, turned his head to look across the water.

White Mask.

I froze, sure he couldn't see me against the brush but feeling his eyes on me anyway. He reached up to itch his face, sticking one finger inside the black eye socket and moving it around for a few moments before turning away.

The man straddling Laura's back—who had to be Red Mask—unrolled another strip of duct tape. "Man, that bitch was *hauling ass*," he said loudly, winding the strip of tape around Laura's legs. The deep, grating voice still didn't spark any recognition.

I kept my eyes on Laura. She still wasn't moving, but if they were tying her up, she must be alive. She had to be.

White Mask didn't say anything—nothing I could hear, anyway. Instead, he took another step away from Red Mask, shoving his hands into the pockets of his hoodie. He looked almost impatient.

"I nearly had her," Red Mask lamented, his voice dipping lower so I missed the rest of what he said.

White Mask muttered something in response I couldn't make out. The profile of the pale mask hovered in the blackness as if disembodied, watching Red Mask while he worked. Even though I couldn't understand what he had said, something about his voice still pinged a bell of recognition in my mind. He raised his hands in an exaggerated shrug. I crouched lower to the ground and strained my ears, desperate to hear what he was saying.

"You know she's ... the road right now. You said we couldn't let them—"

I dipped my body lower, until my ear was nearly parallel to the waterlogged sand and mud. In this position, I could suddenly hear everything on the other side of the riverbank more clearly.

"It doesn't matter," Red Mask replied. "We'll be out of here before she can call anyone. And it's an old plate anyway. Took it as a souvenir when I didn't get my full payment." He laughed, ripped off another strip of duct tape, then deftly wound it around Laura's legs. "Let's go."

I tasted blood on the inside of my mouth and realized I was biting my cheek. Full payment? A souvenir? The important thing was, it was a fake plate. The text I'd sent to Tish was useless.

White Mask didn't say anything else. I wished more than anything that I could see his face. Like it was the thread I had to unravel in order to understand this nightmare.

I squinted at the way White Mask stood, trying to tell whether Ziggy's features were hidden beneath the latex. He reached up and rubbed at his forehead again, causing the pale mask to buckle inward and twisting the black sockets of his eyes upward into dark slits. He wavered where he stood a little longer, staring at the place where Laura lay without moving on the ground. Then, mumbling something under his breath, he turned around and started walking away from the riverbank.

Red Mask bent down, rolled Laura over, and hefted her onto his shoulder like she was a sack of potatoes. "Good girl," he praised. "If you don't want me to drop you, you won't kick me again."

I strained my eyes for any sign of movement from Laura, noticing that her head didn't flop to the side as he lifted her up off the ground. That was good. She was conscious—for now.

Her mouth was taped shut. If she threw up again would she choke? In my mind's eye I could see her thrashing and gagging while Red Mask barked at her to shut up and stay still, until she went quiet and limp.

I could only imagine how terrified she was.

I forced myself to breathe, tamping the paralyzing panic down. *Panic is your enemy. Focus.*

I had several choices to make, and the time to make them was rapidly slipping away.

Three minutes to follow, before they disappear into the brush.

I couldn't see White Mask anymore. He'd already been swallowed up by the darkness on the other side of the riverbank. Soon, Red Mask and Laura would be gone too.

I still held the rock clutched in one hand. Could I cross the river without giving myself away? Maybe. But could I sneak up on Red

Mask and hit him—forcefully enough to knock him out—all without White Mask hearing me? I desperately wanted to believe this was possible but knew with sickening certainty that it was a long shot at best.

I'd have to sneak up on him without giving myself away. At close range, a single crack of a twig might make him turn around. Then there was the problem of my weapon: I couldn't risk throwing it. I had a better chance of hitting Laura or missing him completely but alerting him to my presence. I'd have to be standing directly behind him to hit him with enough force to do any kind of real damage. Then there was the fact that I'd never hit anyone with anything before in my life. The movies made it sound like you just clunked someone once and they went out cold. I had a feeling that might not be true. And if I didn't take him out with one blow, that would be the end of both me and Laura. Even if he dropped Laura or stumbled, there was no way I could unwrap the duct tape fast enough for the two of us to escape together.

The panic percolating in the pit of my stomach threatened to spill over, leaving me floundering on this side of the riverbank while the chance to act passed. I shoved it down again. *Focus.*

Shadows still moved in the brush on the other side of the river. In a few seconds, they would be gone.

Were they taking Laura back to the truck? Were they really going to drag her all the way back up the slope? Why? Surely if they wanted to kill her here, they would have done it on the riverbank.

I forced my mind to work faster, to think through all the choices branching away from me in the precious seconds remaining. If the men had left the truck on the road, it was probably parked near where the Volvo had gone over the shoulder. Could I beat them to the truck if I stayed on this side of the riverbank and hurried up the hillside? I wouldn't have to worry about every twig snap that way. But what if I lost them? The reality was that I had no idea where they had parked the truck, where they were taking Laura, or what they were planning. If I wanted to know where they were going, I would have to follow them.

A long shiver ran through me, and I gritted my teeth to keep them from chattering. None of the swirling questions had simple answers. None of the scenarios I could imagine ended with Laura and I escaping safely.

The final option nagging at the back of my mind was the one I'd just abandoned: Run until I could get out a call. If I left Laura, I could still get help. But how long would it take? What if the battery on the cell phone ran out before I could get a call to connect? How long would it take the police to get here if I finally got through? Tears gathered in my eyes, and I angrily wiped them away. *Focus.*

The man carrying Laura wasn't visible anymore, but I could still hear the branches snapping as he disappeared into the night.

Three minutes.

I moved to a crouch on the riverbank, imagining Laura's face pressed against Red Mask's disgusting, sweaty back, her ears filled with the sounds of his breathing as he dragged her through the darkness.

I imagined the police report, the news reports. *Olivia Heath was the last one to see Laura Atwood alive ...*

I pulled Laura's phone out of my pouch and tried to connect a call one more time.

Nothing. The battery hovered at 10 percent now.

I let the rock slip gently from my fingers. It wasn't going to help me after all. Then I took one awful step onto a flat rock near the river. Then another, and another, until I was back on the other shore.

All I knew was that Laura was still alive—and I was still free. I'd promised I wouldn't leave her. As long as those facts remained, this was the only choice.

18

Earlier, it felt like time expanded while Laura and I inched along the riverbank. Each second had teetered on the brink of so many terrifying possibilities.

Now, as I retraced our steps and followed the men carrying Laura, the seconds sped by too quickly while I tried to come up with an end game. What the hell was I actually going to *do*? If I couldn't answer that question, I was just wasting time I could have spent trying to get a call out. Was there any scenario where I stood a chance in a fight against both of them? The answer to that question was a resounding *no*. I was exhausted, freezing, and weak.

I couldn't win that way. The game felt locked, but I'd made my choice. Now I needed to figure out a way to make it the right one.

Once I caught up with them, I hung back far enough that I could still see their bulky silhouettes bobbing through the brush like shadows made solid.

When they stopped walking, I stopped walking. When they moved, I moved. I kept the sound of their footsteps within earshot without getting close enough to let them hear mine. The two men switched off carrying Laura every few minutes, and whoever brought up the rear with her crashed through the weeds and sagebrush like a bear, breathing loudly with the extra weight on his shoulders.

Much sooner than I would have anticipated, we cut through the brush, back toward the river's edge. The pale shoreline didn't look familiar here: This wasn't the same spot where Laura and I had picked our way across earlier. They must have walked along the other shore for a while before thinking to look for us on the other side.

"You can take the mask off now, dumbass," Red Mask said before he stepped onto the first rock, shifting Laura roughly onto his other shoulder.

My heartbeat zipped faster. If they didn't care about Laura seeing their faces, it was a sign things were headed from bad to worse. Masks meant they cared about staying anonymous. If the masks came off, so did the possibility that they might be willing to let her go after whatever nightmare they had planned.

I squinted into the murky darkness, suddenly realizing that his profile had already changed. The warped, exaggerated nose and chin were gone. He'd taken his own mask off at some point while he walked. I could make out the slope of his real nose along with a mop of shaggy hair.

White Mask balked. "What? Why?" His voice sounded deeper than it had earlier, and I felt sure he was trying to disguise it. *Yes,* I begged silently. *Keep the mask on.* He still wanted to stay anonymous. "I thought we—"

"Keep it on then. I can't fucking breathe. She probably already knows who you are." He laughed. "But drop the big-boy voice. You sound like you're working a 900 number."

White Mask muttered something. He hesitated then lifted one hand to grab at his mask and shoved it into the pouch of his hoodie. I blinked, straining my eyes for any hint of his identity. Mussed, short hair. Strong jaw.

Not Ziggy, I realized with sudden clarity. Ziggy barely had a chin. I would have recognized that profile even at this distance, even in the dark.

The realization crashed over me as a burst of relief and drew back as fear. If it wasn't Ziggy, who was he?

The river was shallow here, more rock than river. Even with the extra challenge of carrying Laura, the two men crossed easily.

I waited until they began struggling to climb the crumbling slope before I stepped out into the open to cross behind them. If they turned around to look, I would be fully visible. I wasn't a sequined disco ball anymore, but my pale arms and legs would stand out plenty.

As I carefully placed my foot on the first rock, my ridiculous shoes slipped precariously on the smooth surface. I gritted my teeth in frustration. I needed to move fast, but I couldn't risk a slip into the water.

Thinking quickly, I took both shoes off and found a foothold with my bare feet. My toes were clumsy and cold, but they gripped the surface of the smooth river rocks much better than the shoes.

When I reached the other side of the river, I slipped my disgusting shoes back onto numb feet and listened for any sign that someone was rushing back down the hill toward me.

They weren't.

I began the ascent up the hill, hurrying to catch up at first, then hanging back to let them stay slightly ahead of me. I felt my way forward at a crouch, staying close to the ground and feeling for loose rocks that might clatter if I made a wrong move.

There was no trail, but it was easy enough to negotiate the gaps between clumps of sagebrush and skinny trees. The two men in front of me weren't worried about sending dirt or rocks tumbling down the slope—so every few seconds, a miniature rockslide of pebbles and small rocks clattered toward me from above. I welcomed the constant trickle of debris that landed in my hair and pinged off my arms. It covered the sound of any wrong step I might make.

With each step, my strappy sandals filled with dirt and weeds, and with each step, I asked myself what I was going to do when we reached the top of the hill.

My brain spit back static in response, no matter how many times I demanded it give me a usable idea.

The static only got louder the longer we climbed. We had to be getting close to the road. I took a few precious seconds to check the phone.

Nothing.

The breeze was picking up, making it harder to hear the footsteps above me. I was clumsy—shaky from the cold, jumpy from the adrenaline.

The sound of footsteps suddenly disappeared. I froze.

"Hey, dickhead, switch me. You take her the rest of the way," Deep Voice called.

Familiar Voice mumbled something I couldn't hear then kept climbing. More small rocks and sand skittered down the slope toward me with each footstep.

The rest of the way. My breaths came faster and shallower as the grade slightly leveled out. We were almost to the road. And the truck.

Tears threatened to spill down my cheeks, and my throat closed up as a wave of despair overcame me. I wiped at my eyes, still demanding my brain find a way out.

She's alive, I reminded myself.

She won't be for long, a knowing voice clapped back. *And you won't be either, if you try to fight them. You can't help her. You should have kept running.*

No brilliant plan had materialized over the last thirty minutes. No flash of inspiration. And no matter how many times I'd flipped through the different scenarios of what might happen when we reached the road, they ended in disaster for either Laura or me or both.

Maybe there was no way to stop them. And now I was even further away from getting help than I had been before. If I'd kept running—instead of backtracking, then following my would-be captors like a lost puppy—I might have even connected with the police by now.

You failed. And now Laura will die, a sickening voice in my gut whispered.

Regret rose like bile in my throat, along with a terrifying burst of understanding. Maybe the survivors, the ones who hung on to tell their stories, weren't stronger than anyone else. Maybe everything they said about miracles and the "will to live" and their refusal to quit being the reason they were sitting in that interview chair was a story the lucky ones got to tell.

I'd really never thought about what the people who *didn't* make it onto *Secrets to Survival* might say if they could sit down in that interview seat. The people who starved, lost their grip, succumbed to the cold, or couldn't fight off their attacker. The ones who didn't make it out alive. What would they say?

I'd always secretly thought they must be a little bit weaker, a little bit less committed to hanging onto life. A little less intelligent. A little less scrappy and savvy. A little less educated in the art of avoiding the bad things. But maybe the truth was even scarier than that. Maybe, sometimes, there was no way out.

Strangely enough, that thought quieted my mind.

Maybe the game *was* locked. But I would keep playing my hand until I no longer had a hand left to play.

I imagined myself watching the truck's taillights disappear as I crouched in the shadows of the brush at the edge of the drop-off. I wondered how fast I could run, once I made it onto the smooth surface of the road. I decided I would take off my shoes again and run until I couldn't run anymore. And then I would try the phone. I would keep doing that until the call finally went through.

The constant trickle of dirt and pebbles from above me had stopped, replaced by the soft thud of sneakers on pavement. Staying low to the hillside, I darted forward until I could see the truck's bulky outline looming above me, its rear end a stark rectangular silhouette against the navy sky.

They had parked along the very edge of the narrow gravel shoulder, so close to the drop-off that the back tires had to be mere inches from the edge. The enormous vehicle looked precarious, almost comical, with its bed tipped over the slope like at any moment it, too, would follow the Volvo's descent.

Earlier in the evening, I was sure I'd seen a sign stating *NO STOPPING ON ROADWAY*. For a brief moment I allowed myself to hope that some civic-minded driver might have passed by the awkwardly parked vehicle and called the police to report it once they got cell reception back in city limits.

The ember of hope faded quickly. Even if a small miracle had occurred and someone cared enough to remember—and then report—the stopped truck, they'd done it too late. Not to mention that the license plate would be a dead end.

All that mattered in this moment was that the road was quiet. And the men would be gone in a matter of minutes.

I inched toward the road's edge, careful to dig my sandals into the loose soil with each step to avoid sending a spray of debris clattering down the hill. I was close enough now that I could hear the men again. I watched helplessly as the man holding Laura lay her down on the shoulder of the road.

He backed up a few steps, as if he wasn't sure what to do now. "Why won't you just tell me where we're taking her? You have to tell me." That familiar voice nudged at my memory then retreated, still unwilling to reveal itself. "This isn't what we talked about."

"We're taking her to the mall for Wetzel's Pretzels," Deep Voice said then laughed, a booming sound that echoed through the stillness.

Familiar Voice didn't join in.

Deep Voice sighed heavily. "My stepdad's cabin, dumbass."

Laura whimpered on the ground. Both men ignored her.

"Why?" His question came out in a guarded monotone. I leaned forward and strained my eyes, trying to piece the glimpses of his face into something recognizable while he stood with his body turned toward me on the road. If I knew who they were, I could give the police something to work with. Something that would help them find Laura in time.

It was too dark. They were specters, boogeymen for all the description I could give police. A gust of wind rattled the sagebrush where I was crouched, stinging my eyes and nose. A skiff of dust swirled over the hill.

Deep Voice bent and picked Laura up, letting her head snap back roughly as he flopped her over his shoulder. I winced. "Because if we stay here much longer, people are going to start leaving the bonfire, and some drunk asshole is gonna plow my truck over the edge," he replied in a patronizing voice. Then he laughed again. "Now *that* would be ironic."

He knew about the bonfire. I'd nearly forgotten about it. While I had serious doubts anyone would be heading home this early in the night, it wasn't completely out of the question. I listened for the sound of another vehicle on the road, trying to manifest the quiet drone of an engine into the periphery of the night.

Nothing.

"You asked for my help, remember?" Deep Voice continued, opening the crew door with his free hand and hefting Laura into the passenger bench as if she were a doll. She kicked out at him, feebly, and my heart beat harder. She was still fighting. She was still okay. For now.

Familiar Voice grunted. "Yeah, and I appreciate it, but what about—"

The car door slammed. "*Semper unum.* Stop being an ungrateful little asshole. Everything is going to be fine."

"But what about—" Familiar Voice insisted.

Deep Voice cut him off again. "We'll take care of her later. Right now, it's Friday night. And I've got a red X on these two. Do we fucking understand each other? I said I'd help you. And I will. Did you think I was gonna do it as a freebie, though?" He laughed. "You of all people know that's not how it works. So, stop it with the holier-than-thou act."

Semper unum. We'll take care of her later. Red X on these two. Everything he'd said seemed important, but none of it made any sense. I begged them to keep fighting with each other, giving me pieces of the puzzle and drawing out the moment they'd drive away with Laura.

"Yeah, okay," Familiar Voice relented, sounding weirdly contrite. Then he opened the passenger's side door and got into the truck.

Deep Voice snorted a laugh and stayed where he was a moment longer, scanning the road's edge. He was looking for me—but from the smirk on his face, he had no idea that I was looking at him. In the dim light cast by the taillights, I could finally see his face clearly.

In some ways, it was even more terrifying than the mask had been. I'd been expecting ugliness that matched the grotesque latex features.

Instead, he was disconcertingly good-looking. Handsome in a way you didn't see often in real life. A face you might flip past in a catalog but stop to admire on the street. Thick, dark brows. Straight, wide nose that curved down a little at the end. Cut jaw, tousled hair that looked messy but was clearly the result of an expensive haircut, full lips, and a dusting of stubble peppering his cheeks.

I didn't recognize him at all. No scars, tattoos, or unusual features.

Basically, tall, dark, and handsome. That was the description I could give the police. It wouldn't help anyone find Laura.

I suddenly realized that if he'd been the one to show up for that MySpace date—instead of Ziggy—I would have been thrilled. I might have let him into my apartment afterward. Hoped he'd text for a second date.

Semper unum.

The words clicked, along with their meaning. "Always one."

They were Deltas.

19

Deltas, Deltas, Deltas.

The word repeated through my brain like an alarm.

I studied the set of his jaw, willing some spark of familiarity to burst into flame.

Nothing.

He scanned the grade edge. At any moment I expected he would make out the silhouette of my body, tucked into the brush. I was crouched so close that if I reached my hand out, it would be illuminated in the red glow of the taillights.

It was just him and me right now. I had the element of surprise on my side. I briefly considered grabbing a rock and leaping out from my hiding spot to hit him. Could I balance on the precarious drop-off with a giant rock in my hand, wearing my broken shoes, fast enough to clock him before he reacted?

I would have one tiny window of opportunity. One chance to aim and take fire. The other man in the truck would hear the scuffle. It would be two against one again in a matter of seconds.

I knew in my bones it wasn't enough to help Laura. Not even close.

Apparently satisfied with what he saw, he shrugged and backed up a few steps. Then he strode toward the front of the vehicle and hefted himself into the driver's seat.

My heart constricted with each crunch of his footsteps. This was it. This was where I'd lose her.

The engine turned over with a throaty roar, and the glare of the taillights cast a pale glow over the sagebrush at the edge of the drop-off, washing it in watery red.

Stop, it warned me.

I obeyed, frozen where I crouched, unable to reconcile the idea that these two psychopaths were actually going to drive away with my best friend while I hid and watched.

Keep looking for a way, I told myself desperately as the futility of the situation hit like a wave break. *You could be halfway down the road right now, calling the police, but instead you're here. So don't give up yet. If there's something to be done, do it.*

The truck's back wheels began to turn slowly, spinning out and searching for purchase on the uneven, gravelly shoulder. I clenched my jaw, squeezing my teeth together hard enough that it hurt.

I had seen his face. I had seen the truck. I knew they were headed to a cabin. I knew they were Deltas. Would that be enough for the police to find them—if and when I could get a call out?

Maybe eventually. Maybe, years from now, when I got a call on a random Tuesday to review lineup photos from some detective who finally caught a break in the case after years of looking for cracks in the Delta Phi fraternity.

Years ago, there had been a scandal involving sexual assault claims at the Delta house. The victim had ultimately retracted her statement, after five fraternity brothers provided an airtight alibi for the supposed assailant.

She'd dropped out after that. Everyone knew Deltas were ride or die.

The tires spun again, spraying dirt and gravel toward me. Laura didn't have time for a drawn-out search. She had hours, if that.

Three hours before they kill her. A shiver ran through me, threatening to throw me off balance on the crumbling hillside.

Find a way, Olivia.

There's nothing I can do. Hot tears burned at my eyes again, and I let them fall from wide eyes as the neon red of the taillights burned auras into my retinas.

Unless.

I blinked past the tears and the floating green shapes, focusing on the angular truck bed, looming above me on the narrow shoulder, tantalizingly close.

It was a terrible, reckless idea. They would see me. They would hear me. They would duct tape my mouth and my legs and my arms like Laura's. And then they'd shove me in the back of that truck with her, sealing both our fates.

They're both Red Xes.

Run.

I clenched my jaw, distantly hearing something pop in the back of my mouth.

With a few quick steps, staying close to the ground, I crossed the short distance to the truck bed and stood up in a crouched position. The vehicle lurched forward then back several inches into the deep rut, making a quiet groaning sound.

The wheels inched forward, spraying me with more dirt and gravel.

Would they see the flash of movement if I hoisted myself up and over the tailgate?

Yes. The angle was wrong. They'd be able to see me.

But there was one other option.

Tentatively, as if making contact with a live grenade, I pulled down on the truck bed's release handle and carefully lowered the tailgate.

20

Time seemed to contract, zooming in on my hands as they hovered on the cold surface of the tailgate.

If the truck rolled back any farther past the rut in the shoulder, the back tires would slide down the slope just like the Volvo had.

The vehicle teetered where it was for a moment, its open truck bed hanging at eye level as I stood in the dirt beside it.

I darted my eyes back and forth, waiting for someone to emerge from the cab. If the vehicle was new enough to have a tailgate-ajar indicator, it would be beeping away. I would have to abandon this ridiculous idea—and fast.

But no one emerged from the truck.

Was the rule of threes still in play?

Three seconds before they pull away. If you're going to move, move now.

No, no, no, my lizard brain screamed.

The tires inched forward again, then dipped back into the rut with a loud, metallic *clunk.*

I stared at the red glow of the taillights, warning me to stay where I was.

I remembered the feel of Laura's arm through mine. Our friendship flashed before my eyes, along with a fresh burst of adrenaline.

The brake lights blazed red, a clear *stop* sign.

Gritting my teeth, I moved toward the warning glow.

If this was a *stop* sign, I was about to run it.

I lifted one knee onto the tailgate and scrambled across the gritty surface of the deep truck bed as quietly as I could.

I could only hope that the soft thump of my body hitting the plastic with each movement would be obscured by the tires negotiating the uneven dirt shoulder.

Part of me felt elated. I'd actually done something. I'd found a way to stop them from disappearing with Laura, without revealing myself.

The other part of me was on the verge of a total panic attack. I'd just knowingly put myself into the truck bed of two psychopaths.

I pressed my body low against the truck bed floor, noting the view through the tiny cab window above my head. When I lifted up onto my hands, I could barely make out the tops of two silhouetted heads in the front seat. It was impossible to see Laura.

What have I done?

I lay down and braced my legs against the back walls of the truck bed, looping my fingers through a bungee cord running the length of the dirty surface and burying my face against a dingy blue Coleman cooler. With the extended cab, neither the passenger nor the driver could see me from this angle. The only person with any kind of view into the truck bed was the backseat passenger—Laura, but only if she'd been able to sit up.

This did nothing to keep me from imagining leering faces suddenly appearing above me.

The gravity of what I had done descended as the truck pulled onto the paved road and started to accelerate. I'd spent all night trying to evade the men in the truck. And now I'd gone and kidnapped myself.

So stupid.

I counted to four with each inhale, trying to stave off hyperventilation.

Opening the latch and getting into the truck bed had been the easy part. Slamming it shut would have been a dead giveaway—so the tailgate had to stay open. Wide eyed, I watched the murky yellow center line turn into a blur.

I turned my face back against the cooler and squeezed my eyes shut. I wasn't following them from the cover of darkness in a vast wilderness anymore. If something went wrong, there was nowhere left to run. My only hiding place now was the bed of their truck. Basically, a box with an open lid. I was one short step away from showing up as a special delivery if—and when—they found me.

The night air swirled around me faster, more violently, as the truck picked up speed.

If I'd been cold before, I was in real danger of freezing now. The wind whipping through the truck bed was unrelenting. I tucked my chin to my chest and curled as tightly as I could into a ball, keeping my fingers curled up in the bungee cord. I wasn't worried about flying out of the back. There was plenty of runway between myself and the open tailgate. But if they heard something bouncing around in the bed of the truck, they'd stop to investigate what it was. And I couldn't let that happen.

For a few minutes, the truck accelerated and braked in a steady pattern, speeding up with each straight section and slowing for the curves. I thought we might be approaching the turnoff to the reservoir at one point, but it was impossible to tell without poking my head up above the truck bed to get my bearings. All I knew was that we were heading deeper into the hills—farther away from city limits.

I imagined our classmates at Coffin Creek, littering the ground with Pabst cans and cigarette butts and warming themselves around a bonfire the freshman had turned into a near forest fire by now. I'd been dreading that scene a few hours earlier. Now I'd give anything to be there with Laura, sipping drinks in the warm glow, listening to someone play guitar.

Each time the brakes engaged beneath my head with a series of metallic *clunks*, I stiffened into a tighter ball, curling my body harder against the Coleman cooler so I wouldn't bump against the truck bed. Something inside the cooler made a soft clinking sound with each turn.

Then, abruptly, the freezing wind died. The truck was slowing down fast.

What was happening? Were they going to stop on the road? There was no way we'd reached their destination so quickly. Did they know I was back here? Had they known the whole time? Had they felt the movement as I climbed into the truck bed? Were they deciding what to do with me right now? Should I jump out? I wrapped my hand tighter around the bungee and hoped my frozen limbs would be able to move quickly.

This won't work. The words ran through my mind like a morbid mantra.

Run while you still can.

The truck came to a complete stop, idling one second, then two, then three. The panic was impossible to fight. I lost track of counting and held my breath instead, waiting in mute terror for the front doors to open above the throttle of the engine.

Whorls of smoke from the exhaust pipe curled into my field of vision. The muscles in my limbs burned as I tensed, waiting to hear the cab doors open.

I prepared to run.

I decided if they caught me, I would scream as loud as I could.

At least Laura wouldn't die thinking I had left her alone with these monsters.

It wasn't survival, but it wasn't nothing.

Beneath me, the truck's engine growled louder, followed by a series of muffled clanks.

Then we lurched forward and picked up speed.

21

There were no more slowdowns.

If anything, the driving got faster and more reckless the deeper we got into the middle of nowhere Idaho. At some point, the curves in the road finally straightened out and we moved downhill again.

When my body began to ache, I shifted to my other side, lying with my back pressing against the cooler and keeping one hand tangled in the bungee cord. I stared at the road behind us, trying to get some idea of where we were going.

The narrow road stayed paved, but the landscape grew rockier and flatter the farther we drove. The rolling hills gradually turned into rolling rangeland dotted with the dark shapes of gnarled trees. I kept my eyes peeled for the silhouette of a rooftop or the glimmer of a porch light. If we were headed to a cabin, maybe there were others out here too.

A sign on the side of the road flashed into view, the white text briefly illuminated in the taillights as we zipped past.

End Sportsman Access.

I cut my eyes to the other side of the road, desperate to know what the sign facing the other direction read. *Sportsman Access*—but how many miles?

We hit a pothole straight on with a bone-rattling jolt, and I winced as the cooler—and my head—bounced then smacked down hard.

I watched helplessly as a small, untethered bungee cord near the tailgate suddenly skittered over the edge into the void. It hit the road with a soft slap, looking like a dead snake in the pale glow of the taillights that came on briefly as we tore around a bend in the road.

I winced, praying that the men were too distracted with whatever sick plans they had to worry about the sound of a rogue bungee cord. When I was a freshman in high school, my family had moved across town. My dad and I had been tasked with ferrying some of the last odds and ends in our pickup truck on moving day. When we arrived, we realized that two of the boxes—the ones that held the bathroom toiletries—were nowhere to be found. When we retraced our path with the truck, we found toilet brushes, loose toilet paper rolls, and prescription medications spilled all over the road in our old neighborhood. We hadn't even heard them fall.

The seconds ticked past, and the truck didn't slow down.

I let go of the cord with one hand to rub at my numb legs. It was like touching bumpy, dead chicken flesh. I thought I had been cold before, in the hills. But with the wind whipping over me in the truck bed, alternately needling and then numbing the fresh cuts I'd gotten from the brush and branches, "cold" took on a new meaning. The icy slap of the wind was unrelenting. I would be woozy and slow when we finally stopped.

When we stopped.

Would that be in one mile or one hundred? It could be anywhere. Every time the vehicle slowed even slightly, I held my breath, praying we weren't stopping yet, even though my fingers were so numb that I glanced at them periodically to make sure they were still wrapped in the bungee. All I knew for certain was that the landscape hadn't changed in miles. Somehow, the night seemed even darker and deeper than it had before.

You should have run, my brain insisted.

I pushed it away, still clinging to the burst of adrenaline that had propelled me into the truck bed.

The farther we drove, the faster it was wearing off.

Once the truck reached its intended destination, my plan—if you could call it that—was a complete blank. *Please help me,* I prayed to anyone who might be listening, careful not to include any curse words this time.

I'd never had any reason to drive this far south past the reservoir before, but I told myself that all paved roads went somewhere. Still, that "somewhere" might be a small town, or it might be miles and miles of undisturbed sportsman access. In Idaho, it was easily one or the other.

I'd been afraid that if I took the cell phone out of my travel pouch to check for service, my numb fingers would drop it, sending it bouncing across the tailgate. But I had to keep trying.

I let go of the bungee around the cooler, hoping we didn't hit a pothole that would send me bumping across the truck bed. My fingers felt like popsicles, so I placed my hands under my armpits for a moment to warm them up enough to bend them.

The truck swung sharply to the right as we tore around a bend, and I shot out a foot to keep myself from sliding along the bed, hoping the sound of my foot hitting the bed wall would be mistaken for the cooler shifting.

I rethreaded one hand through the bungee then reached for the pouch. Careful not to let the contents spill out, I felt for the smaller rectangle of Laura's phone. Making sure I had the warm metal gripped tight, I worked it out of the pouch.

The cell phone's battery still showed ten percent. I breathed a sigh of relief. Unfortunately, it also still showed zero bars.

I moved my frozen fingers to flip the phone shut, but before I could do so, one bar of service flickered onto the screen.

A jolt of adrenaline zipped through me, and I scrambled to hit redial.

The bar disappeared before my finger even made contact with the call key, but the glimmer of hope stayed lit.

We'd gotten a flicker of service. That meant it could happen again.

I shut the phone but kept it pressed beneath my chin, waiting ten seconds before trying again. And again. And again until the phone was down to five percent.

The service bar didn't reappear.

Out of desperation, I curled toward the Coleman cooler then opened the texts on Laura's phone, thinking of the message I had sent to Tish earlier in the evening from my own phone. Had Tish seen the bogus license plate number yet? There was no way to know. I painstakingly typed out another text, spending precious seconds to get the words out right.

SOS. 9-1-1. Coffin Creek. Deltas. Stepdad's cabin.

If she knew that Deltas were involved, she would ask Tony for help—regardless of how awkward it might be. Somebody had to know who had a cabin out in the boonies.

I read the text once quickly before hitting send, imagining Tish getting home from the library and crawling into bed. She'd be wearing her oversized yellow Vandals sweater, the ones that made her blue eyes look almost neon, and her white-blond hair the same shade as Laura's piled on top of her head in a knot.

Love you, Tish, I added, knowing that in a worst-case scenario, whoever found this phone would realize it was Laura's.

I hit send.

A "text not sent" message appeared immediately.

I squeezed my eyes shut, carefully tucked the phone into my travel pouch, and pressed my cheek against the Coleman cooler.

Fuck.

In my mind's eye, I could see the wrecked girl in the truck bed, speeding along the dark highway, numb and clueless. I was desperate to know what would happen to her. Desperate to know whether her getting into the back of the truck was reckless but brave, or reckless in a way that ultimately sealed everyone's fates.

You can still run, my brain insisted. *The next time the truck stops, you can get out.*

I waited for a rebuttal from the part of me that couldn't let the truck disappear with my best friend.

It stayed silent.

Nose-to-nose with the stark reality of survival, teetering on the edge of my adrenaline, the burst of bravery was just that. A temporary burst.

Was I really willing to die for Laura? Or anyone?

If I was being brutally honest with myself, I wished I hadn't gotten into the truck bed, in the same way I wished I hadn't gotten into the roller coaster cart at Silverwood.

I couldn't stop the flood of images that guessed at what might be waiting for us at this "stepdad's cabin." In my head, I saw a reel from *Saw*: torture chambers, hooks, knives, chains, and worse. Did things like that happen to real people?

Of course they did.

I knew all the gory, excruciatingly awful details of what Gary Ridgway—and all the others like him—had done to their victims.

Gary alone had killed more than seventy girls. Nobody knew the exact number. He'd lost count himself, there were so many. He strangled and tortured them, then left their bodies posed in the woods and along lonely highways.

Run, my brain screamed, while I lay frozen in the bed I'd made.

I realized that my armchair fascination with psychopaths like Gary Ridgway had always hinged on distance.

They were all just stories.

I'd always thought of myself as a true-crime junkie. But it turned out, that was only when it happened to other people.

I decided that when the truck finally stopped, I would run.

I would memorize the cabin's location, and then I would fucking run.

22

The road got rougher and bumpier the farther we drove. More pot-holes, more cracks that had never been filled. The truck sped along at a steady clip, anyway, swerving to miss the biggest divots but taking the rest head on.

My stomach started to churn in a nauseous flip-flop, so I opened my eyes and kept them focused on the dusty, grooved surface beneath my cheek and the dim center line trailing behind the open tailgate.

I caught a glimpse of the headlights of an oncoming vehicle only once, the pale glow barely visible at first on the periphery of the truck bed. I turned my head in time to see the headlights flash into view, illuminating the left lane for a brief moment before the other vehicle passed us, speeding away in the opposite direction. By the time I let go of the bungee cord and waved my arm frantically, the taillights had already retreated into the darkness. It was another truck, its bed piled high with shapeless shadows.

I couldn't stop myself from imagining the lumpy tarp covering piles of bodies.

I watched the two glowing red dots until they completely dis-appeared, remembering the man who had flipped us off earlier. Maybe the idea of trying to flag anyone down was a death sentence. I'd have to let go of the bungee and crawl to the very edge of the open tailgate to signal them with any chance of being seen. If we hit a pothole at the right angle, I'd be a goner. And there were no guarantees anyone would even notice me—except, perhaps, the drivers of the vehicle where I was stowed away.

However, if headlights appeared *behind* the truck, that might be a game-changer. I kept hoping I would suddenly be blinded by twin lights that would illuminate my cowering body in the bed of the truck. If that happened, I felt sure I could signal the other driver for help without necessarily giving myself away. Mime calling 9-1-1. Drag a finger across my throat, to let the other vehicle know the situation was dire. I hadn't seen myself in a mirror lately, but from the blood and dirt smeared across my arms and legs, I knew I would be a shocking sight in their headlights. There would be no mistaking that I needed help.

The road stayed empty. No one else was headed this direction on the rural highway, late on a Friday night.

How soon would Tish start messaging the sorority girls who had organized the bonfire, to find out why we'd never come home? How desperate would she have to get to contact Tony?

I swallowed the tight lump in my throat. Even if she woke up at the crack of dawn, that was hours away. What was going to happen between now and the morning? Would there be anything left to find?

I had been curled on the truck bed floor for nearly half an hour now, and my muscles were beginning to cramp. Slowly and painfully, I shifted onto my back, barely registering the dull pinpricks of pain rippling through my legs, which felt like slabs of frozen meat. Then I lay still again, sliding one arm underneath my head to keep it from bouncing on the floor of the truck bed as I listened to the engine purring below the wind.

The sound changed as the truck decelerated and the turn signal ticked in time with the blinking right taillight. I lifted my head up a few inches and watched as we made a right-hand turn.

The smooth zip of the tires on pavement changed, replaced by pings and pops of pebbles as the vehicle slowed to a crawl and turned off the main road.

A flood of adrenaline warmed my frozen limbs. At first glance, we'd pulled onto an overgrown ATV trail. The taillights illuminated a tangle of weeds, along with two barely visible, parallel trails that had been worn down by tires at one point.

Get ready to run.

I rolled onto my side and scanned for any sign of a cabin. Were we stopping on the side of the road now? It was impossible to hear anything that was happening inside the cab.

The truck's nose lurched downward then back up, splashing across a muddy stream and then veering right onto a wider ATV trail.

Right, then stream, then right. I committed the movements to memory.

I tucked my knees beneath me, so I could leap out of the truck at the first opportunity. But instead of slowing down, we picked up speed again, flying down the weed-choked ATV trail. I unzipped my travel pouch and tried the cell again. We had to be close to the cabin.

How far away was help now? Miles farther away? Closer? It was impossible to guess. All I knew was that I needed to be ready to move.

The phone screen blinked to life as I shielded the glow underneath my hands. Not even a flicker. Only three-percent battery left on Laura's phone. The ragged edge of my torn fingernail caught my eye in the phone's light.

I tucked the finger behind the phone and re-read the texts I'd tried to send Tish. "Text not sent" still appeared beneath the little green bubble, like I knew it would.

I put the phone away and rubbed my legs and arms briskly, feeling the bite of the bitter cold start to soften now that we had slowed down. Then I tensed and relaxed my muscles, preparing to run, unwilling to be caught cold and clumsy.

As I stretched and slowly rolled onto my knees, reaching my hands forward in an awkward child's pose, my hand brushed against something hard tucked along the dip at the edge of the truck bed. I stopped moving. Then I inched my body forward, letting my fingers examine the long, cold piece of metal. For the first time, my heart thumped faster in anticipation.

It was a tire iron.

Suddenly, the game had changed again. I had a real weapon.

While the truck bumped along the trail, farther into the sprawling meadow of waist-high grass, I rolled onto my side and gripped the tire iron to my chest.

Take it and run.

Clobber the motherfuckers.

The frantic bickering in my brain started all over again.

The truck slowed, and my view of the landscape through the tailgate shifted. Instead of an endless sea of pale grass, the silhouettes of trees reached high along the edges of the overgrown road. Unlike the scrawny, sparse pockets of trees and brush scattered along the road earlier, these trees were bunched together in a tight, neat line that towered above the dirt road. Cottonwoods, by the pale, knotted trunks.

We were still in the middle of nowhere. But I was willing to bet that if I stood up in the truck bed right now, I'd see the angular silhouette of a cabin nearby.

23

The brake lights flashed on, and the truck finally rolled to a stop.

I tensed and started army-crawling toward the edge of the tailgate, planning to slip into the treeline then follow the ATV trail back toward the road.

The driver's side door opened and the weight in the truck shifted. I froze, unwilling to give myself away too soon but terrified that at any moment I would see a shadowy figure looming over me.

The engine was still running, so why was the driver getting out? I clutched the tire iron tighter and inched closer to the edge of the tailgate, grateful for the fresh wave of adrenaline waking up my frozen limbs.

Instead of circling around the back of the truck, the footsteps moved toward the front. A moment later, I heard a chain rattle, then a long, whining creak.

More footsteps, then a reverberating thud.

The driver's side door shut again, and the truck pulled forward through a wide metal gate mounted between two tall wooden posts. It hung open across the ATV trail, just wide enough to let the truck pass through.

Would they stop again to shut the gate behind the truck? If they did, they would definitely see the tailgate ajar—and then me in the truck bed. I scooted to the very edge of the open tailgate, ready to move the instant I felt the gears shift into park. The metal tire iron, freezing just a moment earlier, now felt slick and warm in my hand.

Positioning my body parallel with the open tailgate, I braced one leg against the side of the truck bed to keep from tumbling onto the ground as the brakes engaged to take a rut in the dirt road. The truck picked up a little more speed.

I kept my eyes fixed on the edge of the open gate, watching it get smaller and smaller in the distance until I lost the shape of the horizontal bars in the darkness.

I could still make out the silhouette of the two wooden anchor posts, their rounded tops peeking out from the cottonwoods lining both sides of the ATV trail.

The truck finally came to a stop.

This time, the engine cut out right away.

I gripped the tire iron tighter and held my breath.

24

Keeping my stomach flat against the truck bed, I rotated my body then let my legs drop over the edge of the tailgate and onto the hard dirt, careful not to let the metal rod bump against the plastic.

Without the drone of the engine, the night was suddenly dead quiet again. For a moment, the only sound I could hear was my own pulse, pounding loud in my ears as I stood there. I was completely exposed, pale skin illuminated in the thumbnail of a moon that had risen above the treeline.

The passenger-side door swung open with a creak, followed by the driver's side.

Panic warmed my icy limbs as I scanned my surroundings, trying to find a hiding place. A shallow ditch ran parallel to the cottonwoods nearby. The treeline ended abruptly maybe twenty yards behind me, where the ATV trail widened into a wider patch of exposed dirt. If I could reach that treeline without being seen, I could hide there until I figured out my next move.

Both doors slammed shut, and footsteps thudded on the dirt.

They were headed my way. If I made a run for the treeline right now, they would definitely see me.

Three, two ...

I finally snapped into action, dropping to the ground and crouching beneath the open tailgate. Flipping onto my side, I scooted toward the back tires, cringing at the quiet popping noise the sequins made in tandem as I wriggled my body farther under the truck.

The footsteps stopped. I rolled over onto my stomach, swallowing a shriek as my bare arm brushed the hot tailpipe.

A pair of shadowy legs shifted in front of me, mere feet from my face. If I'd waited half a second longer, someone definitely would have seen me.

As long as they were both out here, I couldn't risk giving myself away.

And if they went inside the cabin for a few minutes, maybe there was still a possibility that Laura and I could both get away.

All I could do was wait a few minutes longer.

Leave Laura in the truck, I commanded mentally, rubbing my arm gingerly. *Go inside the cabin. Just give me a few minutes.*

I wiped my hand on my shorts to get a better grip on the tire iron. Even with a weapon, the odds of fighting off two of them weren't good. I'd only get one chance to strike, and I had to make the most of it.

Running still seemed like the best option.

My arm throbbed from the burn, but I barely cared. Beneath the hot pipes and warm undercarriage, it was weirdly cozy—and mercifully warm. Despite the legs planted in the dirt a few feet away, I relaxed my tense muscles and let my head drop to the dusty earth, feeling like a lizard as I tried to soak in the reprieve from the cold.

The crew door hadn't opened yet, which meant Laura was still inside the truck. Snatches of conversation drifted above me. It sounded like they were arguing again, but between the soft clanks of the cooling metal on the undercarriage and the wind fluttering the leaves of the cottonwoods, it was hard to make out anything they were saying.

I stayed flat against the ground but turned my head a little and squinted toward the front of the truck. As my eyes made sense of the dark shapes, I could see the bottom steps of what looked like a porch.

If the Deltas went inside the cabin, even briefly, I could open the crew door then use my teeth, my nails, the apartment key in my pouch, to cut through the duct tape binding Laura's legs and arms. I no longer cared about reaching a particular destination. Even freezing to death was a distant concern now. We just needed to get as far away from whatever was waiting for us inside that cabin, as quickly as possible. We'd figure the rest out from there.

I shifted my grip on the tire iron impatiently. Now that I was warm again, I was eager to move. What were they waiting for?

Hurry up. Go check out your stepdad's gross cabin, I demanded, my gaze fixed on the legs. As soon as I had an opening, I would army-crawl to that spot, right underneath the passenger side door, stand up, and quietly open the door. I imagined myself unzipping the travel pouch to grab the apartment key, then ripping through duct tape on Laura's legs as fast as I could.

Give me three minutes, I prodded them, closing my eyes. *Go away, you pieces of—*

"What about Tish…"

My eyes snapped open, focusing on the legs. I wasn't sure I'd heard right, but as I turned the word over in my memory, I was certain that I had.

Tish.

It confirmed the suspicions I'd had since the moment I'd heard White Mask speak on the road. This wasn't a random act of violence. They'd planned this well enough that they knew Laura and I would be the ones driving that beat-up green Volvo. And if they were talking about Tish, there was some reason for it that went beyond the nightmare unfolding tonight.

Why couldn't I place his damn voice?

I tightened my fingers around the tire iron, clutching it to my chest like a security blanket. Part of me was dying to find out the story behind why all of this had happened, but that was a puzzle for

later. Right now, I really didn't care who they were. I would smash
both of them in the face as hard as I could at the first opportunity and
ask questions later.

The crew door finally opened above the pair of legs, blocking
the sound of the wind in the cottonwoods. Suddenly, I could hear
their voices clearly.

"Don't be a pussy," Deep Voice muttered gruffly. "Just relax.
Let it happen." He burst out laughing. "Bet that's a line you've used
before."

"Shut up," Familiar Voice muttered. He sounded flustered—but
like he was trying not to show it. The chilly feeling of familiarity
lapped at the edges of my mind, teasing me into thinking that if I
thought a little more, I could grasp that voice. "Seriously, dude. This
is next level. The whole point was to stay *out* of prison."

Deep Voice laughed again. The truck bounced on its wheels
slightly as the legs took a step closer to the passenger door and
leaned inside. "I've got it under control," he said with a heavy layer
of condescension, as if he were speaking to a young child. "Nobody's going to prison. *Re-lax.*"

Laura whimpered. Half a second later, Deep Voice swore, followed by a loud bang. The truck rocked back and forth above my
head. The second pair of legs moved into my field of vision near the
crew door, and I nearly lost the words Deep Voice said next. "Bitch
has been playing opossum if she can kick like that. You carry her
inside."

Familiar Voice tried to respond, but Deep Voice cut him off so
sharply that I flinched in spite of myself. "If you're gonna be a pussy,
I'm out and you can deal with the Tish situation on your own. Either
relax, or figure it out yourself."

There was a brief silence. I darted my eyes between both pairs
of legs incredulously. *The Tish situation? Figure it out yourself?*
What the hell did any of that mean?

Tell him to fuck off, I mouthed silently. What kind of trouble was he possibly in that this was the solution to his problems? I gritted my teeth.

"Atta boy," Deep Voice said. "Get her inside, then have a beer or two. You need it." Then one set of footsteps crunched toward the cabin. A few seconds later, a door creaked open, and the faint glow of a porch light cut through the murky darkness.

Familiar Voice kicked at the dirt, spraying pebbles and dust into my face. I squeezed my eyes shut, blinking hard and trying not to cough as the dust prickled at my throat. When I opened my eyes again, I could see the white soles of his sneakers along with a red swish, flecked with mud: Air Jordans. Whoever he was, he had money.

"Sorry," he said flatly, loud enough that I knew he wasn't talking to Laura.

The door slammed shut in response.

Familiar Voice kicked at the dirt again, sending another spray of dust into my face. A long silence followed as he hesitated by the open cab door. *Go with Deep Voice,* I begged, biting the inside of my cheek. *Keep arguing.*

Instead, the truck bounced on its wheels as he leaned into the crew door. "Calm down," he muttered. More shuffling and thrashing. The truck rocked in tandem with the muffled screaming as he tried to pull Laura out of the cab. His muddy Air Jordans sidestepped back and forth, flashing red and white in front of my face as he tried to position himself to carry Laura while she kicked at him.

A dark shape hit the ground at his feet with a dull thud and a sharp, muffled cry. Laura's blond hair spilled across the weedy dirt. He'd dropped her. I winced as she curled into a ball on her side, her chest rising and falling in panic. She was so close that if I reached out my arm, I would have been able to touch the back of her head.

A hulking figure knelt beside her. My heart thumped faster as I prepared to scramble out from underneath the truck if the whites of his eyes suddenly focused on me.

He crouched down next to Laura, his voice softer now. "Dammit, I told you to relax. That was your own fault." I leaned a little closer, trying to get a glimpse of his face: Clean shaven. High cheekbones. Strong jaw.

My heart slammed against my ribcage. I had definitely seen that face before, but where?

He shifted onto his heels. "I'm not the bad guy here," he muttered, his hands dangling at his sides. Laura didn't turn to look at him. "Just go with it, keep your mouth shut, and it'll be over soon."

My mouth nearly dropped open in disbelief at the words coming out of his mouth. I still had no idea who he was or what was going on here, but I knew for certain that everything he'd just said was complete bullshit. He was *definitely* a bad guy. I inched toward the side of the truck, itching to clobber him with the tire iron.

Laura, on the other hand, seemed to be listening to him. She didn't fight as he rolled her onto her back, shifting her to a sitting position to lift her up again. I made a note of the duct tape binding her hands, legs, and mouth. If I could get her feet free, we'd both have a chance at escaping.

I shifted a little higher onto my elbows and army-crawled to the very edge of my hiding space beneath the truck, careful to avoid the warm undercarriage above my head. If Deep Voice came back out of the cabin too soon, there was a good chance he'd see me. The moon had risen higher in the sky, casting watery light over the clearing. Even without the sequins, my pale skin would stand out.

Familiar Voice had managed to get Laura to her feet. He bent at the waist and hefted her over one shoulder like a doll. Her hair flopped across her face, the tips waving in the breeze like a sheaf of pale wheat.

When I turned my head, I could finally see the cabin. The wall I'd glimpsed earlier transformed into a small, sixties-style log cabin, its stark silhouette rising up in the clearing devoid of the cottonwoods that ran along the rest of the road. A dim, dirty porch light, half obscured by ropy gray cobwebs and dust, cast an orange glow across the small porch.

A wooden sign beneath the porch light read 67 Deer Flat.

I committed it to memory.

"You can stop making that noise, Laura," he said with more than a hint of irritation in his voice. "It's just going to annoy him."

Hearing him say her name made my stomach clench. I turned the word over and over again in my mind, trying again to fit the tone and the inflections with someone I knew, someone I had met. *Laura.* I felt certain the last time I'd heard that name in his mouth, it had been playful. Warm. I liked this person—or I used to.

Who the hell was he?

The cabin door suddenly banged open, and I shrank back beneath the truck, my heart thudding loud over the soft thump of approaching footsteps.

"The TV finally crapped out," Deep Voice said in irritation and stopped near the crew door. "Guess you're the only entertainment, honey." He made a noise somewhere in between a snort and a guffaw. "I'm getting the beer. Will you hurry up and bring her inside? Or do I need to do that for you, too?"

I tightened my hands into fists as his footsteps circled around the back. I imagined myself swinging it across his face, that perfect nose splitting like a burst seam. I'd never imagined hurting another human being before—I'd always pictured myself as the one being hurt. There was something weirdly powerful about knowing I was the one holding the tire iron.

"Hey, dickwad, you left the tailgate down."

More footsteps crunching.

I bit down on the tender edge of my cheek—the one I'd already chewed ragged—so hard a trickle of blood dripped into my mouth. I squeezed my fingernails into the soft skin of my palm. He knew what I'd done. They would find me now.

Familiar Voice scoffed. He must have turned his head, because part of what he said was lost in the leaves fluttering in the breeze. "... Kyle. I haven't touched it all night. Is the cooler still there?"

Silence. "Yeah." Then laughter.

Kyle. So that was his name. It pinged a faint bell of recognition too. But I'd seen his face. I didn't know him at all, I was sure of it.

Kyle. He looked like a Kyle.

There was a dragging noise overhead as he unstrapped the bungee then lugged the heavy Coleman cooler off the edge of the tailgate. After a moment, his dark silhouette came into view, lugging the heavy cooler.

I slunk to the edge of my hiding spot once again and watched as Fuckboy Kyle stepped into the dim porch light. He struggled with the knob, then kicked at the door with one foot to wedge his body through the opening. "Are you coming or not?" he called over his shoulder, mumbling something under his breath.

Without waiting for an answer, he let the door slam behind him.

Familiar Voice stayed where he was, next to the truck. He stood rooted to the ground for a moment before walking toward the cabin.

I calculated the distance to the doorstep. How long would it take me to reach him with the crowbar before he could make it inside?

Three seconds.

If I was going to strike, this was my moment. If he got her inside the cabin, the window to act would close.

Run.

Help her.

Run. Now.

Laura's hair swung back and forth while he walked, like the ticking hands of a clock. She hadn't tried to fight him again. If it weren't for the quivering rise and fall of her chest, I would worry she'd passed out again.

There were maybe twenty feet of open space I'd have to cover. If he saw me before I had a chance to strike, I'd lose my chance to take aim at his head. If there was a struggle, I had no doubt who would win, and it definitely wasn't me.

As quietly as I could, I pulled myself out from under the truck and rose to a shaky crouch, now fully exposed. If he turned around, or if Kyle opened the cabin door right now, I was completely visible.

There was now a faint light glimmering through the filthy windows of the little cabin, but the door was still shut. Kyle was nowhere to be seen.

Familiar Voice stopped walking and hesitated again at the edges of the ugly orange halo cast by the porch light. He shifted Laura on his shoulder, his eyes fixed on the cabin door a few yards away.

Now.

Gripping the tire iron tightly in my sweaty hands, I crept forward quickly, careful to pick up my feet with each step so my broken shoes wouldn't slap the ground.

I closed the distance between us in a few steps until I was so close I could hear the deep exhale he made, as if resigning himself to whatever was about to happen, before moving toward the cabin.

Laura's head bobbed against his right shoulder. She couldn't see me, either.

I shifted toward his left side, zeroing in on the crown of his head, where his sandy blond hair swirled in a little circle, like a bullseye.

I had a clear shot.

25

I lifted the tire iron and slammed it down on his head.

I squeezed my eyes shut right before the metal made contact with his skull, which made the dull smack even louder in my ears.

I meant to hit him again, but the horror of hitting another human being—even one who was trying to hurt me—took over. White dots swam in front of my eyes, as if *I* had been the one hit on the head. The slippery tire iron fell out of my hand and landed in the dirt at my feet with a quiet *clunk*.

The man holding Laura over his shoulder didn't react right away. I'd hit him pretty hard, but for a terrifying moment I questioned whether I'd done any damage at all. Was I that far removed from reality?

Laura whipped up her head and saw me. Her blue eyes, rimmed by black streaks of mascara, widened in disbelief. She let out a muffled gasp behind the duct tape over her mouth. I glanced at the back of Familiar Voice's head. There wasn't any blood.

I desperately wanted to see his face and finally click the puzzle pieces into place, but there wasn't time for that right now.

He didn't scream. And he didn't whirl around to grab me, like I'd imagined. Instead, he made a strangled moan and took another step toward the cabin door, still clutching Laura's waist with both hands.

Then he crumpled gracelessly onto the dirt, letting Laura slide over his shoulder. I jumped forward too late to break her fall, and she landed in a heap on the ground. She made a sharp, pained sound and struggled to get to her feet.

Hit him again, the peanut gallery in my brain screamed. *Make sure he's dead.*

How many blows would it take? What if Kyle came back outside during those precious seconds?

No. Just get the apartment key to rip the duct tape. I kept my eyes on Laura, not daring to speak yet as I unzipped the travel pouch then knelt next to her legs. Aside from the drone of the cicadas and the wind in the cottonwoods, the night was quiet again. The cabin door was still closed.

I dragged the key across the duct tape where Laura's calves were crossed, grateful when it split in two with a satisfying, quiet *zip.* I didn't bother trying to rip the strips of tape from her legs. She could run. That was all that mattered right now.

I looked up at her in triumph. She resisted when I grabbed her arm to help her up. Why? Her hands were still bound, but she didn't need those to run.

Laura tilted her chin to the side gesturing at the man on the ground. Then she shook her head back and forth, whipping her dirty hair across her face. *No.*

"I don't understand," I whispered frantically, glancing at the cabin door that would fling open at any moment. "Come on, we have to run now."

She shook her head again insistently. *No.* She moved her jaw up and down, wiggling the duct tape and trying to say something.

I darted my eyes toward the cabin door again, feeling sick from the cold and the fear and the pounding in my head. We were sprawled in plain sight. The window of opportunity to run was closing.

"Your mouth?" I asked distractedly, and she quickly nodded *yes.*

Not wanting to waste any more time, I pulled at the corner of the tape and ripped it off. She didn't even wince. "Get out of here, Liv. Now." She gasped for breath and leaned against me. "He has a gun, but he won't use it unless I try to run again ..."

I froze, not hearing the rest of what she said. *He won't use it unless I try to run ...* I didn't ask who "he" was. I already knew it was Deep Voice.

Never, not once, had I heard a story where a barter like this paid off. It wasn't a real promise. It was just insurance for the guy holding the gun—that you wouldn't unexpectedly flip the script. Men like this said things like that to girls like us, knowing we'd been told our whole lives that if we listened carefully and followed the rules, we'd stay safe.

It was a tempting thought. But ultimately, they did whatever they wanted with that gun.

It's hard to make a kill shot on a moving target, my brain whispered.

Ignoring what Laura had said, I grabbed her arm again and hoisted her to her feet. We were not going to let this moment slip away banking on a promise from someone who had ripped out a chunk of my hair. "They're lying," I hissed. "Laura, you *know* they're lying. Listen to me, okay? Please trust me."

Three minutes until Kyle comes back outside. If that.

The man on the ground groaned and shifted in the dirt. My heartbeat drummed so heavily that I could see little white specks floating into my field of vision once again. He was definitely alive. And he was going to wake up any second.

Hit him again.

I looped my arm through Laura's then bent awkwardly to pick up the tire iron. She gasped.

"No, Liv. Don't hit him again. That's *Tony*."

The words didn't make sense at first. *Tony?*

All of a sudden, the name synced with the distinct feeling of familiarity.

Tony. Delta Tony. Sun-kissed, smiling, Band of Horses T-shirt Tony. Tish's ex-fiancé Tony.

I yanked her toward the cottonwoods and away from the porch light, my mind spinning. This time, she let me pull her along.

Tony.

I glanced over my shoulder at the quiet cabin. The figure on the ground—Tony—hadn't moved again. The cabin door remained shut tight.

I felt like I'd just gone down the rabbit hole into a world where nothing made sense.

I tossed the tire iron into the weeds. I had just hit Tony. Tony had run us off the road. My stomach lurched. *Don't think about it now. Just get out of here.*

Laura stumbled next to me, and I tucked my arm tighter through hers. "Are you okay?" I choked. "Can you run? Or walk?"

She nodded. "I blacked out for a minute in the truck. I definitely can't run. But I can walk."

"That's okay," I murmured, hoping it was true. I threaded my arms through the duct tape binding her hands.

We shuffled away from the cabin, toward the ATV trail and the windbreak of trees. If we could just keep going, we'd be completely hidden by the cover of night soon. At least, I hoped so.

We passed the truck, stumbling forward at an agonizingly slow pace. I was exhausted and shaky after lying frozen in the back of the truck, but compared to Laura I was in pretty good shape. She seemed worse than before, less steady on her feet.

"One more step," I encouraged her, as the déjà vu hit me full force. It felt like we'd been dropped right back onto the hills, making a desperate push for the treeline to escape the predators at our heels.

But the truth was, we'd never really stopped running. We were just farther down the same road, with the same truck and the same deadly threat.

Only now, we both knew who was behind the masks.

Tish had spent almost all of her free time at the Delta house. After the breakup—which Laura had only discovered when all of Tony's photos suddenly disappeared from Tish's Facebook account—Tish had disappeared into herself, spending every free moment at the library. They'd never been a "Facebook official" couple. Tish's relationship status had stayed permanently stuck at "single." So had Tony's, even after he proposed to her.

As far as I knew, nobody—including Tish—had seen Tony since the breakup. Was this some sort of revenge? Was he upset with her for breaking things off?

It felt much darker than that. Something else was going on.

Focus, I told myself, scanning for the best spot to cross the ditch. But it was impossible to keep the unanswerable questions from zipping through my mind.

I was suspicious of everything—and everyone—but I couldn't reconcile what little I knew of Tish's ex with what had happened tonight. I'd only ever known him as the hot Delta who was mostly out of Tish's league and supposedly threw epic parties.

Their engagement had lasted only two weeks before Tish broke things off. When Laura cornered her late one night about the missing Facebook photos—after Tish finally came home from the library— Tish had broken down in tears. She just kept repeating that she couldn't marry him. That it was really her fault. And that she didn't want to talk about it yet.

Laura told me we should give her space. She'd come around. Maybe she and Tony would even get back together. They'd been dating since Rush Week, freshman year. Until the breakup, I'd been under the impression that Tish adored him. They seemed so happy in their photos.

But she wasn't my sister, so I took Laura's lead and didn't pry. Now I wished I had.

I wanted to curl up with Laura and Tish on the living room couch with the ratty blue afghan and unravel the whole story. Instead, I shoved the loose threads and unanswered questions away. If I ever wanted to get any sort of answers, Laura and I were going to have to stay alive first.

Laura glanced over her shoulder. "That other guy—the one with the deeper voice. Kyle," she rasped. "The one with the gun. He … he's the guy who sold Tish the Volvo. I didn't recognize his voice. But when he took his mask off and I saw his face …"

Her voice dropped so low I could barely hear her. "While Tony was carrying me, he told me that everything would be fine. That I should just go along with it. That Kyle wasn't that bad."

I didn't respond. Kyle was that bad. And, clearly, so was Tony.

She turned to look behind us. I followed her gaze but could no longer pick out Tony's dark, silent shape on the ground.

When we reached the edge of the ditch, a thought struck me. "Where are the keys to the truck?" The idea that we could drive away from all of this instead of cowering in the weeds made my teeth hurt with longing.

She shook her head no, and I bit back my disappointment. "Kyle has them. He took them inside."

I hesitated, trailing my eyes down the long ATV trail that led to the open gate. The two tall anchor posts were still barely visible in the distance.

If we kept going down the trail, the way the truck had gone, we could move faster. And we wouldn't risk getting lost. But there was hardly any brush cover in that direction. If Kyle came out of the cabin, he'd definitely see us. The only other option was to hide ourselves along the treeline of cottonwoods running beside the ditch, then bushwhack our way through the weeds until we made our way back to the main road.

I made a decision. The gate was too far. And the ATV trail was too exposed.

I nodded to Laura and led the way down the edge of the shallow ditch bank. "Come on, careful with the mud," I stole a glance back at the cabin one more time, itching to be hidden in the trees. The door was still closed, but it wouldn't stay that way. I imagined Kyle inside with an IPA, impatiently waiting for Tony to come inside. I was surprised he'd lasted this long.

"You didn't run for help," Laura said in a barely audible voice as I helped her up the other side. Thankfully, the shallow ditch was nothing compared to the river we'd crossed earlier in the evening. Just weeds, a little mud, and a shallow puddle at the bottom.

I didn't respond. I could tell she wanted to believe I had saved her from whatever was going to happen in that cabin. Maybe I had a plan that went beyond this exact moment. But the truth was that I was flying by the seat of my pants in a way I never had before. I had zero idea what we were going to do thirty seconds from now. All I knew was we had to keep going.

We moved as quietly as we could, parting the tall cheat grass along the other bank then heading toward the tightly knit cottonwoods. I swallowed painfully, the weight of my reckless choice pressing against my airway as I scanned the towering treeline.

Laura shifted her arm, nudging my shoulder and bringing me back from the spiral of ominous thoughts. "Thank you … for not leaving me."

I fought back tears, relieved at least she wasn't upset with me. "I couldn't let them take you. I can undo your hands once we—"

The animalistic howl sliced through the steady flutter of leaves like a knife.

At first, the abrupt noise confused me. I had never heard anything like it.

In what felt like slow motion, I looked back at the spot in the distance where Tony should have been lying.

Now he was standing upright.

26

I stumbled backward, my arm locked through Laura's, urging her to move faster toward the ghostly, knotted tree trunks, even though her breathing was already ragged. Our pathetic party shoes crunched through the weeds loudly now, threatening to broadcast our location as Tony's screams followed close on our heels.

I should have hit him again. And on top of that, I'd been stupid enough to toss the tire iron into the weeds, as if its purpose were complete.

It was much too late to retrieve it now.

Behind us came the wooden *thud* of the cabin door slamming shut. Then a distant, incredulous voice that echoed through the stillness. "What the *fuck*?"

Then again. Louder. "What the *actual fuck,* you dumbass? I go inside for like, one second ..."

I cringed at the closeness of the sound. At the very most, we'd put half a football field between us.

My flats caught on a rock and threatened to tip me onto my knees right as we finally reached the shadowy embrace of the cottonwood trees. Laura stumbled against me, nearly toppling both of us into the lower branches of the first tree.

The dry weeds crunched loudly under our scuffling footsteps in the sudden stillness. Tony had stopped screaming. Kyle had gone silent too.

I'd hoped the trees would provide a thicker, forested cover, but the windbreak past the ditch wasn't quite the dense blanket I'd hoped. The gaps between some of the trees were wide enough that if someone were standing in the right spot on the ATV trail, they would see us easily if they were looking in the right spot for a flash of movement. Thankfully, the tall grass in the fields on the other side of the trees was nearly waist-high in spots. If we could just put some distance between us and the cabin, we could still disappear into the darkness.

"Let's head this way," I whispered, angling away from the tree-line but trying to keep us pointed in the general direction of the main road. It would be easy to get disoriented and move in circles, once we lost sight of the cabin.

Laura didn't answer. She cocked her head slightly to one side, listening with wide eyes. I did the same, already knowing what I'd hear.

The faint crunch of footsteps, coming fast toward us from the direction of the ditch.

Focus.

There were no readily apparent hiding spots on this side of the cottonwoods. But if we could just keep moving through the weeds, toward the main road—without making too much noise—the night would help hide us. I parted the tall weeds with one hand as we moved, looking for the bare patches of dirt beneath where we could place our feet without slapping the dirt.

We got maybe twenty steps before the glint of metal directly in front of us caught my eye.

I gasped and stopped short, pulling back on Laura's arm just in time before she stepped directly into the obscured barbed wire fence.

It wasn't the standard cattle fences that covered most of rural Idaho. Those would have been easy enough to cross with a little effort. This was a tightly strung, imposing fence that made me think of a prison more than a rural cabin. It stood maybe eight feet high, judging by how far the last two rungs hovered above my head. What the hell was this place? Who needed a barbed wire fence that tall?

The images from *Saw* came back to me again, along with the answer. Someone who either wanted to keep something out, or keep something in.

I let go of Laura's arm then knelt and studied the bottom rung of the fence, testing how high I could pull it. There was barely any give in the thick, tightly strung wire that ran a few inches above the dirt.

My brain ticked through our remaining options for escape—none of them good. If we had more time, we could dig our way underneath the bottle rung of the fence, through the packed dirt. I pulled as hard as I could on the thick wire, placing my fingers between the spikes and lifting with my full weight. It resisted with a loud metallic shriek, and I quickly let go. There wasn't room for me to shimmy underneath it—not without getting completely torn up, anyway.

I narrowed my eyes and followed the skeletal outline of the barbed wire fence until it disappeared into the cottonwoods. The gate was on the other side of those trees—and so was Kyle.

"I don't think we can get under the fence," I whispered in defeat, nodding in the opposite direction of the cottonwoods and the gate. "Maybe if we follow it that way, we'll find a broken spot."

Laura stared at the fence, her eyes huge and black.

Behind us, fast, faint footsteps thudded along the dirt road in the quiet night. Except for the patter of the leaves at our left, the night was eerily still. Even the cicadas seemed to have gone silent now. It was much too quiet to hide our footsteps very well. And too quiet for someone who had just been bashed in the head with a tire iron. I'd expected Tony to keep hollering, but Kyle must have told him to shut up. Was he inside the cabin now, thinking of all the ways he'd pay me back? Was he chasing behind us too? Was he dead? I shook my head. That was too much to hope for.

I took Laura's arm again and we moved deeper into the weeds, parallel to the barbed wire. Keeping my teeth gritted to stop them from chattering, I scanned the skeletal fence while we walked. Back and forth, back and forth across the spiky tightropes, looking for a broken rung or a spot where some animal had dug its way underneath, creating a place where we could wriggle through.

If only we'd taken the ATV trail back through the open gate, maybe we'd be free.

The stream of if-onlies running through my head was near constant. If only we'd stayed home. If only Laura hadn't hit her head on the way down the slope. If only the cell had connected during any of the dozens of times I'd tried to call 9-1-1. If only the other driver we'd passed had paid more attention and realized something was wrong, then tried to help. If only I'd hit Tony a little harder. If only this damn fence wasn't here. If only we hadn't been so quick to hide in the trees, leaving us skulking along the perimeter like trapped animals.

I knew it didn't help us. Not really. My brain zipped among the lost chances like a bug in a zapper, still trying to find a way out, unwilling to admit it was already trapped.

Shoo, I commanded all the tattered wings beating at my exhausted brain. I needed to worry about what came next: Not what had brought us here. That was the only way out.

I suddenly remembered the *Choose Your Own Adventure* books I had loved when I was little—the gateway drug to a lifetime of fascination with true crime.

The idea that every choice, no matter how small, mattered had fascinated my anxious brain. Every chapter ended with a choice that set the rest of the story in motion. Sliding doors—the outcome of which either set you free or sealed your fate.

Go to the bonfire: turn to page 10. Get in the back of the truck: turn to page 167.

Cross the ditch, turn to page 39. Stop to cut loose Laura's hands: turn to page 256. Keep moving along the barbed wire, away from the ATV trail: turn to page 35.

I had always cheated while I read them, keeping my finger at the chapter junction and flipping through the pages to see where each fork in the road would lead so that I never ended up in jail, forfeited the pirate treasure, or got hopelessly lost in a snowstorm.

Or died.

The footsteps on gravel were getting closer. *Crunch. Crunch. Crunch.*

There were no takebacks. As much as I wanted to keep my finger in the book while I flipped ahead to see what happened, or backtracked to the last choice I'd made to set a different trajectory, that was simply not an option.

We just had to keep choosing. Keep moving. Find a way to stay ahead of them. And keep hoping those choices didn't end the entire book in disaster.

I hazarded a glance behind us, taking some comfort in the cloud cover overhead that had extinguished even the sliver of moon and most of the stars prickling through the black expanse overhead. Our breathing sounded loud and harsh in my ears, punctuated by the occasional chatter of our teeth, but from the sound of the footsteps on the other side of the ditch, we still had a good lead on Kyle.

A deep voice cut through the night, making Laura and I freeze where we stood.

"I can't see you from here, but I'm sure I'll hit something if I fire."

Kyle.

A faint but distinct click of metal replied in the silence that hung between us.

Laura sagged slightly at the waist, whether in fear or exhaustion I couldn't tell. I threaded my arm tighter through hers, wishing there were a few seconds to spare to cut her hands loose from the duct tape. Then we kept moving along the perimeter of the barbed wire fence, ignoring him.

With each step, I strained my eyes beyond the fence, into the dark fields that stretched toward the crumbling paved road. Was night hunting a thing? Were there other sportsmen—like the ones driving the truck with the lumpy tarps—out here in the middle of nowhere at night? I felt for the whistle, the only other tool at my disposal, in my travel pouch. If I got the chance, I'd use it. It would broadcast our location in a heartbeat. But that was only if we actually wanted to be found.

There was no sign of any other vehicles, houses, or lights.

Even with the slight flutter of the leaves in the breeze, each tentative rustle of the grass and each step we took sounded like a dead giveaway to our location. There was no burbling river to mask our movements anymore. Nothing to hide the crack of a twig or the slap of our shoes, even if Laura could run.

"Dude, where are you?" Tony's voice, clear but farther away than Kyle's had been, broke the silence.

He sounded more pissed than he did injured.

His question hung in the air. Kyle didn't respond.

The tall grass flanking the barbed-wire fence suddenly disappeared, giving way to an expansive clearing. From the absence of grass, the hard ground must have been cleared at some point but had since grown over with a thin blanket of feral ground cover.

But that wasn't the only thing in the clearing.

Laura and I looked at each other in confusion. A contingent of strangely shaped objects stood silhouetted in relief against the navy horizon. Concentric circles glowed faintly on one of them. Two others displayed crude stick drawings of animals.

When I squinted, I could make out more shapes, scattered at intervals throughout the clearing.

The back of my neck prickled a warning, even as Laura and I made a beeline for the nearest object.

Whatever they were, they offered somewhere to hide, at least. A creepy shield.

When we got closer to the hulking object painted with orange circles, I realized it was a thick piece of plywood, propped up in the dirt.

My foot landed on something small and round in the dirt as I reached out a hand to touch the pocked surface of the plywood.

I suddenly knew what this clearing was for.

The plywood was riddled with bullet holes.

The weeds hid scattered bullet casings.

The plywood shapes were targets. And this was a shooting range.

27

Kyle's voice boomed through the silence again—loud, but still not particularly close by. If I had to guess, he was on the dirt road. Maybe that meant he wasn't sure which way we'd gone.

"Do I need to count to three?"

Laura looked at me in terror. He didn't sound particularly upset or frazzled.

He should have been both, since we had outwitted him and escaped.

I had the sinking feeling that this meant we'd done neither.

There was another brief silence. I nudged Laura in the ribs, nodding toward another plywood cutout looming in the dark night. With each step we took, I noticed more shell casings and bullets scattered among the weeds.

The sound of soft laughter blended with the patter of leaves. "Okay, I'll count to three. But after that, all bets are off. You can come out now—and I promise I won't shoot you. Or you can make me play hide-and-seek, and I promise that I won't stop until I hit something. Payback for what you did to my buddy. There's really nowhere to run. Just six hundred acres of weeds."

I locked eyes with Laura again. Six hundred acres? I had no idea how big that really was, but it sounded enormous.

He cleared his throat one more time. "I found you before. I'll find you again."

It was a statement of fact as much as a threat. He would find us.

Laura shook her head and gripped my arm harder but didn't move again when I tried to pull her arm toward the next cutout, away from the sound of his voice.

There was no way to tell for certain without the lay of the land, but I had a sinking feeling Kyle was telling the truth: there was nowhere to hide. I had seen the signs for sportsmen's access and the endless fields. Aside from the windbreak of cottonwoods that flanked the stretch of trail leading to the cabin itself, there were no other trees in sight to speak of. There was nowhere to hide, except the darkness—and the shooting range.

Not a great place to elude someone with a gun. But what else could we do?

From the way Laura wobbled on her feet, she was running on fumes. She should have been admitted to a hospital hours ago. Speed was not a viable option. Hiding was not a viable option. Kyle would find us and then shoot us. But there was no way I was going to just walk back to him and whatever was inside the cabin.

Don't let them take you to a second location. Your chances of surviving an assault at any given location are 97%. Your chances of survival, if you are taken to a second location, drop to 30%.

It was abduction 101. How many times had I spouted that statistic, insisting it was always smarter to keep fighting? A second location meant you were on their turf. It meant they had some kind of plan in mind.

That ship had sailed, of course. We were already at the second location. What were the survival statistics for surrender, versus a deadly round of hide-and-seek?

Three seconds until a bullet pierced the darkness.

Three minutes until it found a target.

"One." He was actually counting.

"I'm going back," Laura said, squaring her shoulders and tilting her chin. Wet trails glinted on her cheeks, and she tried for a tremulous smile. "Maybe … Tony was telling the truth. I just go along with whatever Kyle wants, and it'll all be over soon. And then I'll get to go home."

I stared at her in horror. "No," I choked in a whisper. "No. Laura. He's a liar. He's a psychopath too."

"Two." The word echoed on top of mine, stretching out into several long, loud syllables.

Laura squeezed her eyes shut and wrenched her arm away from me. "I'll slow you down," she whispered firmly. "He'll find us both. I can't keep up. Go, Liv. Now."

I couldn't let this happen, not after we'd both fought so hard. "We can keep going," I scrambled. "There's lots of places to hide—" I gestured to the makeshift shooting range in desperation. "We'll find a gap in the fence somewhere." I scanned the horizon beyond the fence again, frantic to see something I hadn't noticed before. Just one more slim possibility I could grasp that would keep the pages turning in this story.

There wasn't one.

Laura clenched her jaw and backed away a few more steps, out into the open. "Keep running. I'm going back. I don't think they even know you're here yet."

"Laur, no, I left you once—" That was all I managed to get out before Laura whipped around and staggered back toward the cabin.

"I'm coming back!" she screamed hoarsely. "Run," she choked in a whisper as she turned to look at me one more time, tears streaming down her cheeks in earnest, her mouth stretched open in a wordless sob.

I stood where I was behind the plywood target, numb with disbelief. She stumbled away from me, in the direction of the looming cottonwoods.

"Two-and-a-half. Hurry up, it's fucking freezing out here."

Laura picked up her feet, trying to move faster. She took one quick step, then tripped on something in the dirt, landing on her side in the tall weeds. Grass rustled, obscuring her from my line of sight. She yelped, a strangled sob managing to escape as she called out again through the darkness, trying to get back to her feet without the aid of her hands. "I'm coming! Please just don't shoot, okay? I'm coming! Just can't run very fast…" The weeds trembled violently again, before her hunched silhouette reappeared and staggered forward a few more steps.

My throat closed so tight I could barely draw in a breath.

Laura was right. This time there was no question. I should run. *Really* run. I felt sure I could even scale the barbed wire if I really tried—and was willing to get cut up.

I couldn't do jack shit for either of us with my broken, stupid shoes, inside-out-disco-ball halter top, and rape whistle.

"Last chance, girls." He drew out the last syllable in a sort of singsong.

Girls. He knew Laura wasn't out here alone. Of course he did. I imagined the tire iron I'd tossed into the weeds.

Dread rooted me to the ground, and dread forced me to put one foot in front of the other. I waded back through the grass and took Laura's arm. She fought me off at first with a feeble hip check. Then she leaned into my shoulder, breathing hard while her tears fell on my collarbone and mine landed on her hair as we walked back along the barbed wire fence, the way we had come.

"We're coming," I screamed. "Don't shoot."

A few seconds later, we shuffled through the treeline and into the open.

He waited patiently while we stumbled through the mud in the ditch, his arms crossed against his chest. He smiled when we finally struggled up the other side, and even in the dim light I knew it didn't reach his eyes.

As soon as we stood in front of him on the scrubby ATV trail, cowering like contrite children, he lifted one hand. Then he tossed something toward us. It hit the dirt with an unexpectedly light thud and bounced a few times before coming to rest beside my shoes.

I realized instantly that it wasn't a gun.

It was a lighter.

He shrugged and burst out laughing at the expression on our faces. "Don't feel stupid, I've got a real piece in the cabin." He strode forward and grabbed Laura's arm firmly then tilted his chin in the direction of the truck.

When he looked back at me, his eyes were dark slits. "I knew I put the fucking tailgate back up." Shoving Laura toward the cabin door, he shot out a hand and grabbed me roughly by the hair. Tears sprang to my eyes as his fingers dug into the already broken skin of my scalp. I bit my cheek to keep from whimpering.

He leaned close to my ear. "Very MacGyver. I'm impressed that you had the balls. But if you try something like that again, I will give that ugly-ass cabin a fresh coat of paint with your blood."

28

The inside of the cabin smelled like spilled beer and dust.

A cheap throw rug covered the uncarpeted floor of the front room in a blanket of orange shag. The walls were stacked with unfinished plywood shelves lined with dusty canned food and a smattering of tools. A small TV was perched on a plastic rain barrel upended in front of the couch.

The main living room branched into a dark hallway. I couldn't see where it led, but three disembodied deer heads floated in its shadows like sentinels. A badly taxidermied antelope along the far wall stared at us forlornly from its perch next to the brick backing of a squat black potbelly stove.

The target range suddenly made sense.

A dim lamp in the corner stretched our shadows across the rough wood floor. At our feet, faint brownish splotches stood out from the light floor. A thin metal sign near the door, held up with a tangle of wire, read "Big racks only."

Everything in the room was coated in a filmy layer of dust.

Tony was sitting inside the entryway on a threadbare green couch, one hand pressed against the back of his head. Smears of blood and dust streaked the front of his shirt. I felt a tiny burst of satisfaction. He looked almost as miserable as I felt.

"See? If you just ask nice, they'll come right back," Kyle said, pushing Laura toward Tony on the couch.

Tony glanced at Laura but didn't try to break her fall when she landed hard against the arm of the couch, doubling over and nearly flipping onto his lap in a heap.

Kyle laughed while Laura struggled to right herself, finally managing to scramble onto the far edge of the nasty green couch cushions, a few feet away from Tony. She curled her dirty, scratched legs into a ball against her chest.

Tony's eyes bored into mine and his face darkened. He muttered something under his breath. "Bitch," was the only word I could make out.

Kyle laughed harder. "That was your own fault, not hers. She never would have snuck up on me like that." He snorted and shook me roughly so that my head snapped back and forth. I gritted my teeth together and tried not to make a sound.

"Look at her. She's like half your size and dressed like Fuck-me Barbie. Are those sequins?" He let go of my hair to tug at the hem of my shirt.

Tony shifted his glare to Kyle. "Whatever," he mumbled.

Laura slowly looked up from where she sat, and we exchanged a glance. It was no surprise he was pissed off. He'd just been clocked in the head—by me. But there was something else in his voice. Contempt—and not just for me, but for Kyle.

Kyle was clearly the ringleader. Still, Tony was a willing accomplice. Why? Something had prompted him to put on that mask in the first place. But whatever it was, I was more certain than ever of the growing crack between the two men.

"What do you want from us?" I couldn't stop the question from spilling out of my mouth. I hated the way my voice sounded— ragged and small. Powerless and meek.

Kyle didn't answer. He let go of my shirt hem with a last tug then reached behind the ancient-looking TV and pulled something out.

The gun.

"Relax, MacGyver. It's Friday night. And you look like you're ready to party with that outfit. So let's party."

He resumed his vise-grip on my hair. The tender, broken skin screamed under his touch. I could feel his breath, hot and dry, on the back of my neck. Tony looked at Kyle expectantly as if he, too, was less than satisfied by the answer Kyle had given to my question.

I wanted to whirl around and kick him. Claw at his eyes. I didn't feel squeamish about the idea of seeing blood and gore now. Not his, anyway.

Still, he was right about what he'd said. I was dressed like a Fuck-me Barbie. I was half his size. I was exhausted. And I'd tossed my weapon in the dirt like a complete idiot—not that it stood a chance next to that gun.

"Tish has probably already called the police," I tried, which earned me another shake. I felt more of my hair rip at the roots and couldn't stop myself from whimpering. Laura shrank against the disgusting couch, like it might swallow her up if she pressed herself into it long enough.

Kyle chuckled softly, as if reading my mind. "Sure she has. Tish the Bitch is the reason you're here," he said matter-of-factly. Then, "Let's go. I want another beer, and you need a time out for that little stunt you pulled. God, you've made this so much more stressful than it had to be."

My vision narrowed as he yanked me toward the hallway, deeper into the shadows of the cabin, away from Laura. The glassy-eyed deer heads mounted along the hallway watched impassively.

He called to Tony over his shoulder. "Watch that one until I get back. Can you handle that?" Under his breath, he added, "Pussy."

Keeping one hand on the back of my head, he pulled me roughly against his side as I scrambled to keep up down the length of the dark hallway.

We passed one open doorway, where I caught a glimpse of two bunks. At the end of the hall was a tiny kitchen. No fridge or sink. Just a hotplate, more animal heads, and more shelving lined with cans of food.

I caught snatches of Laura's voice, but it was impossible to hear much of anything above the pounding in my head.

Wherever he was taking me, I already knew I didn't want to go there.

He stopped abruptly and swung me around to face another dark room. He lifted one hand along the wall, feeling for a light switch maybe? With my face buried against the fabric of his hoodie, I realized he was wearing some kind of musky, expensive cologne. The smell of it, mixed with his sweat—and the distinctly metallic odor that had to be blood—made my stomach heave.

The light flicked on, bathing the floorboards in an orange glow, and he dragged me across the threshold of what looked like a utility room. I darted my eyes over the tangle of wires, pipes, miscellaneous tools—and a small, grimy window. Could I fit through it if I squeezed?

I took inventory of the tools on the wall: a saw, a hammer, a screwdriver on a tool rack above a crude shelf. A lone spray can with an orange lid sat on the shelf. *Leave me alone in here. Please, god, leave me alone.*

Instead, he shoved me to my knees.

"Please, don't hurt me," I begged, as if he wasn't already doing exactly that.

He gripped my hair tighter and shoved my face against the dirty wood of the floor, ramming one knee into my back. From the next room, Laura shrieked my name louder.

There was a crash from the other room, then silence, except for the sound of my own gasps as Kyle's kneecap dug against my spine.

"Did Blondie come back to life?" Kyle called, shifting his weight and listening expectantly. "You need my help?"

I couldn't breathe with his knee on my back. I tried to shift positions, but it only made him press down harder.

"No." The response that came from the other room was flat and decisive.

Tish the Bitch is the reason you're here. The words looped through my mind as the dimly lit room started to dissolve into black static. What did Tish have to do with this nightmare? What was happening to Laura in the other room?

Kyle removed the knee from my back, and for a moment I thought he had changed his mind about whatever he'd been about to do.

I gasped for breath and tried to roll onto my side. When he pressed the knee lightly against my spine again, I froze, trying not to cough from the dust burning my throat.

"Please," I repeated in a whisper. "Please, I'll do whatever you want, okay? Just don't…" I trailed off, not wanting to put words to the awful possibilities waiting to burst into reality. This utility room wasn't anything like the torture chamber in *Saw*, but I could imagine plenty of awful things that could happen in the next few minutes, regardless.

I craned my neck to look up at him, but he didn't meet my gaze. His hand was stretching toward something on the floor. My eyes followed the movement of his hand in a haze.

A barely noticeable handle protruded from the warped wood.

I watched in horrified fascination as he used his free hand to lift the hatch door to reveal a black void.

It was the opening to a crawl space.

29

"Get in. Now." He gestured to the three-foot by three-foot hole he had opened in the dusty wood floor of the cabin.

Cold air that reeked of mildew and something worse wafted from the opening. A splintering ladder stood propped against the side, the first rung just visible from my position on the floor.

I clenched my jaw against the gag reflex that pulsed in my throat.

He sighed in exasperation, as if I were a petulant toddler refusing to take a nap. "Go on, move," he directed, gesturing with the gun.

"What's down there?" I asked, not really expecting him to answer but willing to do anything to delay my descent into that pit.

"Go find out," Kyle prompted in a singsong, nudging me with his foot and cocking the gun. "I'd tie you up, but this is easier. So why waste the duct tape?"

I stared at him in wide-eyed desperation.

"You seem to enjoy tucking yourself away in clever little hiding spots," he said casually. "So what's the problem?" He glanced over his shoulder and tilted his head, listening. I couldn't hear Laura's or Tony's voice anymore.

When I didn't move, he pointed the gun at my face. "Get down there already."

I crawled to the edge of the dark hole in the floor and peered through the gaping mouth of the trap door. The only thing I could see past the opening was the faint outline of a cement support beam flanked by tattered insulation.

The smell—putrid and sweet, like someone had mixed vomit with sugar—got stronger the closer I got.

Even with a gun pointed at my head, I couldn't bring myself to willingly go down there. I had a sudden flashback to the time I was ten and my dad had crawled under the porch to investigate the distinctly rotten smell wafting across the porch: the same dank, rotten smell wafting from the black hole in front of me now. He'd been in and out in five minutes, while my brother and I waited on the front steps. When he'd emerged, he held a plastic bag full of something hairy and rotten—a raccoon, I later learned. He held it up in triumph then quickly dropped the bag to his side, mistaking our reaction for dismay at the pitiful creature's death. We were actually looking at two enormous brown spiders, legs splayed as they clung to the sleeve of his filthy shirt. He followed our wide-eyed gaze, carefully set the disgusting bag down on the lawn, and flicked the spiders onto the cement with the same stick he'd used to nudge the dead raccoon into the plastic bag.

I had nightmares about the whole thing for weeks.

Kyle kicked my side again, just enough to hurt. "Move," he repeated impatiently. "Or I promise, I'll make you move."

Desperate not to do what he was asking, I wavered too long at the edge of the darkness.

"Did I stutter?" He shoved me with his foot again, harder this time, and I managed to brace myself against the edges of the opening to keep from tumbling down into the trap door headfirst.

The pain in my ribs screamed at me to comply. Things would only get worse if I didn't move on my own, and knew I'd be forced into the crawl space one way or another.

Get into the crawl space willingly, turn to page 165. Live a little longer.

Wait until he shoots you, turn to page 190. Die fast.

"Okay, I'm going now," I said in a wobbly voice, reaching for the rickety ladder.

We made eye contact for a brief second as I rolled onto my stomach and lowered one foot onto the ladder rung. The cold air lapped at my legs, eager to suck me into its depths.

His full lips were partly open against his bright white teeth. I took in the tiny flecks of spittle in his close-cropped dark beard. The mussed but clean lines of his expensive haircut. The wide, black doe eyes with long eyelashes in an otherwise masculine face.

It was so much worse than the mask.

His pinpoint pupils locked in on me. To my surprise, I didn't see any of the rage I'd heard in his voice and in the set of his jaw.

Instead, I saw anticipation.

* * *

The dirt floor of the crawl space was only about six feet below the trap door opening.

Same depth as a grave.

As soon as my feet touched the dirt floor, Kyle pulled the ladder upward, nearly hitting me in the face as the wooden legs clattered through the trap door in the floor.

I took one step backward into the darkness, crouching to avoid the spidery insulation directly above my head. I kept my chin tilted toward the sickly orange light of the opening, like a desperate flower.

There was a hollow *thunk* as Kyle dropped the ladder on the utility room floor above my head.

Then, without another word or even a glance at the girl he'd forced underground, he shut the trap door, sealing me inside the dark, reeking crawl space.

A grave, a grave, a grave, my brain screamed.

But not quite a grave. Not yet. I'd been buried alive.

I crouched on the dirt, pulling my legs in tight and wrapping my arms around my knees. I felt for the shape of the two cell phones tucked in my travel pouch but didn't even bother to pull them out. They were both completely useless and very nearly dead. Just like me.

I stayed frozen on the cold ground for a few seconds, listening to the footsteps above as Kyle dragged something heavy over the top of the hatch door.

"Blondie still playing opossum?" he called overhead as he walked away. His voice carried easily past the floorboards and the tattered insulation.

The footsteps stopped, followed by deep laughter.

Something with whispery legs crawled across my hand. I flung it away, tasting blood as I bit down on my cheek to stop myself from screaming.

The darkness in the depths of the crawl space was not quite as complete as I had imagined while looking down into the terrifying hole from above. But the lumpy, indistinguishable silhouettes surrounding me on the ground were slim comfort.

Each breath I took was thick with the smell of death and decay. My heartbeat pounded so loudly in my ears that I wondered—maybe even hoped—it might finally burst. How long were they planning to leave me down here? Was this really a "time-out"? Or had I seen the sun for the last time?

How long would I survive down here if they decided to leave me for good?

My brain was quick with an answer.

Three days without water.

A violent shudder racked my body. The idea of surviving thirty seconds in this hellhole was barely tolerable. Three days of slowly wasting away, while the spiders and the bugs explored my skin, was impossible to fathom. What would happen if I simply couldn't take the fear and the horror and the whispering legs anymore? Was this insanity? Would my body keep living, increasingly numb to the non-stop terror, while my mind went dark? Or would I feel this panic and despair until my heart really did explode like a spent engine.

More scurrying legs across the bare skin on the top of my feet.

I slapped and scratched at my skin as the tears came hot and furious down my cheeks.

Earlier, I would have said that I was exhausted from running. From the current of adrenaline and fear flooding my body while I did everything I could think of to escape and outwit the men in the truck.

The syrupy anesthetic I felt working its way through my veins now, urging me to go numb and float away from the horror of it all, wasn't about survival anymore. And it wasn't fear.

Fear was a warning, a survival instinct. It meant there might still be a way out, if only you could keep your legs pumping and your brain firing long enough to find out.

This numbness was a shutdown switch, to save me from feeling the full brunt of the awfulness.

It was the same thing an antelope felt when it had run its best—but been caught by the lion anyway. It didn't need the adrenaline anymore to keep its legs pumping. It needed to go numb, so it wouldn't feel every moment of being eaten alive.

I pictured the deer heads on the walls with their vacant glass eyes. The dead doe in the hills with its gaping black sockets.

Same predators, same ending.

Something tickled under my thighs. I shuddered violently and scrambled backward, desperate to escape the legs but equally desperate not to let myself go completely numb. Not yet. But as I put one hand down, I realized in an instant that the surface of the crawl space wasn't dry, cold dirt beneath my fingers anymore.

My palm had landed in the middle of something cold, bumpy, and wet.

The putrid smell in the dank air instantly intensified.

A fresh surge of adrenaline burst through the syrupy numbness, and I drew my hand out of the gooey mess like it had been burned, unable to stop the scream from tearing through my throat.

I blinked hard and whipped my head around to see what my hand had landed in.

My eyes had adjusted just enough to the darkness—and I had moved close enough to a small vent in the concrete wall that let a trickle of dim moonlight into the dank crawl space—that I could see what my hand had smashed.

It was the partially decomposed body of a small animal, its gore and bones now spread through the dirt floor in a dark, lumpy smear where my hand had smashed the rotting corpse.

Deep laughter drifted overhead in response to my screams.

I felt more legs creep across my bare legs and arms, nimble and relentless.

Sour bile rose in my throat. I retched through the tears and tried to wipe away the slimy carnage, using the dim light from the vent to watch where I put my hands.

I backed toward the cinderblock wall thick with spiderwebs until I could go no farther.

The adrenaline that had burst through the haze was already receding, like bathwater through an open drain. I stared into the darkness, unblinking, methodically wiping my hand against the slick lining of my halter top until I couldn't detect any of the slippery wetness.

I closed my eyes and tucked my hands into tight fists on my lap. I couldn't feel the raw edge of the nail that had broken off anymore.

Somewhere above me, there was another crash. The floorboards on the ceiling of the utility room rattled softly, sending a tuft of insulation floating to the floor.

Don't go numb, I begged the off-switch in my brain even as I felt myself drawing closer to the relief the oblivion offered.

This couldn't be the end.

But I couldn't help wondering what was happening in the living room of the cabin.

Was it worse than this?

30

The numbness worked faster than the cold, turning my arms and legs to stone.

A frantic voice in the back of my mind shouted incessant instructions to move, to keep trying, keep fighting, keep looking for a way out.

But I couldn't anymore.

I stayed where I was, frozen in place beneath the tiny vent, my arms and legs pulled close in a rigid ball, letting the static mute the crawling sensations on my raw skin.

There was no question anymore. I'd chosen wrong. I'd failed. And this was the price.

My story—and Laura's—would end here. There were no more pages to flip. No more forks in the road. No more gambles. No more rules of three. No more blogosphere wisdom.

As the seconds ticked past, I gave myself permission to float away, desperate to distance myself from the smell of death in my nose and Laura's distant sobs in my ears.

Something larger than a spider shuffled next to me in the dark, and I imagined myself somewhere else, anywhere else. Back in the apartment, watching *Gray's Anatomy* reruns under an oversized pink quilt with Laura in our pajamas on Saturday mornings. Kayaking with my mom on the Clearwater River back home in Lewiston, scanning for deer on the shore and ospreys in the trees. At the Pie Hole, placing pepperonis onto the pizza dough in circles, trying to end up with a perfect spiral when I reached the center. Flipping through the colorful photos of famous paintings in my humanities textbook, like I did to calm my anxiety when I got burned out on studying for a test. Applying eye shadow in the mirror for a night out, dipping the brush into jewel-colored pots to make the curves and angles of my face shimmer and deepen.

Through the hazy images playing like a movie reel in my head, I realized that the voices above me had changed. Loud footsteps thumped across the wood floor, followed by a scraping sound at the entrance to the crawl space overhead, a few yards away.

A sliver of light appeared in the dingy insulation on the ceiling as the trap door opened a few inches. I lifted my head and stared at it dully.

Kyle's voice—and then Laura's—drifted toward me through the putrid air. It was difficult to focus on what either of them was saying, like I was hearing the sounds from underwater. All I knew was that Laura was begging—like I had—to keep from being forced underground.

More footsteps. Then Tony's voice, tenor to Kyle's bass. He sounded less angry than exasperated.

I dropped the analysis. It didn't matter. Whether he was angry, exasperated, filled with hatred for Kyle, or on the verge of a mental breakdown, he hadn't lifted a finger to help us.

Kyle barked something in response, and then all was silent—except for the sound of Laura's sobs—until the trap door suddenly flipped open all the way.

In the syrupy orange glow that poured into the crawl space from above, I could see that the floor around me was more debris than dirt. Bumpy piles littered the floor. Some scraps of insulation, some dead insects, some dark spots that looked like droppings.

Hundreds of tiny shapes drew back from the light, into the shadows on the floor and along the tattered, decrepit sheets of insulation falling down from the ceiling.

A bulky shadow shifted above the open crawl space, blocking the square of light. Kyle's laugh boomed clearly now. "Don't be a snob," he was saying. "It's not so bad. I really thought we could hang out together, but then you went and spilled my beer all over me ..." The light shifted again. "Now I have to wear this. God, my stepdad was such a redneck."

The shadow crossed the square of light, and Laura sobbed louder.

"Don't worry. it's just for a little while. I don't know about you, but I'm feeling wiped out. When we're all feeling fresh, we'll play, okay?"

My ears perked up. *Just for a little while.* He wasn't planning to leave us down here for good. We weren't going to die down here.

Not here, anyway.

"Is Olivia down there? What did you do to her?" The words came out between sobs.

"MacGyver is just relaxing," he drawled. "Go find her." His voice tightened. "I told you earlier, it's either the hard way or the easy way. But you keep choosing the hard way."

"What's ... what's down there?" Laura stalled, her voice so quiet I could barely make out the words.

Kyle laughed again. "Friends, silly!"

Friends. I swallowed and refused to think about how many *friends* were down here. I was positive he wasn't referring to me.

"Hurry up. Move," he said impatiently. Had a few minutes or an hour gone by since he'd forced me down here? I honestly didn't know anymore.

"Tony!" Laura cried again. From the sound of her voice, she was still in the doorway of the utility room. "I don't care what you did. Please stop him. Please. This isn't you!"

Kyle's laughter boomed again. "Tony!" he mimicked in a frail, high voice. "Sweet Tony! This isn't *you!*"

There was no response.

Kyle made an exasperated sound in his throat, and the shadows above me shifted in tandem with a muffled thud. Laura yelped in pain.

The sound of the yelp finally snapped me out of my daze. Leaving my spot on the ground by the tiny vent, I scrambled to the edge of the orange light, ignoring the debris beneath my hands as I shuffled forward.

"Laura," I called to her from the borders of the patch of light illuminating the dirt, hoping Kyle couldn't see me from this angle. His tennis shoes were just visible above me at the edge of the crawl space. Laura was lying on her side, her blond hair spilling over the lip of the splintering wood cut into the floor.

The bottom rungs of the ladder were mere inches from where I was crouched, tantalizingly close. I stared at the splintered wood dully and called out to Laura again. "I'm down here. I'm okay," I lied. I squeezed my eyes shut, waiting to hear the sound of her footsteps on the ladder.

Instead, I heard more thuds on the floor of the utility room.

I opened my eyes in time to see Laura prop herself up on one elbow, angled away from Kyle's tennis shoes. Another shadow had cut through the dull light, wavering in a dim band across her body. "Please," she whimpered, inching away from the edge of the crawl space so that I could no longer see her.

"I'm done, okay?" Tony's voice again. It had a new edge to it. "Just … I'll see you when you're finished."

It took me a moment to understand that he was directing the words at Kyle, not Laura.

"Do what you want already, and stop dragging this out. My head hurts."

My stomach sank. He wasn't angry on our behalf. He was just tired of being here.

For a moment, nobody—including Kyle—said a word. The shadows above me were static now. I kept my eyes on the bottom rung of the ladder, trying to convince myself there was a point in grabbing hold of it.

I couldn't.

I closed my eyes and waited for another angry exchange. Instead, I heard a sudden yelp from Laura and a scuffling sound above me.

31

The shadows flew into motion, and I caught a glimpse of Laura's dirty, wrecked shoes at the edge of the crawl space as she flew at Kyle. The duct tape still held her arms in front of her, but she was holding something in her hands.

Kyle managed a brief "What the hell—" before a thick *smack* reverberated through the air.

Laura had hit him with something.

Without thinking, I reacted, diving toward the ladder and managing to scale the rungs to the top in a matter of seconds.

When I peered out of the trap door, I saw Tony first. His mouth hung slightly open in shock. His hair was more mussed than I remembered in his photos on Facebook—from wearing the mask, I guess—but in his expensive hoodie and stylishly ripped jeans, he looked like he was ready for a night of partying. I hoped the back of his head hurt like hell.

He didn't meet my eyes. I followed his gaze toward Laura and Kyle.

She was standing next to Kyle on the other edge of the crawl space, locked in a battle for some object.

My heart sank when I saw the expression on Kyle's face as he studied her.

It was the same casual expression I'd seen when I agreed to arm wrestle my dad as a little girl. He'd kept our arms locked briefly on the kitchen table while I struggled with all my might to budge him. At one point, he gave ground a little, and I strained harder, breathlessly wondering if maybe I *was* stronger than I realized. When I'd finally looked at my dad's face, puffing from the effort, he'd grinned and easily pinned my arm to the table.

Kyle was doing the same thing to Laura. I couldn't tell where she'd hit him, but he didn't seem to be hurt.

He glanced down at me in surprise then cut his eyes back to Laura, who was kicking at his leg now. He'd changed out of his hooded sweatshirt and into a dingy, oversized T-shirt that displayed antlers and the words "I Like Big Bucks and I Cannot Lie" across the top.

Laura was kicking him. It had to hurt, at least a little.

He raised an eyebrow at me, as if we were both observing the tantrum of a small child.

Then he twisted whatever Laura was holding and grabbed her by her duct-taped hands. She snapped her head up and struggled against his grip, letting go of the object to claw at his hands.

The object fell to the floor in front of Tony with a soft, impotent clatter: It was a squat black wrought-iron shovel. I flashed back to the little potbellied stove in the hallway—with a small stand of tools tucked behind it. How had she gotten to the shovel without Tony seeing her?

Maybe he had.

"Tony," Laura gasped. Her eyes flicked to the shovel on the floor, willing him to pick it up and finish what she'd started.

I braced on the ladder. The shovel wasn't very big—the size of a garden spade, with a slightly longer handle. Compared to the tire iron, it was a toy.

Tony glanced at it and took a step backward, toward the doorway of the utility room.

Kyle struck like a snake, letting go of her arm and striking it across her face in one fluid motion.

Then he shoved her—toward the opening of the crawl space. Toward me.

There wasn't time to duck away or scramble backward down the ladder. Laura's shoulder hit my chest, and we both crumpled into the hole.

With surprising clarity, I felt the breath whoosh out of my lungs in tandem with a sharp pain at the back of my neck as the force of impact slammed my head hard against the jagged edge of the crawl space cutout. My feet lost purchase on the ladder rung, and I folded downward, the room a swirl of darkness and orange light and Laura's blond hair.

A soft crunch—accompanied by a bright blaze of pain in my ankle—suddenly turned my vision to a sea of black and white dots.

At the same time, Laura landed next to me with a sickening smack followed by a scream. When my vision cleared, I saw that she'd tried to catch herself with her taped wrists. The arm nearest me was buckled at the wrong angle.

I didn't realize I was screaming too, until a booming voice cut through the sound.

"Shut the *fuck* up. Jesus, you two are dramatic."

I bit down on my tongue, tasting blood. The searing pain in my ankle pinned me where I lay, edging out any other fear of whispering legs or dead rats. I was afraid to look at my foot, so I stayed where I was, face up and perfectly still. I couldn't move. I couldn't think.

Kyle said something else that instantly disappeared into the white-hot haze. The numbness I'd settled into had evaporated, making it difficult to breathe. I wanted it back with a ferocity unlike anything I'd ever felt.

"Liv?" Laura cried.

Kyle's voice cut her off, but I could tell instantly he wasn't talking to her. "Did you give her that?" he demanded.

As I lay on my back, vision hazy, I could see his profile floating above me, framed by the crawl space cutout like a badly cropped picture. He was looking at the spot where Tony had been standing a few seconds earlier, before Laura lunged with the shovel. He shifted out of sight for a moment, and I heard the familiar click of the gun.

"I didn't do shit," Tony retorted indignantly. "She must have grabbed it when I wasn't looking."

"Then why didn't she hit *you*?" Kyle asked in a voice that was way too calm for someone who had nearly been whacked with a shovel.

"The other girl already hit me," he boomed back. "Why would I give her a weapon?"

Silence. Then, "Maybe you changed your mind."

Tony snorted. "The weed is making you paranoid. Relax."

I forced myself to stay quiet despite the pain screaming through my ankle. I locked eyes with Laura and saw the same exhausted trauma written on her face—along with something else. Hope? But for what? Surely she didn't still think there was a chance Tony would help us.

Both of us winced when Tony's response was met with sudden, heavy footsteps

The dim light faded, and a shadow filled the crawl space cutout. The ladder, which was precariously balanced on one leg, clattered against the wood as Kyle straightened it. He bent at the waist and peered into the darkness at Laura and me.

The whites of his eyes glimmered as he fingered the gun and leaned into the darkness, studying me and Laura—which meant that, for the moment, he wasn't facing Tony.

Hit him, hurt him, help us. The fireplace shovel was still on the floor. It had to be. Surely Tony could reach it. I was as confused as ever about why he was here, why we were here, why any of this was happening, but I felt certain Laura and I weren't the only ones who got a different Friday night than we'd bargained for. Kyle was a different kind of animal altogether.

Kyle shifted on his heels and looked toward the doorway of the utility room, as if reading my mind. Seemingly satisfied with whatever he saw, he turned back to look at me and Laura, glancing from her arm to my ankle. He shrugged. "I told you, easy way or hard way. Maybe you should try listening."

He waved the gun slowly back and forth, pointing it from Laura to me, then back again. "I'd rather not use it. Not yet, anyway. But something to think about."

He slid the gun into the back pocket of his jeans. Then he stood on the edge of the crawl space, still staring into the hole. He was thinking. Weighing his options. Imagining his *Choose Your Own Adventure*.

He was the villain in my and Laura's story. But in his book, he was the star of this show.

Finally, he squatted down again, resting one hand on his knee and the other on the edge of the cutout. He sighed heavily, as if he didn't have time for this. I knew better. He was relishing every second.

"All right, listen up, girls. It'll take your mind off the owies," he said.

I shuddered, unable to look away from his piercing stare. If anything, the night had had the opposite effect on him than Laura and me. Despite his claims of being tired—hence the beer break—he looked rested. Alert. Alive. His gaze flicked between Laura and I, gauging our response to what he'd just said. I resisted the urge to scuttle into the rank darkness like a cockroach. It would only hurt my ankle more. I stayed perfectly still, staring back at him as long as I could stomach.

"Fuck you," Laura mumbled through the tears streaming down her face. She grimaced and lay her head down on the dirt floor, flicking her gaze toward me again. The dark purple lipstick she'd applied so carefully earlier in the evening was nearly gone. The only hint it had ever been there was a streaky purple wash, rubbed across one cheek. The only reason I knew it was lipstick—instead of another bruise—were the soft sparkles shimmering in the dim orange light.

I couldn't read her expression. Earlier, she'd looked panicked—and dazed. Now it seemed like she was bracing, waiting and maybe even hoping for something to happen. Did she really expect Tony to help us at this point? He'd told Kyle to hurry up and do whatever he wanted. All Tony cared about was washing his hands of whatever had gotten him into the truck at the beginning of the night and whatever nightmare he'd leave behind at the cabin when the night was over.

"Still so spicy." Kyle shifted and glanced over his shoulder and tugged at one sleeve of the oversized brown T-shirt, wrinkling his nose in disgust. "But you're going to want to hear what I have to say. I actually wasn't going to bring it up … it's a little awkward. But I can tell you're confused, and it's time we got a few things straight."

He frowned as if reluctant to deliver bad news. "The thing is, Tony is kind of a pussy." His rich, booming laugh filled the silence. I hated the sound with a ferocity that cut through the static. "Don't get me wrong—I love the idiot. Delta Phi forever and all that shit. But we all have our weaknesses."

He moved his eyes between Laura and I, as if waiting for a response.

When we didn't say anything, he shrugged and glanced to the side. "Like I said, Tony is a pussy. But that doesn't mean he's a good guy. There's a big difference. Which is why he's not going to help you."

As he said the last part, he turned his head to look behind him briefly. "Right, bud?"

Next to me, Laura tried to sit up. She made a soft noise through clenched teeth, equally quiet and violent, like a caged scream.

Kyle sighed. "I know. Bummer, huh?"

"Bullshit. And fuck you," Laura repeated.

"Do you want to tell them, or should I?" Kyle asked loudly, cocking his head to the left.

Tony didn't respond. Was he still standing in the doorway? My ankle throbbed in time with the pulse in my ears. Part of me was hanging off every word Kyle said. But the part that was desperate for the numb feeling to swallow me whole again just wanted him to leave me alone with Laura. The fact that he felt comfortable revealing whatever bomb he was about to drop only meant that he was confident we'd never use it against him.

He had us right where he wanted us. Powerless, trapped, and out of options to fight back. Earlier, I'd wondered why he hadn't shot us in the hills. Surely he'd had the gun with him then, too. Why go to all this trouble, if his ultimate goal was to kill us? I understood now it wasn't his goal. The hunt was.

This story was just another way for him to prolong the inevitable.

Kyle shrugged and shifted on his heels, peering down into the crawl space again. "See? Dude's a total pussy. All right, where to begin …" He tilted his chin and pretended to think hard, tapping on his dark stubble. "I get the feeling Tish the Bitch hasn't told you two *anything*. Am I right?"

Laura kept silent.

"Good. That's what I thought." His lips curled into a satisfied smile. "I mean, I get it. A girl like Tish doesn't have that many options. She's a solid three. Maybe a four, when she *really* tried. You think her and Tony made sense? I mean, look at the guy. He's a Delta. Kind of a god." He gestured to the empty air past our sightline. "He's a little scuffed up at the moment. But besides that." He laughed.

Anger flared in my chest. I pushed it away, desperate not to feel anything. It wouldn't help.

"Stop it." Tony's voice. Abrupt and annoyed. I felt Laura's eyes on me again, but I couldn't bring myself to see the hope anymore. Tony wasn't really telling Kyle to stop what he was doing. He was telling Kyle to shut up. "The more people who know—"

"Shh." Kyle's face broke into a wide grin, a harsh caricature of a smile in the shadows and orange light. He ignored Tony and stared at Laura intently. "Spoiler: It wasn't real. Tish was more of a side-hustle than a girlfriend—"

"You're a liar," Laura spat. "I've seen them together—"

He cut her off. "Where?" He sat down on the edge of the hole in the floor and put his hands on his knees.

"Seriously, Kyle. Knock it off. That's not what happened." Tony again. His voice was closer to the ledge. Angrier now.

I imagined the final pages of this dark, twisted story furling faster toward its end. My ankle wasn't broken. I could tell that much from the way I could rotate it gently. But there was no way I could run or even shuffle very fast. Laura should have been in an ER hours ago. The crawl space was purgatory, and we were just waiting for our final descent into hell.

The only person who could throw a wrench into the trajectory of this storyline was Tony, but it was clear to me that he was little more than a side character along for the ride in Kyle's sick *Choose Your Own Adventure.*

Kyle shifted, turning away from Laura and me to face the direction Tony's voice had come from. "Not what happened? Okay. So what went down at the Kool-Aid party?

Tony made a noise. Kyle cut him off with a wave of his hand. "And the rave. And the toga party. And the banger in the basement."

Tony tried to speak again. Kyle laughed. "Shut *up,* dude." He turned to glance at me and Laura. I couldn't look away. I lay on my back like a dead bug and waited for the awfulness of what he was saying to suddenly become clear. "It was kind of brilliant, actually. Tish got a hot boyfriend—not in public, but still. And Tony got rich. Win, win." He looked away and smiled. "I thought she suspected … but now, I dunno. Maybe she thought it was real all along too."

Kyle raised one hand in a fist bump, still looking at Tony. "Gotta hand it to ya, bro. Although I should get some credit, too. And I should have gotten a cut of the money. It was kind of my idea. But … here we are. This works too—"

Tony cut him off with an annoyed grunt. "I thought you wanted a beer. So let's have a beer."

Kyle smiled. "You go ahead, buddy. Open one for me, okay?"

Loud footsteps fell on the floor, moving down the hallway. Despite my best attempts not to care, I felt the horrified disbelief and curiosity pressing in on my brain, screaming to be acknowledged. I could barely breathe. Beside me, I could hear Laura's fast, hitched breaths.

Kyle raised his middle finger in the direction of the doorway then stared down into the hole in the floor again. "That shitty car you were driving used to be mine. Did you know that?"

When his question was met with more stony silence, he shrugged again. "I told Tish I'd give it to her for a couple hundred bucks if she threw in a blow job." He waited expectantly for a reaction then laughed hard, a dry guffaw. "I wasn't expecting her to actually *do* it."

"She didn't," Laura finally spat, pausing to draw a ragged breath. "She told me about it. About what a disgusting pig you were."

Kyle tapped his chin. "Not quite how I remember it." He peered down at Laura, waiting.

When she glowered at him without responding, he stretched his legs and brushed his hands on his pants, maintaining eye contact while he grabbed the handle to the crawl space. "Tony is probably right. You don't need to know any of this …"

The quirk of his eyebrow called his bluff. He wanted to tell the entire sickening story. And he wanted us to beg him for the details

Despite my resolve to go numb, I had to know.

3 2

"Please. Keep going. Tell us," I blurted, nauseated by how easily I could find the right tone to beg. No matter how much I'd wanted to let the static pull me under, part of me was still eager to find a way out. That part of me wouldn't die until I did.

We couldn't run. We couldn't fight. So what was left? My anxious brain that, despite everything, was still whispering a steady stream of trivia.

Narcissists think they're smarter than everyone else. But that doesn't mean they are. That's how they get caught. They make mistakes. They underestimate the intelligence of police. And they underestimate the intelligence of their victims.

If I could find out what the hell was going on—and why— maybe it would reveal a way out. Or a way to wedge the crack between him and Tony open wide.

At the very least, as long as he was talking it meant we were still alive.

I cut my eyes toward Laura, hoping she'd understand. Whatever we learned—Kyle's twisted version of the truth—would hurt. But knowledge was a weapon, too. And unlike rocks or tire irons or fireplace shovels, Kyle wouldn't see it coming.

Kyle pretended to think, tapping on his beard and studying my expression. "Well, since you asked so nicely."

His face broke into a smile and he glanced toward the doorway again. "You're right. Tish turned me down. But I could tell she was thinking about it." He flashed his perfect teeth. "She's not nearly as boring and vanilla as she looks. So, I offered the money to Tony instead. Just to see what he'd say."

My stomach lurched.

"There were already a bunch of Deltas doing it. There's actually a whole system." He smiled again, not looking at me or Laura anymore. He was remembering. "A few years ago, Delta Phi got busted when some bitch brought the police to the frat house after a party." His face darkened. "Biggest slut around, but the police didn't know that. In the end, nobody got in trouble, and everyone hated her so much that she ended up dropping the charges. And dropping out of school." He looked thoughtful. "But still. Not an experience we were interested in repeating, you know? So we got smarter."

He paused, clearly waiting to be prompted. I pushed the words past the vomit rising in my throat. "So what did you do?"

The dropped assault charges a few years ago were common knowledge on campus. I wasn't naive enough to think they were baseless, but I'd assumed the crime was perpetrated by individuals.

Kyle had used the word *system.*

I could barely breathe.

"Like I said, we had it all figured out. The system was color-coded. Blue meant it was okay to fool around with a girl, but nothing below the waist. Red meant 'anything goes.' Blue paid $100. Red paid $300."

"To the girls?" I asked, keeping my voice measured.

He laughed. "Keep up, MacGyver. To their boyfriends."

Without waiting for a reaction he kept going, lost in the momentum of his revolting story. "We marked all the girls' hands at the door—and we didn't let just anyone in. I mean, it was Delta Phi. If a girl was single, she got a green X. Fair game, but only if she was into it—nothing that might come back to bite the fraternity in the ass, you know?" He shrugged. "If a girl was coupled up tight, in a *real* relationship with one of the Deltas, she got a black X on her hand. *Off limits.* We told all the girls it meant they got access to different VIP drinks, depending on their boyfriends' status in the house. You know, whether he'd won at beer pong or some shit."

I flashed back to a memory of Tish washing her hands in the bathroom sink one morning.

She was scrubbing the back of her hand. I didn't ask why.

Kyle continued, unprompted. "The girls with green and black Xes on their hands partied and got shitfaced like usual. But here's where it gets fun: The VIP drinks we made for the blue and red Xes, well, let's just say they had a couple extra-special ingredients." He smiled. "After a few cocktails, the girls couldn't tell their "boyfriends" from any other Delta. Especially not in a dark room."

I couldn't force any more follow-up questions past the cotton in my throat.

Kyle kept going anyway. "Since all the girls involved in *transactions* were 'dating' other Deltas, none of them got antsy if they vaguely remembered a little drunk action at the party. Everybody won."

He paused before adding, "Tish was a red, if you haven't put that together. She was pretty popular, too. Since she belonged to our man Tony."

Belonged to Tony. I couldn't stop the vomit from rising in my throat this time.

I swallowed it back. The horror leaked out in tears instead that dripped down my cheeks.

The words he'd said earlier—about me and Laura—came screaming back. They made a sort of horrifying sense now.

They're both red Xes.

Red means anything goes.

Kyle turned away from the crawl space and craned his neck. "Tony, bud? How's that beer coming?"

There was only silence.

My brain couldn't process everything I was hearing. Was all of it true? When I tried to fit the white-hot puzzle pieces together, my mind rejected them. Was he making this up to terrorize us? It was too horrifying, too evil.

"Anyway, it worked out great." He sighed. "The money rolled in. But then, like I said, Tish fucked it up. She got pregnant."

33

For a moment, everything froze. My pulse skipped. Pregnant? Laura stopped snuffling and went silent.

Kyle continued, lost in his story. "She was supposed to be on the pill. Had been the whole time her and Tony were 'together.' He kept pretty close tabs on it."

He peered down at us. "Tish wanted to keep the baby, which was obviously gonna be a problem. See, how do I put this ..." Tapping a finger on his beard, he pretended to think. "You've seen Tony. He's straight-up vanilla. Expensive vanilla, but still vanilla. So is Tish. Kroger brand." He laughed at his own joke then cleared his throat, clearly eager to continue. "They're both perfect little Aryans." He chuckled again. "But we've got all thirty-four flavors in Delta Phi, so if the baby came out chocolate, well ... secret would be out."

He gave an exaggerated shrug. "So Tony came to me for help. And good thing. The whole pregnancy was obviously a trap. Tish the bitch did it on purpose to get him to propose to her." His face darkened, as if somehow this was worse than anything he'd told us over the past ten minutes.

He rolled his neck, and his expression relaxed. "Thankfully, she's about as smart as she is hot. So Tony called her bluff. He proposed—told her he wanted to have a whole bunch of kids with her *someday,* but not now. And just like that, she agreed to get rid of the baby."

Turning my head ever so slightly so I wouldn't draw Kyle's attention, I cut my eyes toward Laura. She was so quiet with her eyes shut, that I worried at first that she wasn't conscious. But then I saw her chest shudder. Her arms were pulled up onto her dirty cream shirt. One of them was bent all wrong. Definitely broken. A tear slipped past her closed lashes, dripping into the dust.

Kyle kept going. "If she'd just agreed to get rid of it without a fuss, none of this would have happened."

"You said she did," I said, trying to keep my voice from shaking.

"Nah, that's just what she told Tony. Made up a whole story about going to the campus clinic. Tony even brought her fucking chicken noodle soup while she was 'recovering.' Thankfully, I'm not quite as trusting. And I've got eyes at the clinic: my sister. She's not a doctor or anything, but she has enough access. When she heard what Tish might be trying to pull over Tony with the pregnancy, she looked up the records. And you know what she found? A visit for a blood test. Then another a few weeks later to scan for a heartbeat. Healthy baby, nine weeks along."

"What does that have to do with us?" I couldn't stop the question from tumbling out. I was too exhausted, too horrified to connect the dots myself. All I knew for sure was that Tish had been living a nightmare right underneath our noses.

I believed what he'd told us so far. It was all too specific, too much in line with the way Tish had suddenly holed up at the library, refusing to discuss the breakup with Tony.

Tony was every bit as bad as Kyle.

Kyle was the one holding the gun. But Tony was every bit as eager to tear someone's life apart bit by bit.

He rolled his eyes as if explaining something to a young child. "Think about it for half a second. She was basically a ticking time bomb. If she realized that the baby wasn't Tony's—and chances were pretty fucking good she would—she'd start asking questions. And if she started asking questions, there was a good chance Tony would get busted—and bring all of us down with him."

He waited expectantly then added, "He gave her one last chance to make nice. When he confronted her about whether she'd really gotten rid of the pregnancy, the bitch denied it. And then she had the audacity to break up with *him*. We really didn't have a choice after that."

"But why us," Laura suddenly spat.

Kyle smiled. "I knew you'd have questions. It's pretty simple: We thought Tish was with you. It's her car. She RSVPed on Facebook. And she was supposed to be at the bonfire tonight."

"Bullshit," I hissed, my throat closing over with tears I refused to allow. "You *saw* us. You saw us both—before you ran us off the road. You knew Tish wasn't in the Volvo."

Kyle smiled wider and held up his hands in a "don't shoot" gesture. "Yeah … I realized that pretty quickly. But I didn't give up my Friday night to turn around just because we got the wrong girl. Tony tried to puss out, but he needs my help. We'll take care of Tish another day."

He rolled his neck and moved to stand, brushing his hands against his pant legs. "Anyway, that beer won't drink itself. Hope this helps. Tony isn't your friend. He was your sister's pimp." He lowered his voice, leaning down so that the orange light spilling from the hallway backlit his hair in a sickly halo "And he's *my* bitch, too. He just doesn't realize it."

The crawl space door slammed shut.

34

Snippets of conversation, shifting by the second from angry to jovial, accusing to excited, mocking to almost thoughtful, filtered through tiny cracks of light rimming the crawl space cutout above us.

I heard our names. Tish's name. The phrase *take care of it*. The word *fun*.

I stopped listening and dragged myself toward Laura in the dark, each tiny movement shooting ripples of pain through my ankle. The debris beneath my bare hands barely registered now.

Laura's taped hands were pulled to the side at an angle as she tried to reposition herself, cutting into the broken arm. It all looked excruciating. I reached into my travel pouch for the jagged apartment key. "Hold still, okay? I'm going to cut the tape. Is your other arm hurt?"

She shook her head. "No. It's okay."

As gently as I could, I cut through the tape of her good arm. She flinched each time I jostled her, but once her hands were free she let out a gasping breath and pulled the broken arm close to her chest.

"I had no idea." Laura cried softly, curling her knees to her chest. "I had absolutely no idea. At first I thought he was lying, but …" She choked out a sob. "Poor Tish. They're going to kill her, Liv. And us. How did this happen? How come I didn't know?"

I shuddered as something whispered across my shoulders, but it was Laura's long hair. "We couldn't have known. And Tish couldn't have told us. She didn't know either."

Laura suddenly shrieked, kicking out her leg and wiping her good hand on her shirt. It left a dark smear from whatever she'd smashed. She ignored it, gasping for air. "I should have made her talk to me after the breakup. If I'd tried a little harder, maybe she would have told me about the pregnancy. I could have gotten it out of her if I'd just ..." She shook her head in despair.

"You didn't do anything wrong," I told her softly. "And neither did Tish."

She looked at me fiercely. "Neither did you."

I stopped staring into the darkness and turned my head toward her.

"I know you. You think we're down here—" she looked around the dark pit "—because you messed up."

I opened my mouth to argue then shut it. She was right.

"So maybe we both stop taking the blame for anything these shitheads did?" she whispered, her chest rising and falling faster. "Oh, god. I don't want to die." Her voice broke on the last syllable.

I swallowed painfully.

"I actually thought Tony was going to help us," she said angrily, slapping at her legs with her good arm and whimpering again. "I thought maybe he'd gotten in over his head and was playing along. He came to my parents' house for Thanksgiving last year," she choked. "From the way Tish talked, I thought he was going to be my brother-in-law."

She gasped for breath and looked around, as if fully grasping the horror of our surroundings for the first time. "What's on the floor down here? What's that fucking smell? I can't breathe. What's he going to do when he comes back? We're going to die." She drew in another painful-sounding gulp of air. "Something just bit me. I can't do this, Liv. I can't, I can't, *I can't*." She drew in short, fast breaths, retching a little.

She was in shock. Both of us probably were. "Laur. Stay with me."

She lay her head against mine, rolling her shoulder to protect her injured arm.

"You're right about what you said a minute ago. I didn't mess up tonight," I said shakily. "And I'm glad I came back for you." My voice caught, and my train of thought threatened to scatter to the pain in my ankle and the dark, rank hole in the ground where we were lying. I forced it back. I could give up on myself, but I wouldn't give up on Laura.

"I didn't come back because it was smart. I came back because you're my best friend, and I couldn't leave you. And now I need you to stay with me, okay?"

She let out a soft wail, shaking so hard that I couldn't tell whether she was still hyperventilating.

"Laur? Stay with me," I begged, tears finally spilling down my own cheeks. "Look, there's a little light over there by the vent. It's easier to see. And the smell isn't quite as bad."

After a few long seconds, she nodded against my shoulder and drew in a deep, shuddering breath.

Then, inch by inch, we helped each other across the minefield of dirt, death, and crawling legs.

* * *

The cadence of Tony and Kyle's voices drifted through the floor-boards as we huddled together. If anything, our situation had gone from bad to a hundred times worse. But even languishing in a dungeon with a sprained ankle was just bearable if I wasn't alone.

"How's your head? And your arm?" I whispered, tilting my chin toward the faint moonlight streaming through the vent, tantalizingly close to the fresh outside air—and encased in a thick wall of cinder block and cement.

Laura shrugged against my shoulder. "I'd kill for that gross ibuprofen bottle in the Volvo," she whispered after a few seconds.

A bubble of laughter I didn't expect or understand rose in my throat, even as something scurried across my foot.

To my surprise, Laura started laughing too.

I clutched my stomach. Every movement hurt, even laughter. Tears rolled down my cheeks fast and hot, salty and stinging the scratches on my bare thighs.

After a few seconds, Laura stopped laughing and let out a long, shaky exhale. Then she whispered, "When Kyle left me alone with Tony in the living room, he told me he didn't know any of this was going to happen tonight."

I frowned. "Do you believe him?"

She hesitated. "I don't know what to believe after what Kyle told us." She looked around the dank crawl space. "Part of me just wants them to get it over with," she added dully. "They're going to kill us, right?"

"Maybe," I replied softly. "Tell me what else Tony said."

She went quiet. Then she said, "He thought they were going to scare Tish on the way to the bonfire. Teach her a lesson. He didn't say anything about a baby or ... or human trafficking. He just said he was pissed about the breakup."

I shook my head. "He's lying. He hasn't done anything to help us. He's not on our side."

"I know he's not," Laura murmured. "But ... he stopped talking when Kyle came back into the room. His whole face changed. For a minute, he was Tish's Tony. When Kyle came back into the room, he disappeared."

She leaned closer. "When Kyle came back with the beer, he sat down next to me and tried to pull me onto his lap ..." She shuddered against me. "Tony just kind of looked away. I ... I'd told myself I was going to go along with whatever they wanted. So maybe they wouldn't hurt me, or you, anymore." She drew in a wheezing breath and shivered hard. "But I couldn't. That was when I spilled the beer all over him."

I squeezed her good hand.

She squeezed back. "When Kyle went to change his shirt ... and Tony brought me into the utility room ... I swear he knew I was going to take that fireplace shovel. He kept staring at it while we were sitting on the couch, rubbing his head where you hit him earlier."

I closed my eyes and tried to fit these new puzzle pieces into the messy picture.

Laura kept talking. "Tony didn't grab my arm until we got to the hallway—where Kyle could see both of us. Before that, he didn't touch me. He led me right past that fireplace. When I grabbed the little shovel, he didn't even look back at me. At first I thought he was just out of it—from you clobbering him earlier—but then I convinced myself he was going to help us. How stupid am I?"

"You're not stupid," I whispered.

"I wish I'd hit Tony instead," Laura added quietly. "Tried to finish him off. I could have. Then at least there would be one psychopath upstairs—not two."

I flinched as something new crawled across my skin. The motion jostled my ankle a little, sending a fresh jolt of pain through my leg. I was suddenly aware that my stomach hurt, too. I vaguely remembered a bright flash of pain near my belly as I hit the ladder on the crawl space floor before flipping onto my back. "Maybe he'll—"

I stopped talking as a memory zipped to the front of my mind: The crunch I'd heard.

The sound replayed in my mind, distant and strangely inorganic.

It hadn't come from my ankle. It wasn't broken, so a crunch wouldn't make sense.

It had come from the travel pouch at my waist.

"Fuck," I whispered shakily. Careful not to jostle my ankle again, I grasped the zipper of the pouch.

"What? Oh god, what?" Laura asked.

With shaking hands, I found the smaller rectangle of Laura's phone and flipped the screen open.

"Oh my god, you still have my phone? Do we get service here …" She trailed off when she saw the screen: not just black and cracked, but hanging slightly askew.

Laura's phone wasn't dead. It was broken.

"What about yours?" she whispered urgently.

I reached into the travel pouch again, prepared to see another black screen. It had been at one-percent battery hours ago. There was absolutely no way it was alive—and even if it was, there was no way we got service here, in the bowels of the crawl space, of all places.

But I was wrong.

When I flipped open my phone, the screen glowed blue.

Still one-percent battery life. Still no service. It wasn't nothing, but it wasn't going to get us out of here.

I moved to close the phone, but Laura reached out with her good arm. "No, wait! Look."

She pointed frantically at the screen.

One bar blinked in the corner like it had earlier—a lifetime ago.

"Did you see that?" she whispered. "There's gotta be a cell tower somewhere around here. Try to make a call. If we can get it to connect, even for a second, they'll be able to find us. That's how 9-1-1 works, right? They can find us if we call and it connects?"

I honestly didn't know. I'd heard stories of the police showing up after an accidental butt-dial. But would that apply all the way out here, with just a flicker of service? How many seconds of battery life did we even have left before the phone crapped out completely? Definitely not enough to make call after call, like I had before.

There might not be enough juice to make even one call. Or any more failed texts.

I pulled up the call screen, my thumb hovering over the little green button as Laura and I both stared at the *No Service* message, waiting for that elusive bar to materialize one more time.

As the seconds ticked by, there was a shuffling sound from above. Then footsteps. Then voices, closer than the steady mumble from the living room.

The bar suddenly flickered onto the screen.

"Go, go, call!" Laura hissed.

I hit the call button.

The pixelated message on the screen displayed the word *Connecting.*

35

My stomach flipped violently while the call tried to push its way through the ether.

As quickly as the adrenaline rush rose, it crashed.

An *End Call* error message appeared as the service bar disappeared.

"We have to get the phone higher—onto the main level," Laura whispered, seeming unrattled by the failed attempt. She drew in a sharp breath and clutched her arm as she moved to grab the phone. "Did you see any service bars when you were in the truck outside?"

I shook my head miserably. "I didn't look." The cell phones had stayed zipped inside my travel pouch from the moment the truck had pulled up to the cabin. Every moment felt like it was one breath away from my last.

"Hand it to me," Laura whispered, moving to a crouch beneath the disgusting sheets of insulation hanging above her head. "I'm going to hold it up by the crawl space door. If we can just get that goddamn bar back …"

I got a better look at her injured arm as she reached out for the phone with her good hand. It bent past the wrist, bumpy and bowed where it should have been straight. The darkness hid most of the bruising on the side of her face, but even in the dim light the lump near her temple looked painful and ugly. I realized that one of her eyes had nearly swollen shut.

My stomach recoiled. I knew I didn't look any better. The pain in my ankle was starting to subside—mercifully—but one glance told me that it wasn't because it was getting better. The skin on my calf, already broken and filthy, had swollen to nearly twice its size.

I tore my gaze away from my ankle and watched as Laura picked her way across the dirt floor. She crouched beneath the insulation, trying to avoid the worst of the debris—including the dead thing I'd smashed earlier.

My nose, like my ankle, was numb enough that I couldn't really smell anything anymore—unless I breathed in too sharply.

When Laura was directly beneath the crawl space entrance, she held the phone up to the cracks of light surrounding it. Fumbling with one hand, she opened the phone and peered at the screen.

She frowned. Then she turned her head and toward the opposite wall of the crawl space. There was no vent to the outside air along that wall, and the darkness was nearly complete. She held the cell phone in front of her a little ways, and I stopped myself from calling out to her. The phone would die any second.

"Laura," I hissed. "Shut it. Hurry."

The muffled voices above us were still carrying on. I thought I'd even heard a sharp click that might have been the pull tab of a beer. Were they getting drunk in preparation for round two? What were they waiting for?

Laura closed the cell phone, cutting off the dim beam of blue light that she'd angled into the darkness.

She didn't try to make a call. And she didn't say anything for a few seconds. But I could hear her breathing, faster and heavier like it had been before.

Something had changed. Something new was wrong.

"Liv," she finally choked out. "There's something over there along that wall."

36

"What do you see?" I hissed, craning my neck in a futile effort to see anything except Laura's dimly lit, crouching silhouette beneath the crawl space opening. "Do you get service?" I added hopefully.

Whatever was along the wall of that crawl space couldn't be more important than getting that damn call to connect.

She made a soft gagging sound. "No bars. But the smell is really bad over here. The closer I got, the worse it got. So I flipped the light into the corner, and ..." She trailed off.

Another mouthful of bile rose in my throat as I remembered the slimy, bony body I'd crushed under my bare hand earlier. The smell had been awful, and the air was still thick with it. I was surprised the entire cabin didn't reek. What else was down here?

"Liv," Laura said so quietly I could barely hear her. "It's really big."

My stomach twisted. "What do you mean, it's *big*? How big?"

Laura's silhouette took a hesitant step farther into the darkness, toward the back wall. "I can't tell for sure unless I open up the phone again. I'm just going to get a little bit closer so I don't waste any more battery."

"Okay," I managed.

Her soft, hesitant footsteps crept into the darkness until I couldn't see her at all anymore with the dim light of the vent. Her voice, so quiet I nearly missed it, floated through the blackness. "Liv, can you keep talking to me? I'm afraid to look."

I tried to think of something even remotely comforting to say. All I could think to respond with was a quiet, "I'm here." I got to my hands and knees and tentatively put a little weight on my ankle. It protested but held. "Hold on. Don't open the phone yet. I'm coming over there," I whispered.

Gritting my teeth, I inched my way back to the middle of the room. By this point, the path was familiar enough that I managed to avoid the worst of the debris in the dirt.

I quickly realized that Laura was right. The smell was significantly worse over here than by the vent. Especially with the crawl space door closed. When I opened my mouth, I could nearly taste it.

The closer I got to Laura, the worse the smell got. My pulse thudded in my head, and my breath came in ragged gulps that forced the putrid smell deep into my lungs. Fear trickled down my back like a warning. I wasn't willing to go any closer unless we had some light.

Laura opened the phone, filling the small room with a faint blue glow.

The wall was closer than I'd imagined. In the dark, the crawl space seemed to stretch on in all directions. In reality, there was maybe ten feet between where we stood and the far cinder block wall.

The beam of light from the phone was just bright enough to illuminate the object Laura had seen—crumpled in the dirt, slumped against the cinder blocks.

The shape came into sudden focus as the fear prickling across my skin turned poker hot.

They were human remains. A girl, from her long braids.

I registered the legs first, pulled up to her chest and peeking out from underneath a dirty skirt. The limbs were a brownish yellow, sinewy and thin in the blue glow. Her arms were wrapped tight around the base of the skirt, fingers interlocked in a permanent embrace.

Neither Laura nor I spoke, but the blue light wavered like a strobe as her hand holding the phone began to shake.

My eyes took in the rest of the woman's body frame by frame: the face—less a skull than a leathery, rawhide skin that clung tightly to the hollows of her cheekbones and eye sockets. Her mouth gaped open, revealing rows of yellow teeth.

Her ebony hair, shockingly neat, hung in two dark braids, woven through with ribbons of different colors.

"Liv, look at her dress," Laura choked.

I dragged my eyes away from those perfect, neat braids to look at her tattered clothing. I wasn't sure what Laura meant at first. The pale skirt was filthy. The loose material looked almost old-fashioned—loosely bunched up where her arms encircled her knees.

"I—what?" I could barely breathe.

"Her chest," Laura managed.

Suddenly, I saw it. Through the dim, shaky light, I realized that the shadows on the remains weren't actually shadows.

A dark hole gaped in the center of her chest.

Spreading out from it was a jagged red X.

37

Laura let the cell phone go dark.

A buzzing sound had started in my ears, like a frantic alarm bell. As the darkness blanked the crawl space once more, I blinked fast and forced myself to breathe. With each breath of the cold, putrid air, I pictured the girl's leathery, mummified face.

Who was she?

How long had she been down here?

How had she died—and more importantly, who had killed her? Had it been Kyle? Did Tony know?

And had we just gotten a preview of our own fate?

For a few seconds, the two of us stayed frozen where we stood.

Without saying a word, Laura reached for my arm. Then we helped each other over to the vent, as far away as possible from the dead girl with the braids—and the X on her chest.

"It's her," Laura rasped so quietly I nearly missed it even though she was right next to me.

I didn't understand. Another deep wave of nausea rolled through my stomach. "Her? Who is 'her'?"

Laura swallowed, a painful, sticky sound that was louder than her voice.

"The missing girl. You said her name before."

My mind spun, trying to grasp the meaning but distracted by the sound of footsteps overhead. The back-and-forth of distant voices suddenly cut out, and I strained to listen. The footsteps got closer, louder, then stopped above us, in the utility room.

"Lightweight. Are you buzzed already? Have another beer, dude. It's barely ten." It was Tony's voice.

I braced, waiting for the crawl space door to open.

"Shit, shit, shit," Laura whispered.

The footsteps thudded back into the hallway.

Dizzy relief flooded my senses. I sagged against Laura for a moment—before sitting upright so fast my ankle bumped against her leg. I bit down on my bottom lip to keep myself from crying out.

I suddenly knew who the dead girl was, too.

"Ava Robles. Coffin Creek," I whispered.

38

It was the braids that jolted the memory to the front of my brain.

Those neat, black braids strewn with colored bits of ribbon.

I'd seen them in a post that was shared in a flurry across campus after Ava Robles went missing three years earlier.

I probably wouldn't have recognized her face in a lineup. She was absolutely gorgeous in an almost generic way that described all the girls who earned a spot in a sorority before the semester had even begun: full, pouty lips; dark lashes for days, skin belonged in a Neutrogena commercial. But those braids were something else. The photo that circulated had been taken the night she disappeared—red lips pursed in a sultry smile, eyes glowing bright in the flash, and her hair a riot of colored ribbons.

"He killed her," Laura whispered.

Her words hung heavy in the air. She was talking about Kyle.

I knew she was right.

Kyle's words from earlier, sickeningly smug, ran through my head yet again. I understood them even better now.

Red meant 'anything goes.'

Anything, including murder.

I swallowed, trying to process this information. How many times had I rolled my eyes at the mention of Coffin Creek? How many times had I recommended the blog that combed through the case from every angle—all of them dead ends? How many times had Laura and I called each other while walking back to the apartment after a late class—just in case a prowler was stalking the campus that night?

Ava hadn't been killed by a stranger lurking in the shadows.

Her killer—or killers—had been strutting around campus this whole time, flashing perfect smiles while they preyed on girls like Ava and Tish. Girls who carefully wove ribbons into their braids for the honor of spending the evening in his company. Girls who felt special to be chosen—even if only in secret.

I couldn't stop myself from imagining what Ava's last moments must have been like in this hellhole. Bleeding out. Terrified. Alone in the dark. I could barely breathe past the hard lump that formed in my throat.

Aside from Kyle—and possibly Tony—Laura and I were the only people alive who knew what had happened to her.

But not for long. That number was about to drop by two.

Maybe this was the last rule of threes: The looming, worst-case scenario that left three skeletons, side by side, in a lonely crawl space.

"Do you think Tony knows about Ava?" Laura whispered shakily.

"He probably helped drag her out here at the very least," I mumbled, remembering what Kyle had said: *He's my bitch.*

As far as I could tell, Tony hadn't lifted a finger—or even protested—when Kyle ran us off the road. Then followed us into the hills. Then forced us into this hellhole. The most he'd done was sulk over getting whacked in the head and tell Kyle to hurry up—and then insist that he wasn't quite as scummy as Kyle's story made him out to be.

All Tony cared about was Tony, no matter the cost. He just didn't like getting his hands dirty. He was happy to let Kyle do whatever he wanted, as long as it kept him out of jail for his role in the Delta Phi horror show.

Laura didn't respond at first. A sudden, loud crack slammed through the steady murmur of voices overhead, followed by laughter.

Both of us flinched. It sounded like a gunshot. I pictured the gaping hole and red X on Ava's chest.

"I don't think he knows she's down here," Laura said abruptly, turning to look at me in the dim moonlight streaming through the tines of the vent. She glanced down at her arm, hanging limply next to her chest. With her good hand, she reached up to touch the dark lump on her head. "I know that sounds crazy," she added.

When I didn't respond, she continued. "I want to kill him. And Kyle. And all of the Deltas who were involved with this. I'd bet my life that some of them saw Ava with Kyle that night she went missing a few years ago." She stared into the darkness of the far wall and then cut her eyes toward me again. "Liv, do you trust me?"

I stared back, not sure what she was asking. "Of course I trust you. But why do you think Tony doesn't know she's down here? Why does it matter? If he was going to try to stop Kyle from hurting her or us, he would have done something by now. They're up there drinking IPAs and laughing together, while you're down here with a concussion and a broken arm—a few feet from a dead girl."

This time, it wasn't adrenaline that cut through the haze numbing the feeling of spider legs on my skin. It was white-hot anger. It sparked and ignited in my chest like some kind of primal pilot light.

The ghosts of the crime bloggers, survivalists, and news articles I'd been counting on to get me through all night shouted in unison: *He's a monster. And he definitely knows.*

Laura continued, drawing in a slow breath. "Just … hear me out. Maybe you're right. But I keep thinking about *why* Kyle told us that story. It wasn't to help us make sense of all this." She laughed bitterly. "I think he wanted us to stop trying to get Tony to help us. He wants us to think that Tony is every bit as evil as he is. That he's been in on everything. That he knows exactly what happened to Ava Robles—and maybe even helped put her down here—the same way he knew exactly what was happening at the Delta parties. The same way he helped drag us out here."

I stared at her. She had a point about Kyle's little story time act. I hadn't thought about it in that light. "I knew you were a sleuth at heart," I murmured, squeezing her arm.

She shuddered. "Maybe. I might be wrong, but I swear to god that he knew I would grab that fireplace shovel. We were alone together for maybe a minute on the couch. I barely looked at him. But when I did, I saw pathetic human trash. Not somebody who's along for the ride. I genuinely don't think he's having a good time."

She stopped to catch her breath. "When I look at Kyle, it's like looking at a shark. He's enjoying every moment of this."

Everything she was saying made sense. But was she right?

More footsteps overhead.

When I didn't say anything, Laura kept talking in a rush. "When Tony told me that I needed to calm down—and that everything would be okay if I went along with it—I really think he believed himself. He's still telling himself we're going to get out of this alive. That it'll be sort of like those girls at the parties. Like Tish. Kyle will fuck us up, scare us so bad we don't tell anyone, then let us go. We need him to understand he's wrong."

"But what's going to change his mind?" I gestured at my ankle, her arm, then toward the dark corners of the crawl space where Ava's skeletal remains were hidden from view. "Things are really bad. He has to know Kyle won't really let us go after all this. After everything we know."

Even as the words left my mouth, I thought about the other side characters in the endless horrible stories I knew by heart. Most of them didn't have memorable names, but they had one thing in common: they helped their spouse, boyfriend, roommate, fiancé, lover, parent, or friend get away with murder.

Most of them claimed willful ignorance. They helped dig graves, wash bloody clothes, dump garbage bags full of evidence, create alibis, and collect on insurance money—while clinging to paper-thin excuses and alibis. "It was an accident." "I hit a deer." "I slept at the office last night." "I was hunting." "The police are targeting me, and I need you to vouch for me." "If I go down, you go down too."

On message boards, that cast of side characters earned as much venom as the killer himself. How could anyone be so stupid? They knew exactly what they were doing. It was a less frightening possibility than the alternative: that sometimes we married, dated, befriended, or shared a roof with monsters.

It was a less frightening possibility than the idea sometimes, when the lure of money or power or revenge was strong enough, we even became monsters alongside them.

Like Tony had.

Laura's words echoed on repeat through my mind. *Trust me.*

I wanted to. But if I was being honest, I still suspected that Tony knew about the body down here.

It was the way he'd looked at me earlier, before Kyle marched me down to this pit. I'd hurt him, and he was glad to let me suffer—even though he was the whole reason I was in this nightmare.

I was pretty confident he knew exactly what had happened to Ava Robles.

And I was pretty confident he knew exactly what was going to happen to us.

Even if Laura was right—and he didn't know—I still didn't see a way out. Maybe Tony wasn't interested in getting his hands dirty—not like Kyle. But he clearly saw Kyle as his ticket out of the mess he'd created with the Delta's human trafficking ring.

Tony was a hyena, not an alpha predator, but that didn't mean he cared what happened to us. Or that he was going to stick his neck out to help, especially when it meant putting himself in jeopardy. I'd hit him in the head with that tire iron before I even knew about Tish. He might be stupid, but he wasn't stupid enough to let me—or Laura—walk away from this, thinking we'd keep silent about what the Deltas were doing. What he'd done to his own girlfriend.

Trust her, my gut whispered. *This is her story, too.*

I swallowed hard. "Tell me what you think we should do."

39

The crawl space door opened with a thud, sending a shaft of the sickly orange light onto the dirt floor, along with the brighter beam of a flashlight.

The hollow clunk of the ladder followed a moment later.

"Ready or not!" Kyle's voice rang out, with the slightest slur. He might not be completely drunk, but he was definitely buzzed.

I squeezed Laura's good hand.

I didn't know if this would work, but I also didn't know what else to do. We were hurt. We were trapped. We were at their mercy—unless we could press on the cracks between Tony and Kyle hard enough. At least long enough to get us out of here.

I heard the rush of air as Laura filled her lungs next to me. Then she screamed, tilting her chin and letting her voice fly toward the beam of orange light. "Kyle killed Ava Robles."

I drew in a breath as soon as the last syllable left her lips. "She's down here. In the crawl space."

The words left a bitter taste in my mouth.

A pair of legs appeared on the first rung of the ladder, and the flashlight beam swung in a slow, searching arc. "Ava Robles, huh?" Kyle said after a moment, descending another step. He laughed. The flashlight landed on Laura, then me. He kept the beam on our faces until we squinted and looked away. "Is Elizabeth Smart down there, too? How about Freddy Krueger?"

He laughed again. "One, two, Freddy's coming for you."

I stared in shock as he took one more step down the ladder. He'd hesitated a moment too long before his flippant response.

Laura was right: Tony *didn't* know about Ava.

I couldn't think of any other reason Kyle would try to pretend she wasn't down here with us.

The question now was who Tony believed. And whether or not he drew the line at murder.

Laura sat up straighter. "Tony!" she screamed. "He's lying. Ava's down here. She's … he shot her. There's a red X on her chest." Kyle was moving faster now, the flashlight beam shuddering as he ducked beneath the vapor barrier and insulation. His sneakers hit the floor. Tony was nowhere to be seen. Was he hearing all this?

As Laura's voice broke, I screamed again as loudly as I could while Kyle's hulking form moved toward us with the flashlight. "Remember the missing person photo that went around campus? Her braids? The colored ribbons?" The words tore through my throat and I tasted blood, but I didn't care. "She's down here. Look for yourself."

My every instinct screamed for me to run as the erratic beam of the flashlight, and the sound of Kyle's footsteps drew closer.

But there was nowhere to go. Nowhere to run, even if my ankle could hold my weight.

"Keep screaming," Laura hissed as my voice died. Then she leaned close to my ear and shoved something against my side: the cell phone. "Take this. I don't have pockets," she whispered.

I shoved it beneath the waistband of my shorts and into the travel pouch, just as the flashlight beam landed on Laura's face. She squinted into the blinding light but didn't cower. I went silent as a slight movement from the crawl space cutout caught my eye.

Tony was up there. Had he heard everything? My pulse hammered so hard that for a second I thought I might pass out. What was he thinking? What would he do now?

Kyle slowly moved the beam to Laura's injured arm. In the light, it looked even worse. The bone hadn't broken through the skin, but from the angle of her forearm—buckled sharply beneath the skin —it had come pretty close.

Glancing between me and Laura, Kyle swung the flashlight in a wide circle around the room until the beam came to rest on the far wall.

"Ava? Where ya at, girl?" he called. The beam illuminated the corpse even as he said the words, throwing a wash of light onto Ava's skeletal remains with her perfect braids and dusty ribbons.

Now that I knew what I was looking at, I took in every detail of the red lines running across the center of her dingy toga dress. The gaping black hole in her chest was a few inches off from the center of the red X. Dark brown, blotchy stains discolored the white fabric at the edges of the hole.

Laura screamed again. "We're looking right at her, you shit-head!"

Kyle swung the flashlight back to her face, crouching deeper to avoid the hanging insulation. "Now you're just hurting my ears. So shut up, already."

The shadows at the top of the crawl space shifted again, and another pair of legs moved to the top rung.

Tony was coming into the crawl space. "It sure smells like something's dead," he muttered. "Dude, it *reeks* down here."

Kyle laughed and shifted the flashlight so it landed on the putrid corpse of the rat beside his foot. From the looks of it, it was the one I'd smashed earlier. "Look, it's Ava Robles," he guffawed.

Tony was on the crawl space floor now. I watched his dark silhouette duck to avoid the insulation, then hesitate by the ladder.

I suddenly realized he didn't have a flashlight with him.

I opened my mouth to scream again, but Kyle flicked the beam of light onto my face, careful not to shine it across the back wall. "I said, shut *up*. And move. Now." He gestured toward the ladder then let his hand trail over the butt of the gun he'd shoved into his waistband. "I'm more than happy to drag you, but it'll hurt less if you move your own asses. God, you two are extra."

"Let me see the flashlight." Tony's voice cut through the darkness.

40

"Why?" Kyle grunted after a moment. "You actually think Ava Robles is down here?"

Laura glanced at me quickly while Kyle's head was turned away, toward Tony. I gave her hand a quick squeeze. This was good.

Tony took a step into the darkness beneath the crawl space, toward the flashlight beam that was still blinding Laura and me. He didn't answer Kyle's question.

Kyle flicked the flashlight beam to Tony's feet, where a few tiny shadows and legs scurried away from the light. Then he swung the beam to Tony's face.

Tony stopped walking, squinting into the light. It struck me again how handsome he looked, with that baby face and rumpled blond hair. How innocent.

So deftly I almost didn't realize what was happening, Kyle reached for his waistband. Through the red and green halos burned into my retinas, I watched in horror as his hand grasped the handle of the gun and slowly moved it in front of his body. If I hadn't been right next to him, I wouldn't have seen the movement.

My mind spun. If Tony wasn't supposed to find out about Ava Robles—or that Kyle definitely planned to kill Laura and me—then it was game over for all of us. Tony included.

At this point, I still relished the idea of the gun going off with Tony as its target. A quick, painless death was the least of what he deserved. But if he died, we died too.

I calculated the distance between myself and Kyle. If I made a move on Kyle, would Laura and Tony jump into action, too? He was distracted. But I remembered all too well how easily he'd taken the shovel from Laura.

I gritted my teeth. *No.* Kyle would fire the gun. And in this small space, I had no doubt he'd hit at least one target. Probably all three.

"Come on girls, let's go," Kyle flicked his gaze toward us again, keeping the flashlight on Tony's face.

"Where are we going?" Laura asked fearfully.

"You wanna stay down here longer?" Kyle laughed. "Let's go. You too, bro. Unless you wanna poke around for Ava Robles?" he added lightly.

The question hung in the air, a gauntlet.

Would Tony demand the flashlight? If he did, it meant he'd flipped on Kyle—and we'd all die right here.

If he backed off, he might live to see another day. But Laura and I wouldn't.

The last page of the book fluttered in the silence.

Turn to page 200, you die.

Turn to page 300, you die.

It turned out there was a third option I hadn't anticipated.

41

"Why? Are you scared I'll tell? Who's the pussy now?" Tony's tone was mocking. Loud. Scary.

He suddenly sounded exactly like Kyle.

I kept my eyes on the dark shape of the gun in Kyle's hand while my stomach recoiled violently. "We're just gonna get rid of them, right? They've seen our faces. You told them the whole story about Tish the bitch. So what's the fucking problem? I want to see Ava. Why are you holding out?"

Kyle lowered the flashlight from Tony's eyes a little. He barked out a laugh. "Nah. You don't have the balls. You've been dead weight all night, ruining the fun, after everything I've done to help you. It's like you *want* to go to jail. Maybe you belong down here with these two." In the dim light from the vent, I watched his lips stretch into a half-smile, showing a sliver of those ultra-white teeth that almost glowed in the dark.

"Fuck you. I just needed a few beers to loosen up," Tony slurred, taking a step closer, careful not to step on the oozing rat. "You know that's how I am. I overthink it. Anyway, you were right. We can't let them go. So we might as well have some fun." He laughed, then pointed into the darkness as he blinked into the flashlight beam. "I get to end the one who hit me though. My head still hurts like a bitch."

Laura looked at me in terror.

Either Tony was a much better actor than I'd given him credit for, or a much worse person than we'd calculated.

Kyle lowered the flashlight a little more.

He believed Tony.

And so did I.

That meant it was really and truly over for Laura and me. I felt for her hand again in the cold dirt. Her fingers were freezing, but they weren't shaking anymore.

I imagined the missing photos they'd post of us—and Tish, sooner or later—that would make the rounds. Just like Ava's had.

We hadn't actually made it to Coffin Creek, but we'd gotten close enough to fuel more legends of ghosts and bloodthirsty vagrants or cougars up the canyon. Close enough that they'd tell our story, or what little they knew about it, on blogs and during Rush week for years to come.

They'd be right about one thing: We'd met the same fate as Ava.

Kyle dropped the flashlight beam to Tony's feet, but he still didn't lower the gun.

Instead, he cocked it with a metallic *click,* sharp and precise in the murky darkness beyond the beam of the flashlight.

Tony froze.

Kyle laughed. "Fine, let's have some fun, then. Go get the tire iron." Then he pointed the gun at Laura and me. "Move," he snapped. "Back up the ladder." Then, so softly I almost missed it he added, "Or I'll shoot you right now. You know I will."

Laura had already struggled to her feet.

I did the same, tentatively putting a little weight on my twisted ankle. It hurt like hell, but it held.

I gritted my teeth and limped toward the ladder, hearing Laura right behind me.

Neither of us spoke. What was there left to say?

As we approached the ladder, Tony's hunched form suddenly backed away from us, into the darkness.

Kyle reacted, swinging the flashlight beam toward Tony—and briefly illuminated the far wall of the crawl space.

For a fraction of a second, Ava's beautiful, dark braids—and her screaming, skeletal mouth—flashed into view.

She was gone before I could flick my eyes back to Tony. Had he seen her?

"Where are you going, dumbass?" Kyle demanded.

"Sorry. I just don't want them to tag-team me. You know, like they did before."

He sounded contrite. A little embarrassed. Not at all like he'd just seen a dead girl in a crawl space. And if he had, he didn't care.

Kyle sighed impatiently. "If you let them go first, they'll shut your ass down here. With the rats," Kyle replied matter-of-factly. "So get up the ladder."

Tony didn't hesitate.

He clambered up the ladder and stood at the top, staring down at me while I struggled to follow him, favoring my ankle.

I stole a glance at his face while I reached for the top rung, trying to find some indication that he wasn't all monster. He stared back at me without flinching. He was holding the fireplace shovel in one hand.

I stopped before pulling my body past the ledge of the trap door, into the floor of the utility room.

There was only one question still running through my mind. Was it better to go out fighting, or cowering like a cornered animal?

If I let go of the ladder and rushed Kyle, he would probably shoot me. But wasn't that better than whatever "fun" they had planned? I desperately wanted one more minute alone with Laura. Was she thinking the same thing? Did she have any other ideas?

I gripped the top ladder rung harder. There were no guarantees Kyle would shoot to kill. And even if I knew with complete certainty that he would, there was still some part of me that screamed *no*. That as long as we were alive, there was still a slim chance something would turn in our favor. That the balance of power might shift long enough to give us another opening if I could hold on a little longer.

I remembered the nearly dead phone in my travel pouch.

Our chances for survival were as slim as the ghost of a battery that remained.

I pictured the dark screen that, against all odds, had lit up a few minutes earlier with that ghost of a bar.

I couldn't give up before that battery.

42

Tony backed away from the crawl space ledge while I rolled onto my side in a heap, drawing in gulps of fresh air.

I could still feel his eyes on me, but I refused to meet his gaze anymore.

When Laura reached the top of the ladder, she lifted herself onto the opposite side of the hole, toward Tony. Her wide blue eyes were pleading, desperate. She held her bruised, bent wrist slightly away from her like a bird with a broken wing.

It was clear that, despite everything Tony had just said, she still thought there was a chance he might help us. That what had happened down there in the crawl space was an act.

He stared at her for a moment, then took a step toward her. I watched him dart his eyes between the crawl space ladder and her face.

I groaned and rolled onto my stomach. Then I reached into the open travel pouch to pull out the cell phone, palming it and tucking it under my arm before struggling to a sitting position next to a dusty chest freezer pushed against one side of the room.

I just needed one bar. Then a few seconds to hit the call button—when nobody was looking.

Basically, I needed two miracles.

The ladder thunked against the crawl space opening as Kyle began to climb. My stomach lurched. There wouldn't be time.

Tony was standing above Laura now, staring down at her impassively while she mouthed something to him.

Suddenly, he reached down and grabbed her by the arm—the one she'd broken.

She let out a piercing shriek, sobbing for him to let go of her arm. That he was hurting her.

Ignoring her screams, Tony pushed her toward me, barely missing Kyle's head as he emerged through the crawl space. She landed hard on her good arm. Her shoe kicked into my ankle as she fell. I screamed too, the sound tearing through my raw throat as she collided against me.

"Atta boy. Let's go." Kyle laughed and pulled himself fully out of the hole in the floor.

Call now, my mind insisted, a sharp demand that cut through the pain in my ankle. I shifted closer to Laura. "Don't move," I whispered through gritted teeth. In response, she slumped against me more deeply, her pale hair spilling across my hands.

I buried my head into her hair, breathing in sweat and a familiar whiff of the BedHead shampoo we shared. The smell brought with it a longing for home and safety so intense it was difficult to breathe. The idea of taking a shower, of tucking my weary body into my soft, clean bed, made me nearly dizzy with desperation.

I fumbled to get the phone out from under my arm, then opened the screen in front of my face.

The service bar flickered in and out in the corner of the screen —still erratic, but steadier than anything I'd seen since we lost service in the hills.

Would the battery last long enough for a call to connect—for a dispatcher to understand what was happening, who was calling, and where we were at? How would I explain where we were at, even if I had the time? I couldn't say anything. I couldn't reveal that I even had the phone.

Not to mention that the phone would die at any moment. Just like us.

Following my gut, I opened my text messages.

There was no way Tish had gotten the messages I'd sent before, from Laura's phone. Even if she had, it wasn't like she could find us based on what I'd sent. I hadn't even known their names—or that Tony was involved at that point. The license plate was useless.

I typed six words and hit send.

911 Tony Kyle 67 Deer Flat.

The message hovered in limbo for a heartbeat. Then "message delivered" appeared in tiny letters beneath the bubble.

I nearly gasped. The message had sent.

I thumbed to the emergency call button.

But before I could press it, the screen went black.

Part of me wanted to scream in triumph. I'd done it. That text would be read. Tish would unravel this nightmare. Which meant Tish would survive. And Tony and Kyle and the rest of the Deltas might go to prison for what they'd done.

Another part of me quietly let go of the last bit of hope I'd been holding onto.

The police would find Laura and me—but not in time to help us.

We were at least two hours into the hills. I could feel the end coming much sooner than that.

Laura's sobs shuddered against me, but she didn't move. Kyle shut the trap door to the crawl space with a thud that sent one last blast of putrid air wafting through the utility room.

When he spoke, his voice was full of newfound glee. "You think we need to tie them up? Blondie seems a lot perkier than she did when we first got here, but her arm is wrecked. I don't think Barbie #2 can walk."

"Nah, they aren't going anywhere," Tony responded, his voice fainter as the sound of his footsteps disappeared down the hall—presumably to get the tire iron I'd dropped in the dirt outside.

I shuffled closer to the old yellow chest freezer against the wall in the utility room. A thick layer of dust coated the ground beneath it. From the way it sat silent—no electric hum—I knew it wasn't on. I darted one hand beneath it, through the dust, and set the cell phone just out of view.

It was clear enough from the grime, the smell, the disrepair, that the hunting cabin wasn't used regularly, if at all. And that nobody had been down in that crawl space for a very long time. Three years, at least. That was when Ava had gone missing.

When the police finally made it out here and searched the cabin, they would find the phone. The unsent texts would be read. They'd open up the crawl space and find Ava Robles—and us, too.

As I thought through it, tears pricked my eyes.

It wasn't survival.

But it was something.

43

"Stand up," Kyle instructed, pointing the gun at our faces. "And face the wall."

We obeyed.

I imagined the feel of the tire iron crashing through my skull. Would I feel it, or would my vision suddenly go black? Would I wake up to something worse? Would he use the gun afterward, too, like he had on Ava?

The seconds ticked by, accompanied by the sound of soft clanks and rustling from the utility room shelves.

It sounded like Kyle was looking for something in the cabinets and cupboards. My tongue felt like sandpaper in my mouth as I tried to swallow, and my ankle throbbed hard. The straps of my shoe were starting to cut off circulation as the swelling intensified.

Next to me, Laura slipped her good hand into mine and squeezed.

I squeezed back.

The porch door slammed, followed by Tony's footsteps and a sudden, loud bang from behind us.

I jumped and hazarded a glance over my shoulder, nearly losing my balance—and toppling Laura—in the process.

Tony was standing next to Kyle near the doorway to the utility room. He was holding the tire iron in one hand, the tip still resting against the hollow utility room door. He laughed. "Oops."

Kyle grunted then I heard him next to me. "There it is." He moved to the shelf to our right and snatched the canister with the orange lid. Before I could get a good look at it, he shifted his eyes toward me. "I said, face the wall." He lowered his voice and moved away from us, clearly talking to Tony now. "Check it out."

There was a strange sound of something metallic rattling. Footsteps crept up behind us again, I braced myself for whatever was coming.

Laura squeezed my hand tight.

But instead of impact, I felt a cool mist on my arm. Then more on my legs. My back. My butt.

The smell of spray paint filled the air with a sharp chemical bite.

"Um, what are you doing?" Tony laughed.

Kyle didn't respond. Instead, he moved on to Laura's back, sweeping the can of spray paint in short strokes until he coughed and stepped back. I tilted my head to the side to see what he'd done.

Laura's legs and torso were covered in a series of neon, reddish orange Xes.

I pictured the X on Ava's chest, the faintly glowing spray paint on the target range outside, and my knees threatened to give way.

More jagged puzzle pieces of what Kyle had planned for our last act.

"Turn around and face me," Kyle instructed. "You'll probably want to close your eyes, but don't let me tell you what to do. God knows you refuse to listen."

I had barely squeezed my eyes shut before I felt the paint sting my face.

Short, fast slashes across both of my cheeks.

When I couldn't hold my breath any longer, I sucked in a shallow mouthful of air—then started coughing hard. Laura did the same a few seconds later.

Both men laughed.

"Dude, seriously. What the hell are you doing to them?" Tony asked, taking a step closer with the tire iron.

Kyle looked at him for a moment before answering. Then a smile lit up his face. "There's a big range out back—my stepdad set it up a few years ago—before he landed himself in jail." He held up the can of paint and shook it again. "It's actually kind of sick. It glows in the dark."

My eyes were streaming from the paint fumes, but the look on Tony's face was clear enough. Confusion, then surprise, then pure admiration. "So … you're saying we're gonna do some target practice?"

Kyle grinned. "Look who's got balls after all." He tossed the paint can on the floor and waved the gun at Tony. "Have you ever even used one of these?"

"Nah. But I learn quick."

Kyle's laugh boomed through the tiny room. He stepped backward, nearly tripping on the spray can. "You two had better pray he does," he said as he looked between me and Laura.

I already was, more fervently than I'd ever prayed. Just one word, again and again.

Please. Please, please.

I wasn't sure if the prayer was meant for God or to my own lizard brain, begging for a swift end to this nightmare.

Either way, nobody responded except Kyle. "You know, you really should have run earlier." He looked thoughtful for a moment. "I guess you tried. Twice." He sighed. "But you were so, so bad at it, both times."

He shrugged. "Don't beat yourself up too much. It was all part of the fun."

In my peripheral vision, I saw Tony lift the tire iron.

For a moment, I thought he was going to do it: bring the long, narrow piece of metal down on Kyle's head, exactly like I'd done to him earlier.

Instead, he stepped next to Kyle. "I still get first shot at her, right?" He locked eyes with me and pointed the tire iron at my face.

Kyle snickered. "Sure, whatever. She's gonna be slow with that leg. Let's bring them into the living room for a minute. The paint won't glow until it's dry. If they try anything, or say anything—hit them. Just ... not so hard they can't run. I'm gonna grab some more ammo."

Laura was squeezing my hand so tightly my fingers had gone numb. I didn't pull away.

Tony hit the door frame with the tire iron again as he backed through the door.

"You heard him. Move."

44

Tony and Kyle both slurped yet another beer while Laura and I limped in front of them, our bodies glowing a faint white. Each step sent dull waves of pain rippling through my body. From the sound of Laura's jagged breaths—and the way she was holding her arm—I knew what Kyle knew: we'd be easy to catch.

We were the perfect targets.

Tony belched loudly. Then, as if reading my thoughts, he said, "They can walk okay. What if they run again—and like, find a way out?"

Kyle took a loud swallow of beer, then let out an even louder belch. "Dude, look at them. Anyway, everything except the gate is fenced. They can't."

I imagined the imposing barbed-wire fence glinting in the moonlight and took another step forward, watching my glowing skin with a kind of morbid fascination. Was this what he'd done to Ava? Would we run like they wanted—moving targets, fish in a barrel, drawing out the end as long as possible—or would we stand arm in arm until the bullets made us fall?

As quietly as I could, I whispered to Laura under my breath. "I got a text out. To Tish."

I didn't look at her, but I heard her breath catch. She nodded ever so slightly and lifted her chin, like the words had given her the strength to keep moving.

I didn't tell her about the dead screen or that I'd sent that text instead of calling 9-1-1 with those last, precious seconds of battery life.

It felt like the least I could do—to let her hold onto that hope a little longer even if I couldn't.

The quiet, mournful yip of a coyote sounded in the distance. A few seconds later, a chorus answered her. For some reason, it made tears prick at my eyes as I took another step.

I wanted to howl too. For my family. For Laura's family. For Tish.

The sound of another loud belch made me grit my teeth. Both men were tipsy and giddy, oblivious that they'd be caught soon. They weren't even being particularly careful. I hadn't seen either of them wear a pair of gloves. And why would they be stressed? If it weren't for the text I'd managed to squeak out, they probably would have gotten away with this. Nobody had discovered Ava's body over the past three years. Why would anyone find us, either?

Despite Laura's arm through mine, I felt alone in a way I never had before.

Survivor, victim, prey. The lines between all the labels blurred together in my mind.

What it came down to was this: We were all targets.

Even if you made the right choice, followed the right rules, took the right risks, kept your cool, made the right friends, didn't walk alone home after dark, kept a rape whistle in your pocket, and guarded your drink at bars.

I'd always thought I could skip the bad parts of life if I tried hard enough. If I was smart enough.

But sometimes the trouble came to you—for the simple fact that it could and it wanted to. When you were the one caught in the crosshairs of the gun, the biggest factor that determined whether you survived, escaped, died—was the person with their finger on the trigger.

Maybe it had never been our story at all. Like Tony, we were just side characters in Kyle's plot.

The neon Xes on our arms and legs blurred into fuzzy flashes of dead light as the tears spilled down my cheeks, burning when they touched the spray paint.

Red means anything goes.

The silhouettes in the target range loomed into view as we threaded through the tall weeds, taking a path behind the cabin this time instead of cutting through the ditch like Laura and I had earlier. My ankle protested with each step, but Laura kept her good arm locked through mine to steady me.

Every few steps, she tilted her head to the side, listening for the sound of sirens I knew weren't coming.

The cloud cover had lifted in the past hour, and the sliver of moon sent just enough light onto the clearing that I could see a few of the tall, skinny fence posts spaced along the barbed wire fence. As I took in the enormous shooting range, I realized Kyle had never really been worried we'd get away before. It was just another way to drag the hunt out, like a cat with a mouse.

When I'd stowed away in the bed of that truck, I wasn't thwarting any of his plans. Not really.

My presence was a bonus. Two targets instead of one.

"Whoa," Tony slurred. "Your stepdad made this whole thing?"

"Part of it." Kyle belched. "I've added some," he added proudly.

"Whoa," Tony repeated. "Why is the fence so high?" He threw his beer can at the nearest plywood board. An illustration of what might have been a deer glowed faintly on its surface. "Do these come alive at night or something?"

Kyle snorted. "He put it up for the deer. There's a million of them out here. The fence is high enough that they can't jump it if they wander in through the gate. Easy hunting. One time he got a twelve-point buck right over here."

I imagined the sound of frantic hooves and gunshots. In my mind's eye, I could see the glassy eyes of the does on the wall in the cabin.

Had Kyle dragged Ava out here, too, or had he shot her in the crawl space?

I suddenly decided I wasn't going to run—like a cornered animal.

Kyle saw himself as an alpha predator. He chased, we ran. And ultimately, we died.

I knew I couldn't escape, but that didn't mean I had to act the part of prey.

Laura turned her head again, scanning for red-and-blue lights to crash down the ATV path. My heart broke. I needed to tell her.

"They're not coming," I whispered in a low voice I hoped Kyle and Tony couldn't hear as they tramped along the path a short distance behind us.

She kept her face forward. "What?"

"I got the text out. But the phone died before I could make a call," I breathed.

Something hit the ground near my feet with a flimsy pop: a beer can. "No more scheming, MacGyver," Kyle slurred.

The tall weeds flanking the trail had tapered off, yielding to the hardscrabble cleared ground of the range. The footsteps behind us stopped as Laura and I walked into the range. The first target was maybe ten yards away.

I stared at it, deciding that was where I would stop. Far enough away from Kyle and Tony that I could whisper my goodbyes to Laura. Close enough that I'd ruin Kyle's sick game.

Laura gripped my arm tight. With each step toward the first target, I willed my short life to flash before my eyes: The house I'd grown up in with the big backyard and towering catalpa trees. My first kiss with David Abrams in eighth grade, after the spring dance. My mom taking the day off work to watch *Harry Potter* with me on the sofa bed when I got strep throat. Dancing to MTV with Laura in Tish's old satin prom dresses. Sneaking into the luxe apartment complex off campus with Tish to sip cheap blackberry wine in the hot tub. The porch swing in my backyard at home in Lewiston, where I liked to read.

Laura leaned close to me when we were a few steps away from the first target: a tall, narrow piece of plywood that displayed a badly drawn bear. Its eyes had been painted as Xes, like the ones covering my body. Like it was already dead.

I scanned the other ghostly, spray-painted shapes in the target range behind the bear. There were so many. Then I looked at Laura. Even with the bump on her head, the purple stain across her chin from the smeared lipstick, and the debris tangling in her pale hair, she was beautiful.

She managed a smile. "You can never be my dream boy if you don't see me, boy," she whisper-sung, so quietly it was nearly lost in the breeze.

My throat tightened, and my pulse thumped faster. This was it. "I'm not running," I whispered to Laura. "Tish has the address. In the text." The words caught in my throat. "They'll find us here. Like this." I squeezed her hand.

She squeezed back and let out a slow breath. "I'm not running either. Love you, Liv."

"Love you too, Laur," I rasped back.

Howls rose again in the distance, the sound alien and wild.

"Show me where …" Tony's voice—and Kyle's soft laughter—mingled with the chorus of howls.

"Go ahead," Kyle called to us. "Run along. Lots of hiding spots." He lowered his voice and said something to Tony. I couldn't hear what either of them were saying anymore.

The howls swelled, then petered off into silence as the pack gathered. Maybe they were hunting something, too.

A metallic *click* broke through the quiet ruffle of cottonwoods in the distance.

I gritted my teeth and watched my breath swirl in frosty puffs. Instead of running, Laura and I turned in the direction of the *click*. I squinted but couldn't see Kyle or Tony.

My heart pounded, and my legs itched to move. Instead, I wrapped my arm around Laura's shoulder. She did the same.

"I'll count down from three, okay?" came Kyle's disembodied voice. "Give you a head start." My eyes scanned the darkness to our left and right, but all I could see were the plywood silhouettes.

Three. I nearly laughed at the word.

Instead, I relaxed my jaw and lifted my free hand in front of my face, along with my middle finger.

A neon *fuck you.*

"Three." His voice boomed.

Laura drew in a quiet breath.

"Two. Better move, ladies."

I shifted my weight to my uninjured leg and closed my eyes, letting my mind go blank and drawing in a lungful of the cold night air that tasted like dust and sunbaked grass. I held the breath as long as I could, knowing it would be my last.

"One."

45

The gun went off with a violent pop the moment Kyle's countdown ended.

I squeezed my eyes shut tighter, waiting for the bullet to pierce my skin, hoping he'd aimed to kill.

Instead, I heard a muffled thud. The sound came from somewhere in the distance—nowhere near me or Laura. Had he hit one of the plywood targets on the other edge of the range? Was he still trying to get us to run? How many shots would it take to finally end this? I clutched the hem of Laura's shirt in my fist, hoping for the impossible: that we'd both go at once.

I knew better. They were drunk. And they were enjoying this too much.

The acrid smell of gunpowder wafted on the breeze.

"Liv," Laura whispered. "Listen."

A harsh, repeated hissing sound pierced the stillness. For a moment, I wondered if those drunk bastards had hit a gas line somehow. I hoped so.

But, no. There were words in the hiss. I listened harder, trying to make them out. Laura tilted her head toward the sound and took a step away from me.

Suddenly, I made sense of the hissing syllables: "Shit, shit, shit, shit."

"Tony?" Laura called softly.

I stared at her in confusion as she took another step away from me. I wanted to reach out for her arm, to keep her next to me.

She peered into the darkness, wavering in the moonlight that reflected on the strips of duct tape still stuck to her arms in tatters. She glanced back at me quickly, her eyes wide. Then she moved faster toward the sound.

The fresh trickle of adrenaline that had been pumping through my veins crashed as she moved toward the cabin. I could only brace for impact so long. I couldn't take any more twists. I just wanted this endless nightmare, this fucked-up game, to fade to black permanently. I didn't want to feel the wrecked tendons in my twisted ankle, the scratches down my arms and legs, the dried gore in my hair anymore.

My body was shaking so hard that when I took a step to follow Laura, I nearly fell.

She walked faster through the weeds, the glowing Xes slashed across her body forming a mesmerizing blur of movement that reminded me of a Cirque du Soleil show I'd seen in Vegas. It was almost beautiful. "Tony?" she called again.

I moved faster to catch up with her, ignoring the sharp protest of my ankle. With each step, I waited to hear another *pop.*

When we reached the edge of the target range—where Tony and Kyle had stopped following us—I stared in disbelief, trying to make sense of what I saw.

Tony—not Kyle—was holding the gun now.

It glinted in his hand as he held it off to one side, like he might drop it at any moment. He didn't react as Laura and I approached him.

All of us were staring at the crumpled body on the ground:
Kyle.

46

"Shit," Tony repeated in that same fast, hissing whisper. He didn't look at Laura or me. Instead, he lowered the gun to his side and inspected the body on the ground, his wide eyes fixed on the motionless form.

I couldn't look away, either. Other than Ava, I'd never seen a dead body before. And this one had been alive a few seconds ago.

"I shot him," Tony said, then repeated the same words incredulously as if trying to convince himself he'd really done it. "I shot him."

Kyle was lying face down in the dirt, maybe three feet away from Tony's dusty Air Jordans.

I couldn't see where the bullet had gone in, but I could already see the blood seeping into the dirt beneath Kyle's chest.

His body twitched a little. I froze, trying to recall some reassurance from my true-crime trivia files that this was something dead bodies did. I remembered something about involuntary movements after death—as air left the lungs, as muscles relaxed then contracted when rigor mortis began to take hold. He wasn't making a sound. I couldn't see his chest rising and falling from where I stood, but did that mean he was really dead?

Would he suddenly reach out a hand or jump to his feet the moment we turned away? Was Tony about to turn the gun on us, too? My tired mind spun. The only thing I knew for sure right now was that I needed to find out whether Kyle was dead.

I edged closer to the body on the ground, even as Tony and Laura took a step backward, watching my movements in frozen fascination and horror.

I studied the pool of dark blood seeping under his folded arm. It was spreading fast, widening into a puddle that swallowed the squatty weeds poking their way through the hard ground.

His chest hadn't moved again—I was pretty sure, anyway. It was difficult to tell in the dark.

Keeping my eyes fixed on the position of his arms, I crouched awkwardly beside his body and reached one hand toward the back of his neck.

The last thing in the world I wanted was to touch his skin with my bare hands, but I had to know.

I clenched my jaw and jammed two fingers against the side of his throat, doing my best to separate the pounding of my own heart from any movement beneath his skin.

Nothing.

I concentrated, feeling for any flicker of his throat.

Again, nothing.

I felt down the side of his face, where his nose was pressed into the dust. His mouth was slack and still. There were no puffs of air moving in or out. He was really and truly dead.

Still in shock, I wiped my hand against my scratchy sequins and stumbled back from the body, turning to stare at Laura—and Tony.

"Why did you do that?" Laura asked slowly, breaking the silence.

Tony's head swiveled away from me, toward her. I braced, no longer sure what was going to happen next. Five minutes earlier, he'd been Kyle's bitch, chugging a beer and getting ready to take aim at two girls he'd helped put through hell.

He'd suddenly made this his story.

And I didn't understand.

Tony ignored Laura's question. Instead, he glanced at the gun in his hand and mumbled something unintelligible.

"What did you say?" Laura demanded, louder this time. She sounded almost angry. A spark of her outrage lit something inside me as well, burning away my resolve to die with dignity.

He blinked fast, as if suddenly coming to his senses. "We need to get out of here."

Neither Laura nor I moved. My eyes kept going back to Kyle's unmoving body on the ground. The pool of blood had stopped spreading, congealing in the cool air. I knew I should feel at least a little relieved that he was dead and we were alive, but until we knew why Tony had done it, we were still standing in the middle of nowhere in a shooting range—marked as targets—in the dead of night, when we both should have been in the hospital.

As I shifted on one foot, I noticed something glinting in the weeds next to Kyle: The tire iron.

Tony followed my gaze. "You wanna take another swing at me?" he spat. "*I'm. Helping. You.* Okay?" he said, enunciating each word so aggressively that I re-ran the sentence through my mind to make sure I'd understood him.

As if to prove his point, he wiped the gun on the edge of his shirt—spending extra time on the crevices of the trigger—and tossed it into the shooting range. It hit the bear target with a soft clunk then disappeared.

"Come on. The truck keys are in the cabin," he muttered.

* * *

Tony held the screen door open for us while we limped up the steps to the cabin behind him.

Something brushed against my bare leg as I crossed the threshold and I quickly whipped my hand down to bat at it—thinking it was a spider that had been clinging to my clothing since the crawl space.

Instead, it was a corner of mesh, flapping loosely in the broken screen door. Tony eyed me warily and gave me a wider berth as I passed him. I avoided his eyes as I crossed the threshold into the cabin, still unwilling to let myself feel relief.

I caught a brief glimpse of my reflection in the living room windowpane as I limped through the entryway and stood on the shabby rug near the dusty couch. A trickle of blood from my scalp had turned into a dark smear across one cheek, blending with a wash of black mascara rimming my eyes. An angry red scratch bloomed on my chin, just visible beneath a layer of dust and grime. I reached up to tug at a large leaf covered in cobwebs entangled in my hair.

When I glanced at Laura, I could see that she was studying her reflection in the same windowpane. She reached up to touch the lump on her head. A fine layer of dust from the crawl space covered most of the reddish purple color, but one of her eyebrows tilted sharply upward from the swelling near her temple.

Tony let the screen door slam shut. He let out a sigh and tried to brush past Laura to get to the kitchen—nearly running into her injured arm. She took a step back and glared at him. "Why did you do that?" She repeated the same question she'd asked while the three of us stood around Kyle's body.

"How about a *thank you,* first?" he muttered. "What happened to 'help me, Tony'?"

I nearly laughed out loud. After everything that had happened tonight, after everything he'd done to Tish, and to us, he was upset we hadn't *thanked* him properly. That we weren't more *grateful* for his generosity and heroism. I couldn't quite believe he'd flipped on Kyle. And I couldn't quite believe we were alive. But I wasn't about to tumble all over myself thanking Tony for anything.

How about an apology to us? How about acknowledging that you are still a supreme piece of shit?

I pictured the sneering expression on his face as he slammed the crowbar against the doorframe. The way he'd grabbed Laura by her broken arm—tossing her toward me on the utility room floor while she begged for him to help us. The way he'd drunk beer after beer in the living room with Kyle while we scrambled over dead rats —and dead bodies—in the crawl space below him.

Still, here we were, impossibly alive. I swallowed back the rage and the exhaustion and forced the words out. "Thank you," I managed, not wanting to antagonize him any more than he already was. "But we don't understand."

He looked at me incredulously, as if I were the one with the explaining to do. "He took it too far. I'm not like him."

Laura and I exchanged glances. The look in her eyes was crystal clear. *Bullshit.*

He caught the meaning, too, and his expression darkened. "Fuck you. I'm not a bad guy. I had no idea about Ava Robles until tonight. But I had to pretend like I was into it until I could get my hands on that gun."

I let the words sink in. Laura's instincts were right. Tony was a piece of shit, but he was a different kind of monster than Kyle. He just didn't realize it until tonight.

I flashed back to what he'd said to Kyle at the top of the crawl space: *I still get first shot at her, right?* He'd wanted to get that gun in his hands before Kyle took a shot at us. Which meant he had to play up how bad he wanted to use it—especially after what happened with the shovel.

Kyle wouldn't have believed him if he half-assed that performance.

Laura slowly nodded. Tony stared at her, giving her a chance to offer up her own *thank you*. When it didn't come, he sighed heavily and walked away. "Sit down before you pass out. Jesus. I'll get the keys."

Laura and I looked at each other. I wasn't sure how much longer I could stand, but I sure as hell wasn't going to sit down on that disgusting couch or relax. Not until we were safe. Actually safe.

Kyle was no longer around to remind us, but the fact remained that Tish was still out there, pregnant with somebody else's baby. Tony had to know that we would tell her—and help put his ass in jail for what he and the Deltas had done.

There was no amount of redemption that would make up for that. Tony wasn't stupid enough to think we'd all shake hands and walk away. He didn't want to go to jail, and he couldn't let Tish have that baby. What that meant for us, I didn't know, but I sure as hell wasn't ready to kick up my feet and relax on the couch.

"Should we call the police?" I asked lightly to gauge his reaction as he moved toward the kitchen. In the light of the living room, I saw the back of his head clearly for the first time. The matted, dirty-blond hair swirled around a painful-looking dark spot like a messed-up halo. I hoped it hid a lump at least as big as the one on Laura's forehead.

At the word "police," he turned to face me, his expression soured. I instantly regretted bringing it up. He wasn't thinking that far ahead yet—which was a good thing.

"There's no service," he said flatly.

I thought of the cell phone tucked beneath the old chest freezer in the utility room and the flickering service bar that had squeezed out a text to Tish. Tony was wrong, but there was no way to gauge whether he knew that or not. "Yeah, of course. Sorry."

He studied me, and I felt a smile creep onto my lips despite wanting to scream. *Act more grateful,* my gut instructed. I glanced at the deer heads in the hallway above his head, and the word I needed offered itself up: *Fawn. Make him think he's a good guy. That he's in charge. Don't talk about Tish.*

I moved a little closer to Laura and squeezed the fingertips on her good hand. She squeezed back, then glanced at the couch and shrugged. We were both bone tired and about to collapse. Maybe it wouldn't be so bad to sit down after all. Compared to the crawl space, the disgusting couch was the Waldorf Astoria.

"Yeah, of course," I said. "Duh. Thank you again. Seriously. And ... I'm really sorry I hit you earlier. I didn't understand what was happening."

Laura cleared her throat. "Yeah ... thank you. I'm sorry I was so aggressive before, too. My head really hurts. I understand it all now. Kyle did this."

He nodded, and the set of his jaw relaxed a little.

As he disappeared down the hall, Laura turned to me. "Should we stay here—instead of trying to leave? The police have the address. How long has it been since you—"

My eyes widened, and I shook my head frantically, begging her to stop talking. She looked at me quizzically.

Tony had reappeared in the hallway, beneath the deer. The set of his jaw was rigid again. He lifted up one hand to rake it through his hair, stopping before he reached the wound on the back of his head. "What did you say?"

Laura fumbled for the right words. "I just—I thought maybe we should stay here ..." She trailed off, cutting her eyes toward me.

"Why would we do that?" he prompted.

Laura darted her eyes toward me again, begging for help. My mind was blank. I wasn't sure how much he'd heard or how he would react if he knew I'd gotten a text through to Tish. Even the idea that I'd already called the police seemed preferable to that. I had to assume he'd heard everything Laura had said.

"I got a call out to the police," I lied. "Before. In the crawl space."

He stared at me in disbelief. "You what?"

"The phone died," I said truthfully. "Let's find the keys. We can't count on the police coming here." I hated that this part was true, too. It had been maybe half an hour since I'd sent the text to Tish, but I had no idea whether she'd seen it between the time she'd left the library and gone to bed. It might be morning before the police knew to look for us at 67 Deer Flat.

Tony took a few steps closer and sat down on the edge of the couch. "Maybe we should get a few things straight before I get the keys."

My gut clenched. *Pretend you don't know what he's talking about,* it instructed. "Huh?" I asked distractedly, exaggerating my limp as I moved to sit beside Laura on the couch. The coarse, dusty fabric felt like sandpaper on my bare legs, and the springs squealed in protest.

"I want to know what you two are going to tell the police."

I nodded, as if considering this for the first time. "We'll just tell them what happened. What you explained. That Kyle tricked you into coming out here. He was the one driving the truck. He was the one with the gun. He was the one who shoved us into the crawl space. You couldn't do anything—until you got the gun away from him." *Yes,* my brain praised. That version of events sounded believable enough to get us to the police. And that was all we needed right now.

Tony frowned. "I mean, about what Kyle told you," he said evenly, bringing his arms across his chest. He wasn't in a rush anymore, and the shock of what he'd done to Kyle was clearly wearing off. He was thinking farther ahead now, about how all of this would play out. I nodded, trying to figure out what he needed to hear. What he'd believe.

"All we care about is getting out of here," Laura said quietly.

Tony frowned. It had been the wrong thing to say. "Bullshit. What are you going to say when the police ask why your sister's boyfriend was involved? They won't believe it's random. What are you going to tell Tish? She'll figure it out. And the baby…" He raked his hand through the front of his hair again. "Shit. Shit, shit, shit."

I could see his mind working frantically to find a way out. His face twisted, and he peered out the side window of the cabin—in the direction of the shooting range. If I had to guess what he was thinking, it was *Maybe Kyle was right all along.*

"We'll convince Tish to have the abortion," Laura suddenly blurted out.

His head swiveled toward her, his eyes wide with surprise.

"It's the best thing for all of us," I added quickly, trying to infuse as much earnestness to the words as I could.

I swallowed my disgust and studied the deer heads on the wall again. "You aren't a bad guy. We know that. It was just a mistake, and nobody got hurt at the Delta parties. Without you, we'd be dead right now." The words tasted like acid in my mouth but came out like sugar.

He considered this. "Yeah," he finally said gruffly.

I scooted closer to Laura. She picked up where I'd left off weaving the ridiculous story about how nobody had been hurt—even while she swayed against me for support, cradling her broken arm. "Olivia is right. I don't want Tish to know about the parties. It'll only hurt her. And she already thinks Kyle is disgusting—back from when he sold her the Volvo. She'll see that you're a hero, too."

I kept the expression on my face soft and open, but my insides had turned to steel. Tony wasn't the only one who could put on an act.

47

Tony made us go over the story we'd tell the police—and Tish—
three more times, watching us carefully while we answered.

Kyle had been right: Tony was weak, but he wasn't a dummy.
And he wasn't planning on going to jail for anything he'd done
tonight or in the past. Kyle would take blame for everything. Conve-
niently, he couldn't object.

When Tony ran out of questions for the third time, he sighed
loudly and stood up, kicking at the couch leg in frustration. "Let's go
over everything one more time." He furrowed his brows and scruti-
nized me, then Laura carefully, as if he could see our real motiva-
tions if he looked hard enough. His gaze didn't linger on Laura's
broken arm or the lump on her temple. And they didn't pause to take
in my swollen ankle or scraped-up body. He watched our eyes, trying
to determine whether we were allies or liabilities in helping him
cover up the mess he'd made.

He was asking the same questions again and again. I could
think of a dozen more that would point back to Tony as much as
Kyle. But I wasn't about to go there. "We've got our stories straight.
But I just thought of something."

His eyes narrowed and he stopped kicking the couch. "What."

"You need to get rid of the masks. There are two. If the police
find them, it'll look like you knew what Kyle was planning all
along."

Tony's mouth opened slightly. Then he nodded once. "Yeah, that's good. Yeah. They're still in the truck. We can toss them somewhere."

We. He was mentally including us in his plans. He believed us.

Encouraged, I kept going. "If there's any alcohol here, wipe the masks down first. You don't want your DNA on them."

He shot me a grateful look. "Yeah, okay. There's some whiskey on the shelf back there." He pointed down the dark hallway with the deer. "Come on, let's go."

He insisted Laura and I accompany him into the dusty kitchen to get the keys and the whiskey, walking a few steps behind us like he'd done earlier when he'd marched us onto the target range.

"Sit there if you need to." He waved a hand at a card table and plastic chairs against one wall of the tiny kitchen. More shelves lined with dusty cans of food covered the wall behind the table. A rack of antlers hung dangerously close to the single burner of a hotplate on the butcher block counters.

My eyes landed on four badly taxidermied antelope heads, their faces distorted and lumpy, arranged above a stack of mugs, dishes, and loose silverware. The expression on their faces was almost comical. I didn't know anything about taxidermy, but this looked like a DIY job.

There was no sink. On the lowest shelf, several jugs of water sat next to a grimy bottle of whiskey.

Tony grabbed the whiskey then walked to the Coleman cooler that had been wedged into the corner of the kitchen, beside a freestanding cabinet with a squatty door.

"He put them in here when we first..." He tried to pull out the dusty wooden drawer, but it stuck at an angle. He peered into the narrow opening, brushing his fingers along the edge, trying to grasp the keys.

"I can feel them ..." As he said it, I heard the soft jangle of metal coming from inside the drawer.

Laura nudged me when he looked away to focus on the contents of the stuck drawer. She shook her head quickly and cut her eyes toward the drawer. Then her expression turned blank again.

I wasn't sure what she was trying to tell me, and there wasn't a way to ask.

I kept my mouth shut and forced myself to look away. Tony couldn't see us exchanging glances—not if we wanted him to believe we were solidly on his team.

I didn't dare breathe as he fished for the keys. Were we really going to get back into the truck with him? Did I want him to find the keys?

"Got them," he muttered finally, and dragged a small tangle of keys out of the drawer.

My heart flip-flopped as soon as I saw them.

Those weren't car keys. Those were door keys.

Tony's face fell too. "Um, I think they're in there." He tried pulling on the drawer again, but it stubbornly stuck. He stared at it, then suddenly lifted one foot and kicked.

The drawer shattered, spilling its meager contents onto the warped linoleum.

Laura and I watched in silence as he scrambled on the grimy kitchen floor, swearing softly when the search proved fruitless. The keys to the truck were nowhere to be found.

"I swear he put them in here," he muttered, glaring at us as if we were somehow responsible for this oversight. "But it must have been the door keys ..."

He slammed a cabinet door. "Come on, help me look," he demanded.

* * *

Laura and I limped through the tiny cabin, leading the way from room to room while Tony peered behind the dusty canned food on shelves and even ran his hand along the wings of a taxidermied pheasant, searching for the keys. The sparse cabin didn't have many hiding spots.

He stared at the trap door in the utility room for a few long seconds.

Please don't make us go back down there, I begged mentally even while I steeled myself to feel the cobwebs and whispering legs all over again. Laura wobbled against me, clutching my hand tight.

Both of us let out an audible breath of relief as he turned away from the trap door and poked around on the floor instead. My breath caught as he felt underneath the old yellow chest freezer and pulled something out.

My phone.

I kept my face impassive as he turned it over in his hands, flicking his eyes toward us and opening the black screen. "Is this yours?" he asked gruffly.

I nodded. "Yeah, I told you. That's how I made the call."

"Did you call anyone else?" He stared at us, suspicious all over again.

It took all my concentration to keep my eyes from drifting to the tools on the wall behind him. I fantasized about hitting him again but didn't bother running the scenario through. Too risky. If anything could get us out of here alive, it was the tenuous trust we'd built.

I shook my head. "No, I just tried to call the police. That lines up with everything we went over."

He nodded slowly but turned the phone over in his hand one more time, looking at the port before tucking the phone into his pocket. "There's a charger in the truck, once we find the keys. We'll see."

I smiled, trying hard not to let my true feelings show on my face. If he saw that I'd texted Tish, he'd know I lied to him. And he'd know he was going to jail.

As we circled back to the kitchen, Tony suddenly stopped walking. His eyes went wide. "Fuck," he said softly. "I think I know where they are."

He walked a few steps to stare out the filthy window. The outer glass was covered so thickly in dust and cobwebs that I knew he couldn't see anything out of it. But the window faced in the direction of the target range.

"They've gotta be in his pocket," he said slowly.

His face went white, and I understood why. The idea of walking back out to that target range in the dark to sift through a dead person's pockets was more than I could stomach.

"Come on," he said, pointing down the hallway.

Laura hesitated, pointing to my ankle. "Can we wait here? Please? She can barely walk. And I really need to sit down again. I'm not okay." She lifted her hand to point at her face.

He seemed to consider this, then shook his head. "We stay together. Come on. It'll be fast."

Laura reached for my hand to help me walk, giving it three quick squeezes as she did.

When we made it to the living room, she began to sway, gasping for air.

I grabbed her elbow to help her stay upright, but she sagged against me and onto the couch.

Her mouth went slack, and a thin line of drool dripped out one corner down her purple-glazed chin.

"Laura!" I shrieked.

Her chest heaved, and she convulsed on her back, one leg drooping over the armrest. The couch cushions creaked in protest as I wedged my body beside her, trying to keep her from falling off the edge. Was she having a seizure? Was this the end?

Tony was saying something behind me. I didn't catch the words, but he sounded panicked.

The screen door shut with a bang, accompanied by the sound of footsteps rushing away.

He was going to get the keys, but it was too late.

Laura had gone completely still.

* * *

I let out my breath in a wail—that abruptly cut short.

Laura struggled to sit up, her eyes flashing. "I didn't think I'd fool *you*."

Blondie playing opossum. Kyle's words floated back to me.

You bet your ass, Kyle.

"Grab that, now," she demanded in a whisper, pointing to something black lying on the floor beside the couch cushions.

I didn't ask questions. I grabbed it and recoiled. It was a hoodie—and it was soaked through with something sour.

Beer.

My confusion turned to a fresh shot of sweet adrenaline when I heard the faint sound of something tinkling in the pocket.

This was Kyle's hoodie. And those were the keys to the truck.

48

"Laura, you genius," I gasped. She was already on her feet, moving toward the door while I followed.

"When Tony was looking for the keys, I suddenly remembered I heard something hit the ground. It was when Kyle took off the hoodie," she whispered. "The more I thought about it, the more I was sure it was the keys. Can you drive? I feel terrible."

I nodded. My right foot was fine. I'd push the gas pedal with my hands if it came down to it.

Tony would be back any minute, and we needed to get the hell out of here before he returned to the cabin, empty-handed.

I hurried to open the latch on the screen door for Laura, closing it softly behind me. We crept onto the porch and down the steps as quietly as possible. The truck's bulky silhouette loomed a short distance away.

I listened hard, but all I could hear was the wind in the cottonwoods.

The coyotes had gone silent.

I pictured Tony standing next to Kyle's body, trying not to get blood on his expensive shoes while he gathered the nerve to reach into Kyle's pocket and search for the keys.

I hoped he'd linger there, trying to gear himself up to touch the corpse that had gone cold in the night air by now.

Even though I'd felt Kyle's pulse—or lack thereof—with my own hands, years of scary movies had me imagining Kyle popping up like Michael Myers as soon as Tony got close enough.

I pushed the image away. In real life, once you were dead you were dead.

My hands shaking, I fit the key into the passenger lock. I didn't want to hit the auto unlock button, afraid it would make the headlights flash. But would inserting the key make the car alarm go off?

I studied the key. The ridges looked more functional than decorative.

I held my breath and pushed it into the keyhole. It slid in with a quiet, satisfying click.

Laura didn't hesitate. She hefted herself into the passenger seat with her good hand and reached for the interior lock on the driver's side.

"I can't reach," she said desperately. With the wide extended cab, she'd have to lean her body over the console and wriggle over to the driver's side to unlock the other door.

It would be faster if I went around the truck and unlocked it from the outside.

"It's okay, I'll be right there," I whispered.

I held my breath and quietly shut Laura's door behind her with a soft *click*. The soft burst of air that whooshed from the truck's interior as the door closed smelled like the cologne I'd caught a whiff of earlier. Expensive and disgusting at the same time.

Almost there. Almost there.

I ignored my ankle's protests and crept around the back of the truck, toward the driver's side door. Each footstep landed too loudly in the silence. But within seconds, I could see the outline of the driver's side door handle, dimly through the darkness.

Three more steps. Two more steps. One more step. My ankle throbbed in time with my pulse. My spray-painted legs flashed with each movement.

In a few minutes, we'd be home free. Tony would be stuck here with Kyle's body, without a way to follow us.

I inserted the key in the driver's side door and turned it with a quiet click.

I'd just grasped the door handle to open it when I heard another click.

49

I froze, my fingers still locked on the door handle.

My eyes stopped on a tall silhouette standing at the edge of the clearing, maybe thirty yards away.

I could just hear his ragged breathing through the pounding in my ears. Gasping gulps, like he'd been running.

His arms were raised in front of him.

I couldn't see the gun, but I didn't need to.

For a brief, terrifying second I thought it was Kyle, back from the dead.

But as the shadow took a step closer toward the truck, I saw the shape of the dark hoodie and the flash of the white on his Air Jordans.

Tony.

I suddenly remembered the sound the gun had made as it clunked off the plywood target and into the weeds. He'd gone back for it. In case he needed it.

As it turned out, he did.

My fingers tightened on the door handle, hoping he couldn't see the movement this far away.

"If you move, I shoot," he said, his voice shaking with rage.

He took a few strides closer. *Twenty yards away.* Would he hit me at this distance if I dove inside the driver's seat?

He's too close, my gut replied. *He can make a kill shot from there. Especially since you're still painted like a target.*

I didn't dare turn my head to look at Laura, inside the passenger seat. But I knew she must have followed my line of sight by now.

"You knew where the keys were all along," he growled. "This is how you thank me? I killed my *friend* to save *you*. What the fuck is wrong with you?"

He sounded like Kyle again. Only this time, it wasn't an act.

He moved closer. *Ten yards.* I could see the gun in the dim moonlight—and the hand holding it.

A smear of something dark glinted on his skin.

Kyle's blood.

"We didn't know where the keys were. Laura remembered when she woke up—"

"Shut up," he interrupted, taking another step closer and steadying the gun.

Sick regret mixed with the terror. I should have given Laura the keys. Driving with a broken foot was nothing to being gunned down where you sat.

I tried again. "If you shoot me, the whole story we went over goes to shit. We can still—"

"You weren't going to stick to the story," he scoffed. "You were going to leave me here and tell the police about Tish."

"Tony, think it through." I insisted, louder. "If you fire that gun at me right now, the police—"

"The police will think Kyle did it," he insisted, his voice cold. "It's my story against yours. And you won't be around to tell it anymore. You ungrateful little bitches." He lifted the gun higher.

I heard a soft *click* to my right, accompanied by a slight movement beneath my hand, still touching the driver's side door handle.

The truck door had just cracked open.

Laura. She must have angled herself over the console to open the driver's side door from the inside.

Move. Now.

I gripped the handle hard and flung the door open, ducking at the same time. Then I threw myself onto the driver's seat, waiting to hear the loud pop of the gun.

"Hurry, shut the door behind you," Laura gasped. She was hunched over the console at a painful-looking angle. She must have had to lean on her broken arm to get the driver's side door open a crack, while still leaving enough room for me to tumble onto the seat.

I fumbled for the door handle behind me and pulled it shut. Laura shifted into the passenger seat and hit the locks with a quiet *click.*

There was a *pop*, followed by an ear-splitting *crack* as the bullet hit the driver's side window.

I shrieked—then blinked in surprise. Unlike the rock that Kyle had smashed onto the Volvo's windshield earlier, the bullet had left only a small, glassy crack. I'd had worse rock chips.

I raised my head slightly to see over the steering wheel. I could see Tony's face through the window. Five yards away.

Point blank range. He barely has to aim. Just start the truck.

I fumbled for the keys, still clutched in my right hand. Out of the corner of my eye, Tony was on the move again.

"Hurry," Laura gasped. "Stay down."

I felt for the ignition, fingers flying over the unfamiliar shape of the truck's steering column.

Laura cringed into the leg space of the passenger side, bracing for impact.

The second bullet hit the front windshield dead-on with a deafening *crack.* This time, it broke cleanly through the glass.

I felt the impact as the bullet jolted the seat rest behind me. If we didn't get out of here soon, he was going to hit one of us. I'd expected him to keep firing from the driver's side, but it seemed like he was moving around the front of the truck.

He's hoping he hit you. He needs to hit Laura, too.

I finally found the ignition and turned it. The truck roared to life.

I pushed my good foot down on the gas, shifted into reverse, then raised my head a few inches, just enough to see through the bottom part of the windshield.

The headlights looked strange.

First, they were milky yellow. Then they turned red. Then blue.

Tony stood in their glare. He slowly backed away from the truck. I watched in disbelief as he raised his hands and dropped the gun onto the dirt.

"Oh my god," Laura whispered, rising from a crouch and twisting around to look through the back windshield.

A police cruiser, its lights flashing, had come to a stop behind the truck.

An officer leapt out of the front seat. The red and blue flashing lights glinted off his raised weapon.

I whipped around to look at Tony, craning my neck to see through the spidery glass of the windshield. He was kneeling in the dirt illuminated by the truck's headlights, his hands high above his head.

"Keep those hands where I can see them. If you reach for that gun again, I will shoot," the police officer bellowed.

Tony stayed where he was, hands in the air and eyes trained on the officer's gun.

A car door slammed.

The officer barked another command. "Stay in the vehicle, ma'am!"

Was he talking to Laura and me? Had he even seen us yet?

Laura began to sob. "Oh my god."

I turned around to look at the police cruiser again.

The passenger door was open.

Next to it, wearing an oversized yellow Vandals sweatshirt and frantically craning her neck, was Tish.

50

When Tish locked eyes with Tony, she froze.

She opened her mouth. Closed it. Then moved one hand protectively to the middle of her sweatshirt and made a beeline for Laura, who had already tumbled out of the passenger side of the truck and was rushing toward her.

I cracked the driver's side door to join them, then stopped. An overwhelming rush of relief slammed into a wall of dread.

Tish was about to learn that she'd been part of this nightmare for much longer than tonight.

Ignoring the officer's repeated instructions for both girls to get in the squad car, Tish pulled Laura into a fierce embrace. She drew back in horror when Laura whimpered. "Oh my God, Laur. Your arm. What ..." She turned her head to see the truck's half-open driver's side door, where I sat motionless.

The officer was hauling a handcuffed Tony inside the cabin.

"Olivia? Are you okay?" Tish flung open the driver's side door fully and gently helped me down.

I couldn't stop the choked howl that tore through my throat when I felt her arms tighten around me.

* * *

All of my texts had gone through. Some of them more than once, even though the messages on Laura's phone had all showed "text not sent."

Tish had left the library early, feeling tired and nauseated.

That's when she saw my first text about the truck's license plate.

She ignored it—like I knew she probably would. *Just Olivia being Olivia.* She'd ask me about it in the morning, if she remembered. But before she tucked herself into bed, she checked her phone one last time.

That was when she saw the SOS message from Laura's phone. And that was when she called the police, with the license plate.

An officer came to her apartment. He'd run the plate—which didn't exist. When he found out Laura and I were partying at a bonfire near "Coffin Creek," he seemed skeptical that this might be some kind of prank. It had happened before.

By that point, Tish was frantic.

She even called Tony. No answer.

Then she told the officer that she was going to drive into the hills herself right then, if he wouldn't.

She didn't have a car to do that—since we'd taken the Volvo—but she must have been convincing, because he reluctantly agreed to let her ride with him in the patrol car.

That was when the address pinged on her phone: 67 Deer Flat.

EPILOGUE

It took days for Laura and me to get the spray paint off our skin, no matter how much we scrubbed.

Even after the last traces were gone, I could still see those Xes glowing faintly when I closed my eyes.

Eleven Deltas—including Tony—went to prison for what they'd done to Tish and so many others.

The story stayed in the headlines in Idaho and beyond for the next year as the case went to trial.

In addition to human trafficking, kidnapping, and two counts of attempted murder, Tony was charged as an accomplice in Ava's death. That charge didn't stick. His defense team subpoenaed both Laura and I to testify that he didn't know Ava was down in the crawl space.

Tony stared at us pleadingly while we took the stand for the defense. He refused to meet our eyes when we testified for the prosecution, to tell the jury what had happened right before Tish and the police officer showed up.

The attempted murder charges, kidnapping charges, and human trafficking charges all stuck.

The other Deltas got twenty-five years, with the possibility of parole.

Tony got life.

* * *

Ava Robles' body was finally laid to rest in Boise, where she'd grown up. Classes were dismissed for the funeral, and half of campus attended.

The girls, and some of the boys, wore brightly colored ribbons braided into their hair.

In the end, Tish, Laura, and I decided not to go. We'd all seen too many comments on the Facebook invitation celebrating Ava Robles Day—and the break from classes. And we'd all seen the photos circulating online: an image of Ava in the crawl space, her ribbon-woven braids and the dark X across her sunken chest visible in the flash of the camera. Someone had leaked it, and while Ava's family had succeeded in getting many of them taken down online, they still popped up all the time.

I didn't read the extensive blogs that popped up in the aftermath, despite the relentless interview requests that found their way into all three of our email inboxes.

I wasn't interested in hearing anyone else's telephone version of events or a play-by-play of that long night. And I didn't want to hear whether any of us were brave or brilliant or a cautionary tale for other college girls.

It was my story. And Laura's. And Tish's. And the girls who'd had red and blue Xes marked on their arms.

Nobody else's.

The three of us decided to finish the school year online. We rented an apartment together in Nampa.

Even with what she knew, Tish decided to keep the baby, a girl.

She named her Chloe: Goddess of new beginnings.

282

NOTE FROM THE AUTHOR

If you enjoyed this book, a positive review would mean the world to me. Like other small-press authors, I rely heavily on word-of-mouth recommendations to reach new readers.

I can promise you that I read every single review. Because each one is a new window into this story. And because if you loved this book, *you're* the one I wrote it for—which is why I'm placing this note *before* the acknowledgments.

One last thing: If you want to find out what happened to Ava Robles, find me on Instagram @noelleihliauthor. You'll find a link to a free short story in my highlights called *Red X.*

ACKNOWLEDGMENTS

Thank you to everyone who gave their time, talents, and support to this book.

Thank you to Stephanie Nelson, Anna Gamel, Sara Ennis, and Jeanne Allen. Your insights, edits, and encouragement made this book so much stronger.

Thank you to my editor, Patti Geesey. I'm always grateful for your time and keen eye.

Last, but not least, thank you to my husband Nate for being my final reader, my cheerleader, and best friend.

ABOUT THE AUTHOR

Noelle's two great passions are murder and horses (separately, never together). *Run on Red* is her third suspense thriller.

She lives in Idaho with her husband, two sons, and two cats.

When she's not plotting her next thriller, she's scaring herself with true-crime documentaries or going for a trail ride in the foothills (with her trusty pepper spray).

Read on for a thrilling excerpt
from Noelle W. Ihli's novel *Ask for Andrea*

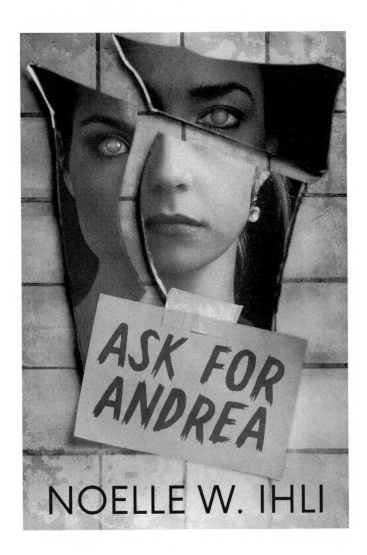

1. MEGHAN

OQUIRRH MOUNTAINS, UTAH

1 YEAR BEFORE

Despite the crushing weight of him, my brain screamed at me to run.

Run, it demanded as he grunted and pulled the scarf—my scarf—tighter around my neck.

Instead I lay frozen, like a mouse under a cat's paw, until the vise of pressure and pain suddenly released.

He looked at me for a few seconds as he got to his feet, his mouth turned down in disgust. He was breathing hard. His pale face hovered above me in the darkness, the distinctive mole on his cheek a stark punctuation mark.

He let the limp, pink-and-green scarf fall to the ground beside me.

Run, my brain roared again. *RUN!*

I still didn't move. I didn't even blink.

He turned toward the car he'd precariously parked on the shoulder of the rutted dirt road.

I could only imagine what he'd left in the trunk. But if I didn't move, I knew I'd find out.

So that's when I finally ran, bolting into the shadows of the pines that beckoned with hiding places, if not safety.

I scrambled down a steep embankment toward a dry stream bed, pushing myself faster and willing myself not to fall, no longer even conscious of the pain in my throat.

I wasn't sure where I was going. All I knew was that I needed to put as much distance as I could between myself and the spotless blue Kia Sorento. And more importantly, I needed to get away from the soft-spoken, fine-as-hell man who drove it: *The needle,* I'd called him when I told Sharesa about our upcoming date. As in, the needle in a deep haystack of bachelors on the MatchStrike app: divorced dads with kids, complicated custody agreements, and cringey gym-bathroom selfies.

Jimmy was different. With his dark amber eyes, a close-shaved beard along his angular jawline and a hard-part haircut, he was a dead ringer for Chris Hemsworth.

When I showed Sharesa his photo, she'd actually squealed.

I, on the other hand, had kept my expectations in check. I wasn't new to the online dating scene. I'd taken an Uber to Gracie's Spot in Salt Lake after my shift and braced to meet Chris Hemsworth's creepy cousin. I even texted Sharesa on my way. *Call me in an hour with an out?* I could see the text bubbles appear immediately after I hit send. *Whatever, you know you're thirsty.* I rolled my eyes. More bubbles. ... *I'll call <3.*

We talked in the back booth of Gracie's until last call at eleven. I texted Sharesa from the bathroom that there was no need to rescue me after all. She'd replied immediately, like always: *Thirrrrrsty.*

As I washed my hands, a paper sign taped to the bathroom mirror caught my attention. "On a date that isn't going well? Do you feel unsafe or just a little uneasy? Ask for Andrea at the bar. We'll make sure you get home safe." I smiled as I dried my hands, grateful I didn't need to ask. Not tonight. Not with him.

I stopped looking at the sign and studied myself in the mirror. I'd taken extra time with my hair, which I usually let fall in a blunt line across my shoulders. Earlier, I had coaxed it into waves that looked like spun gold in the restaurant lighting. I reapplied some of the deep pink lipstick that had become my signature accessory over the years and pressed my lips together, wondering if he'd kiss me later.

I had two beers over the course of the evening. Not enough to get me drunk or anything. Just enough to take the edge off my nerves. Because he did not in fact look like Chris Hemsworth's creepy cousin. He was thoughtful and funny. Even the large mole on his cheek somehow made him all the more attractive.

He drank ginger ale. It didn't faze me. I lived in Utah, after all.

The last thing I remember was feeling a little bit too warm. And really, really happy. The syrup-colored lights blazing in the trendy sputnik chandeliers suddenly had these little auras surrounding them. So when he suggested that I let him drive me home instead of waiting for an Uber in the cold, I didn't even hesitate.

The car had those crinkly paper covers on the seats, like it had just been cleaned.

That's the last thing I remember. Until I woke up with his hands—and my scarf—around my neck. The warm lights of Gracie's were gone, replaced with the bite of pine needles and dirt under my hair and the swirling dark of the freezing night air.

For a few seconds, I couldn't understand what was happening. I couldn't scream. I couldn't move. I couldn't even tell where I was. All I knew was that everything hurt.

The memory of our date crashed through the haze when I saw his eyes glinting above me. They weren't warm or even amber-colored anymore like they had been in the booth at Gracie's. These eyes were cold. Wide. And full of rage.

I thought about the sign in the bathroom at Gracie's. *Ask for Andrea.*

Andrea couldn't help me now. No one could.

I moved faster than I'd ever moved in my life, the pounding in my head and my chest and the crushing pressure of the scarf forgotten.

I didn't care where I was going. All that mattered was putting as much distance between us as possible, even if it meant running headlong into the looming woods.

I thought I heard someone call out as I dove down the rocky slope of the shallow stream bed. It sounded like a woman.

I ignored it and kept running.

He didn't follow me.

He didn't need to.

Because when I finally stopped running, I realized to my amazement that I wasn't out of breath.

Just as quickly, the amazement turned to horror.

I wasn't breathing hard because I wasn't breathing at all.

2. BRECIA

2 YEARS BEFORE

I first realized I was dead the same way you realize you've been dreaming. Except backward, I guess. Because the bad dream was real.

I didn't know it had happened at first. Not for a few seconds. Not until I stood up—while my own body stayed put. I looked at the soft chambray pajamas I'd changed into after getting home from work, now dirty and damp. One of my slippers was kicked off, so you could see the chipped peach polish on my bare toes. My long, dark hair was streaked with something darker and sticky. I couldn't feel the throbbing in my head or the awful pressure on my neck anymore.

He was looking at me, too. Not at *me*, me. At my body. At my unblinking, bloodshot hazel eyes. He was breathing hard, expressionless. He was still holding the extension cord.

He'd grown out a Joaquin Phoenix beard that nearly—but not quite—obscured the dark mole on his cheek. It made him look ten years older than the last time I'd seen him. If he'd been sporting the beard back then, we probably wouldn't have gone out in the first place. Don't get me wrong: I'll swoon for a good five-o-clock shadow, but this thing was fully bird-nest material. It took him from a comfortable nine to a very solid three.

A year earlier, we had dated for exactly one week. How do I know that? Because he was upset when I spent our "one-week anniversary" with my girlfriends. I couldn't understand why it bothered him so much. It was Lanelle's birthday. And like I said, we'd been dating for *one week*. Still, I talked about him the whole time. I hadn't dated much since my last breakup a couple years earlier, and it felt good to say the word "boyfriend" again. It felt good to answer all the juicy questions over watermelon margaritas about whether he was a good kisser (yes), good in bed (no idea, early days), and how we'd met. That one, I fudged a little. I wasn't proud I'd finally gotten desperate enough to make a profile on MatchStrike. So I dodged the question. I decided that if we lasted, I'd fess up.

When I ran into him on my way out of the restaurant after Lanelle's party, I didn't know what to think at first. He smiled his pretty smile and acted like it was a wild coincidence. That's how I played it off to Lanelle and the rest of my friends. I could tell that they thought he was cute. That I'd done well. So I pushed aside the uncomfortable feeling in my gut as I tried to remember whether I'd mentioned the name of the restaurant to him earlier. I was pretty sure I hadn't.

I let him drive me home, even though that meant leaving my car in the Barbacoa parking lot. At first, he just seemed happy to see me. But when I asked who he'd met up with at Barbacoa, he sort of dodged the question. So I asked again. That was when he just kind of blew up.

He went on and on about me brushing him off to hang out with my friends. Then he ranted about me not even being glad to see him at the restaurant.

I texted him later that night to tell him I thought we should break up. He tried to call me immediately. When I didn't pick up, he called again. And again. And again. I put the phone in airplane mode and went to bed, still feeling the watermelon margs and wishing I hadn't told Lanelle or the girls about him yet.

When I woke up the next morning, I had twenty-two text messages waiting for me. They started out sort of sweet. He'd had a terrible day yesterday and just really wanted to see me. He understood why I was upset. Could he have another chance? By the last text message, I was a fat bitch. A fat bitch who had wasted his time. As soon as I had finished reading that one, another text came through. He could see that I had read his texts, so why wasn't I responding? I'd wasted his time, broken his heart, and now I wouldn't even write back.

The texts trickled in for the next three days, even though I didn't respond. I finally blocked his number and reported his profile on MatchStrike, figuring that maybe I'd save other girls the trouble.

When the texts stopped, I pretty much forgot about him.

I redecorated my duplex. I got a new job and a raise. I got bangs and highlights in my hair. I deleted MatchStrike after a handful of duds who didn't even make it past a second date. And I adopted a cat: a fire-point named Frank.

So when I took the recycle bin out to the side yard in my pajamas that night, he was the last person I was expecting to see.

I didn't even recognize him at first with that awful beard. He was standing there almost casually, like maybe it was some kind of coincidence. Just like he had that night at Barbacoa. Except this time he was standing in my side yard. Behind my fence.

I almost screamed. I only caught myself when I recognized his eyes. Honestly, I was a little relieved that he wasn't a stranger.

Then I got mad. It had been an entire *year.* What the *fuck* was wrong with him, showing up like this? Scaring me like this? Did he think I was going to take him back now?

That was when he pulled out the extension cord. My extension cord. I recognized it in slow motion as he came toward me. I hadn't bothered to bring it inside yet after using it to plug in the Christmas lights I'd finally goaded myself into putting up.

If you want to know, it takes a long time to strangle somebody. I'd heard that on an episode of *Investigation Discovery* once. I can tell you it takes even longer when you're the one being strangled. My throat was on fire. My head was on fire. My chest was on fire. Even my eyes felt like they were burning. I couldn't make a sound. I couldn't even see, as the tears poured down my cheeks.

I guess it was taking too long for him, too. Because in the end, he smashed the side of my head against the pavement. After that, everything went dark. The unbearable fire was suddenly gone, along with the chill in the air and the feel of the wet, rough pavement.

When I caught my first glimpse of, well, I still didn't know what to call it—my soul? My spirit? My echo?—it was sort of like looking at my reflection in a mirror. I wasn't wafting in the breeze or anything. I wasn't see-through. I just wasn't alive anymore. I was still wearing my pajamas and slippers, but they looked clean, the way they had a couple minutes earlier.

As soon as he realized I was dead—which was a hot minute after *I* realized I was dead—he booked it through my back gate. I was left standing beside my own body and the recycling bin I'd just wheeled out of the garage.

I followed him, finding that I could keep pace with him easily—something I never could have said of myself while alive. I actually grabbed his arm and watched as my own fingers rested lightly on top of his shoulder. I sort of expected them to slide right through.

He didn't react, exactly. However, he did walk faster, down the dark driveway, down the sidewalk, until he reached the blue Kia he'd left at the end of the street.

When he opened the driver's side door, I dove inside the car headlong with him. I wasn't going to risk letting him go if that car door slammed shut in my face.

As I watched him hurry into the car, I knew that I couldn't do anything for the girl who was lying on the pavement with blood in her hair. I couldn't do anything for Frank, who was probably still asleep on the big tufted chair in my bedroom.

Nobody else was looking out for me tonight. Nobody else was going to realize that I was missing, let alone dead, until I didn't show up for work tomorrow. Nobody could do anything to help me now.

Before he drove away, he used a packet of wipes to clean his hands. Carefully. Almost lovingly. Like he hadn't just used them to wrap a dirty extension cord around my neck by my recycle bins in my side yard until I finally stopped fighting.

In hindsight, that was when I decided I was going to haunt him.

I studied him from the passenger seat while he drove. His amber eyes, black in the darkness of the car, stayed fixed on the road while we made the twenty-minute drive back to his place.

It wasn't the apartment he'd told me about last year—down to the roommate who left his socks in the kitchen. Instead, it was a little brick 70s-style rambler in Broomfield with one porch light burned out.

I followed him up the front walkway of the house, past a Big Wheel bike tipped over into an overgrown flower bed and a tangle of half-naked Barbies on the steps.

The lone porch light flickered a little as he turned the knob and went inside the house, shutting the door behind him and leaving me standing on the porch for a little while longer, staring at the toys and the riot of azaleas in the flowerbeds I just knew he hadn't planted.

I found that I couldn't just walk through the front door, once he went inside. So I was glad I'd gotten into the car when I had the chance.

I stood outside on his porch for a while. Because despite all the scary movies I'd watched, I had learned zero useful information about being dead. Could I make the doorknob move if I focused really hard? No. What would happen if I screamed? I tried it. I could hear myself just fine, but based on the reaction of the guy walking his dog across the street, nobody else could.

Well, that's not totally accurate. The dog—a little gray schnauzer—stopped walking and looked straight at the front porch.

I got my hopes up. "Hey, buddy! Hey!" The schnauzer growled a little. He sniffed. Then he kept walking. The owner didn't even look up from the blue glow of his smartphone.

I turned away from the useless dog and sat down on the porch. I studied my hands—the reflection of my hands. I watched the way they rested on the reflection of my knees. The way my feet rested on the cracked concrete. Barely touching, as if I were made of something just heavier than air.

I swiped hard at a leaf on the step and watched it move so imperceptibly it was impossible to tell whether it had been the night air.

You're dead, I told myself firmly. *Feel sad.*

When my favorite aunt had died in a car accident, the cushion of denial lasted a solid hour. It was too big. I couldn't take it in. When it finally hit me, I felt like the wind had been knocked out of me. It felt like that. Only this time, the impossibly awful thing had happened to me.

I could see blurry shapes moving behind the pebbled glass of the kitchen window above the flowerbed. I stepped into the azaleas and watched my reflection scatter through the spaces between the leggy blooms. The plants didn't move. *I* did.

It would have been completely fascinating if I hadn't just been murdered; however, it did give me an idea. I couldn't walk through walls. Or grab anything. I seemed to have had all the power of the night air. Not the wind, even. *The air.*

I sat with this idea for a while, watching the azalea leaves shiver in the slight breeze. I lifted my hand toward the nearest flower and reached for a cluster of blooms. This time I watched more carefully as my hand slipped, sort of like smoke, between two large magenta blossoms.

I wasn't wind: I was air. But air could go places. And that gave me an idea.

I walked around the house until I got to the side gate, which was closed. I could see the side yard—and his recycle bins—through the slats. I focused on the air between the slats and moved forward.

Easily enough, I scattered right through the fence.

My gaze settled on a cat door, slightly ajar, leading into the garage. I went through that too. No problem.

The light was on, illuminating a neat garage and a few rows of stacked boxes on one side, a minivan on the other. I gave the boxes a cursory glance. They were labeled with kitchen, bathroom, bedroom, etc. A stack of labels and a permanent marker sat on the topmost box.

He was moving.

I heard a clattering noise behind me and turned in time to see a little calico cat scurry into the garage through the cat door.

"Hi, kitty," I said softly, and I swear he sat down and stared right at me for a few seconds—then settled in front of a bowl of cat food. I followed him and crouched beside him as he ate. I thought of Frank with his chirping meow. He was probably tearing up the carpet at the bottom of the stairs in protest that I hadn't fed him yet.

I knew I couldn't cry actual tears. Even so, I felt the familiar prickling feeling in the back of my eyes and sadness that spread through the center of me. I wouldn't ever feel the downy fur underneath Frank's chin or his rumbly purr as he flopped down on the bed beside me with his eyes closed again.

As the feeling got bigger, I heard a quiet pop that plunged the garage into sudden darkness.

I froze, listening to the quiet tinkling of the filament in the bulb.

"I think I did that," I whispered to the cat, who continued crunching away.

There were little pinpricks of light surrounding the door to his house. I moved toward them and the sound of the muffled voices inside.

An hour ago, he had taken everything I had.

I didn't know how, but I planned to return the favor.

3. SKYE

NOW

He came into the Daily Grind coffeehouse a lot when I was on shift that summer.

It didn't bother me. I looked forward to it, actually. He tipped. He was cute. He was one of the few white folks in Idaho who didn't try to make small talk about where I was *really* from or take the opportunity to test out their fledgling Spanish. (Much to my mom's disappointment, I had taken exactly one year of Spanish elective in middle school.)

He called me "Dolly," on account of me wearing a Dolly Parton shirt the day he first came in for a hot chocolate. Never coffee. Always hot chocolate. That was a little unusual, so I remembered his order. I started adding a little smiley face on the cup, next to his name. *James.*

"Thanks, Dolly," he always said with a grin that made me blush. So of course I mumbled something awkward and turned around to prep the next order. His amber eyes—I swear, they looked like dark, liquid gold—lingered on me while I pretended not to notice.

My manager, Ken, teased me about him once in a while. He told me I should write my number on his cup next time he came in. "The hot chocolate dude that looks like Chris Hemsworth is totally flirting with you," Ken said, wiggling his eyebrows. "Ball's in your court, honeybun."

I almost did. I rolled the idea around in my head sometimes while I was toasting somebody's bagel or adding exactly 5.5 pumps of caramel syrup to a Frappuccino. I was embarrassed to admit—even to myself—that I had never been on a real date, let alone made the first move. I told myself that's what college was for. When I got there in the fall, somehow I would shed my skin and lose my awkwardness when I crossed the threshold of campus at Idaho State.

It wasn't unusual for me to see him three or four times a week that summer; however, a few weeks before I was set to drive to ISU, he suddenly stopped coming by. I felt weirdly sad about it. Like I had missed my chance or something. I pictured his face while I worked, feeling wistful that I'd probably never see him again. He was older than me by a lot—late twenties, if I had to guess. Honestly, he was so good-looking with those caramel eyes, dark hair, and dramatic celebrity-style beauty mark that I didn't really care.

It felt like fate when, on my last day at work before I left for ISU, he walked through the doors with a big smile and ordered his usual. I could feel my cheeks go red as I tried to bully myself into writing my number on his hot chocolate cup. I told myself it was practice, I guess. To prove I was ready for college (I wasn't). But I chickened out. I reasoned that I was leaving for school in two days, so what was the point?

I told him in a mumbled rush that today was my last day. He probably wouldn't see me at the Daily Grind again. He looked genuinely disappointed and then sort of shrugged. "Well, I'll miss you, Dolly."

My cheeks flared even hotter, and I pretended that the espresso machine was spilling over until he left. *Idiota,* I thought to myself. I remembered the curse words.

I finished my shift at four and turned in my apron and employee door tag. I gave Ken a hug, promising I'd text him. Then I walked to the bus stop. I was about to hit *send* on a text to my mom about dinner—pupusas at our favorite food truck? I had skipped lunch and was starving—when I saw a car slow down beside me in the shopping center.

It was him.

He gave me that smile, like he was as surprised as me. Like it was serendipity. Then he said, "Hey, Dolly. Want a ride?"

I didn't even hesitate. The universe had given me a second chance after I'd punted earlier—and all those other times. I easily batted aside the voice that quietly piped up to wonder why he was still in the sleepy shopping center two hours after I'd last seen him.

"Sure, why not?" I said, pleased that my voice sounded so easy-going, even when I could feel my heart pounding hard against my chest. *It's not a big deal,* I told myself. *It's not like he's a stranger.* I smoothed down my curls, which were a mess like they always were after work.

Then I got into the blue Kia and buckled my seatbelt.

"You maybe wanna grab something to eat first?" he asked. I felt my heart calm down a little.

"Sure, I'm starving," I replied, blushing and making eye contact with the dark mark on his cheek. This meant it was a date. I couldn't wait to text Ken later. He'd be so proud of me.

He grinned. "Well, then I'm gonna take you to my favorite place, okay? It's kind of out of the way, but it's worth it."

The voice in my head piped up again. I'd lived in Kuna all my life. There weren't many places I'd never been. Especially when it came to food. "What's it called?" I asked.

He shook his head. "You'll see."

As we drove, he asked me questions. Questions about my family. Whether I'd ever visited El Salvador (once, when I was a baby). What kind of music I liked. What I wanted to study. Whether I was a morning person or a night owl. Question after question. Like I was the most interesting person in the world. All with that smile. Stealing glances at me while he pulled onto the interstate toward Boise.

I told myself to relax. Boise was a thirty-minute drive, but it did have more restaurants.

I focused on what he was saying and tried to enjoy myself. He was telling a story about one of his roommates, who had gotten a growler instead of a pony keg for their last party. I laughed, not really sure what the difference was either but unwilling to reveal that. He seemed kind of old to still be partying, but what did I know?

Five minutes later, he signaled to leave the interstate. I looked up at the sign. Blacks Creek. Kuna-Mora Road. My stomach turned over. He didn't miss a beat as he continued telling the story. I had been on Blacks Creek Road once, on a hike. As far as I knew, there weren't any restaurants this way. Just hills and canyons.

My stomach started to hurt. "Is this the right exit?" I asked, as lightly as I could. I was still worried I would blow it. Hurt his feelings. Disappoint him. Reveal that I was a baby who had never even been on a real date or kissed a boy. That Ken—who himself had a boyfriend— was the only boy I ever spent any amount of time with.

"You haven't been to Moe's?" he asked, glancing at me with genuine surprise. "And you grew up here?" He shot me a sly smile, and I believed him.

Just in case, I decided to send a text to my mom. "Oh, Moe's?" I bluffed. "Oh yeah, I've always wanted to try it." I swallowed as I pulled my phone out of my jacket pocket. "I'm just going to text my mom, let her know. I told her I'd be home soon."

As I said it, I looked at the screen and saw zero bars.

My thumbs hovered over the text message box as I read my mom's last text message again and again. *Te quiero, mi'ja.*

The sick feeling came back. And when I looked up at him, I saw that he had been watching me. I plastered a fake smile on my face.

He took it in stride. "There's no service for a couple miles—but just past that hill, you'll get three bars. No problem. You want me to stop there so you can text her?"

The whiplash from dread to relief made me feel dizzy, and I mustered up a real smile. Maybe Moe's *did* exist. Maybe everything was fine. I was getting worked up over nothing. Like I always did. "Sure," I said, as casually as I could. "She'll worry if I don't."

A few minutes later, we took a bend in the road. There was a "Ranch exit" sign just ahead, and he slowed the car and signaled onto what looked like little more than a dirt trail. I looked down at my phone as the tires crunched and rumbled along the uneven, rocky surface.

Still no service.

He spoke as if he had read my mind, pointing outside the car. "If you still aren't getting bars, that spot down by the creek should do it." He smiled. "Found it by accident when my friend Greg had to take a leak on the way out here."

I laughed a little and got out of the car, my eyes on my phone as I walked toward the creek.

Still no bars.

I held the phone up and took a few steps forward and tried again.

Nothing.

And that's when he grabbed me from behind. One hand roughly pulled my head back by my hair. The other closed around my throat as he pushed me to the ground. I landed hard on my stomach, but the only sound I could manage was a muffled grunt as his knees pinned me down.

I tried to scream. Tried to twist my body around to get him off me. Tried to fight.

All I could focus on was trying to get his hands off my throat.

When I was in fourth grade, the little boy next door—his name was Dewey—drowned in the hot tub on his back patio. He tried to get in it while his mom was making lunch, and the cover shut on him. After that, I sometimes had a hard time falling asleep at night. I couldn't stop thinking about what it must have been like for him.

Drowning was the worst way I could imagine dying.

Until now.

It couldn't have been more than a couple minutes before I lost consciousness, but the seconds seemed to expand as I tried—and failed—to find a way to make him stop.

When the darkness finally closed in, the pain and the pressure disappeared with the light.

When the light reappeared, I could still hear him grunting behind me. I could still see the dirt and gravel beneath my face. Everything else had gone numb.

To my amazement however, I rolled away from his grasp.

To my horror, he didn't even notice. Because the girl with the dark, messy curls lying face down in the dirt didn't move at all.

I'd seen those *Dateline* specials about people who had out-of-body experiences. Near-death experiences. I quickly decided that's what was happening.

"GET OFF ME," I screamed, launching myself at him.

My fists landed on his back with all the force of a butterfly wing.

"Stop, stop, stop," I cried. I knew he couldn't hear me. I wasn't sure I could even hear myself.

The girl on the ground—me—wasn't putting up a fight anymore. Her lips were a deep lavender. There was a long line of drool coming out of one corner of her mouth. Her eyes weren't closed, but they weren't open, either.

The distant sound of a vehicle on the interstate was what finally made him let go. It wasn't close, but there was no cover out here, aside from some scrubby sage and the shallow creek.

I watched as he finally stood up and inspected his hands then walked back toward the blue Kia.

He didn't look back at the body on the ground.

As I heard his tires crunch along the road, I waited for it to happen. For my soul to reunite with the lifeless, dusty body in the dirt.

I sat down and got as close as I could to my body. "He's gone," I whispered. "You can wake up now."

I imagined reuniting with my body, focusing as hard as I could on what it had felt like in the moments before everything went dark. I lay down next to myself, hoping that all of a sudden, I'd feel the pain again, the desperation to breathe. That was what happened in the *Dateline* episode. You saw yourself outside your body, and then wham, you came roaring back. Or some kind of loving being appeared to tell you it wasn't your time to meet God yet.

"Come back," I whispered. I thought about my mom, already home from work and wondering why I hadn't beat her home. Why I hadn't texted. Whether I wanted two or three pupusas.

My phone was lying in the dirt beneath me. I could see one corner, pinned underneath my thigh.

It was still and silent.

Just like me.

Made in United States
Orlando, FL
06 March 2024

44450227R10186